Murder for Beltene

A Beltene Family Mystery
(... dressed like a mystery, with fantasy lingerie ...)

by
Sandra L. Brewer

A Write Way Publishing Book

All the characters, the city of Sevyrn, Brennen County and any rituals contained within this book are the products of the author's overactive imagination and are not to be construed as real (Sorry, Trystan). Any resemblance to actual events or persons, living or dead, is entirely coincidental.

Copyright © 1999, by Sandra L. Brewer
(email: rbeltene@ismi.net)

Write Way Publishing
PO Box 441278
Aurora, CO 80044

First Edition; 1999

Queries regarding rights and permissions should be addressed to Write Way Publishing, PO Box 441278, Aurora, CO, 80044; email: writewy@aol.com

ISBN 1-885173-67-9

1 2 3 4 5 6 7 8 9 10

DEDICATION

*To Lois Johnson, for all the red ink, encouragement
and especially for Stratford.
And to Robin Lynch & Deidree Devlin,
for their faith, patience and friendship.*

Acknowledgments

I would like to thank the following people for their assistance: Doug Kelly, for providing me with all that wondrous information about embalming; Dave Teggerdine, for answering all my questions about how a small sheriff's department in Michigan would run; Christine Ecarius, for all the illustrator shortcuts; Robin Lynch, for letting me use Liam & friends; the Renegade Writers for all their support; and all those for whom Trystan is real—thanks.

The Beltene Family

Aranrhod (Aran-hrod), student; Rhiannon's sister
Branwen (Bran-ooen), wife of Pwyll; Rhiannon's mother
Cristin (Krees-teen), druid; Rhiannon's cousin
Daffyd (Daf-eed), apprentice druid; Rhiannon's brother
Dylan (Dee-lan), artist; Rhiannon's cousin
Grandmama, druid; Rhiannon's grandmother
Gwendolyn (Gooen-doleen), nun; Rhiannon's cousin
Gwenddydd (Gooen-theeth), family historian; Rhiannon's cousin
Gwydre (Gooee-dre), druid; Indeg's husband
Indeg (Een-deeg), Gwydre's wife
Morgan, priest; Rhiannon's uncle
Morfudd (More-veethe), county clerk; Rhiannon's aunt
Olwen (Ole-ooen), teacher; Rhiannon's cousin
Pentraeth (Pen-treyeth), doctor; Rhiannon's cousin
Puck—Siamese kitten
Pwyll (Powee-thl), mayor of Sevyrn; Rhiannon's father (Branwen's
    husband)
Rhan (Hran), county commissioner; Tangwen's husband
Rhiannon (Hri-annon), novelist and the Beltene
Rhodri (Hrode-re), doctor; Rhiannon's brother
Rhys (Hrees), district court judge; Teleri's husband
Righdhonn (Righ-dhone), mercenary; Rhiannon's cousin
Taliesin (Tal-iesin), bard; Rhiannon's cousin
Tangwen (Tang-ooen), county prosecutor; Rhan's wife
Teleri (Tel-eri), comptroller forMetalworks; Rhys' wife
Trystan (Trees-tan), artist; son of Rhan and Tangwen; Rhiannon's cousin

Glossary

Babalawo—high priest of Santeria
Cariad—Welsh, love
ISP—Internet Sevice Provider
Torc—necklace
Uffern dan—Welsh, damn it

Citizens of Sevyrn

Lesley Benedict—Sam's wife
Sam Benedict—owner of Sam's Black Abbey; Lesley's husband
Jessie Blackthorne—owner of ojibway.net
Henry Branton—repatriated Gwynn O'Keefe, driver for Superior
    Deliveries
Pete Conwy—companion to Trystan
Elaine Dalton—photographer, wife of Tom
Roseanne Davidson—nurse, wife of Eric
Elise de Maria—owner/Gypsy Witch Café
Gray de Maria—son of Elise
Erin de la Marchiere—wife of Jody
Jody de la Marchiere—high priest of Santeria, chef/Beltene
    family, husband of Erin
Eula—the Beltene's secretary
Lars Morrison—farmer, Lesley's and Philip's father
Philip Morrison—student, son of Lars Morrison
Diuran O'Keefe—head of the Gwynn O'Keefes, father of Niall
Niall O'Keefe—repatriated Gwynn O'Keefe

Members of Sheriff's Department

Rachel Conwy—sheriff's department dispatcher
Tom Dalton—deputy for Brennen County, husband of Elaine
Eric Davidson—detective sergeant for Brennen County,
    husband of Roseanne
Doc Hellers—County Medical Examiner
Marilyn Hunter—deputy for Brennen County
Lucas St. John—investigator for Michigan State Police
Daniel Thorpe—new sheriff of Brennen County
Lige Williams—outgoing sheriff of Brennen County

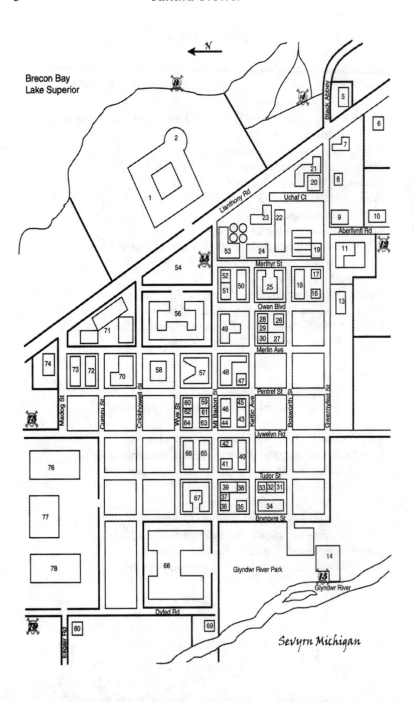

City of Sevyrn

1	Beltene House	40	Eaton Furniture
2	Rhiannon's Tower	41	Lidell Shell & Hop-In
3	Cave of the Paintings	42	A&W Rootbeer
4	1st body—Tuesday	43	Grotta Pets
5	Sam's Black Abbey	44	Tudor Century 21
6	Herman Brothers' Ford	45	Lane's Fix-it Shop
7	Gustafson Outdoor Leisure	46	Our Little Launderette
8	Rosati & Son, Builders	47	Gypsy Witch Café
9	Cole Well & Septic	48	Keltia Bank
10	Rebbeck Lumber	49	Brennen Cty Sherriff's Office
11	Patchett Veterinary Clinic	50	IGA
12	5th body—Saturday	51	McEvers, Beltene & St. John;
13	Self Service Car Wash		Attorneys at Law
14	Rhaedr Mill Comm. Center	52	ojibway.net
15	3rd body—Thursday	53	Beltene Mill & Co-op
16	Old-n-New, Antiques & Gifts	54	St. David's Cemetery
17	MacInnes Sporting Goods	55	6th body—Sunday
18	Sevyrn Cinema	56	St. David's Cathedral
19	Knighton Florist & Greenhouse	57	Brennen Cty & Sevyrn City Off.
20	Edinger Auto Parts	58	Brennen Cty Library
21	Mitchell John Deere	59	Bower's Video
22	Fuelgas	60	Edwin Parker, CPA
23	Chun Chevrolet	61	Little Caesar's Pizza
24	Buchanan Excavating	62	JD's Liquor
25	Brennen Cty Farmer's Market	63	Marx Books & Cards
26	Dairy Queen	64	Fine Feathers Clothing
27	Sevryn Hardware	65	Post Office
28	Jade Music, Beauty Salon	66	State of Michigan Offices
29	Escoffier Bakery	67	Doctor's Office
30	Dalton Photography	68	Brennen Cty Hospital
31	Down's BarberShop	69	Lige William's home
32	Sinberg Jewelry	70	Conwy Funeral Home
33	Bodilan Travel Agency	71	Beltene Woodcarving & Mtlwks.
34	Brennen Cty News & Hamilton Graphics	72,73,74	Morrison's Meat, Dairy & Farm
		75	2nd body—Wednesday
35	Country Cooking Restaurant	76,77, 78	Brennen Cty Schools
36	Roth Pharmacy	79	4th body-Friday
37	Farm Bureau Ins.; T. Morrison, Agt	80	Beere's Tavern
38	Rowland Appliances		
39	Trefulin Grocery		

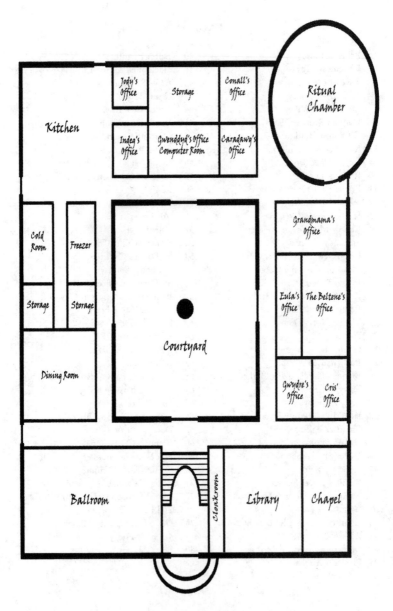

Beltene House - 1st Floor
Sevyrn Michigan

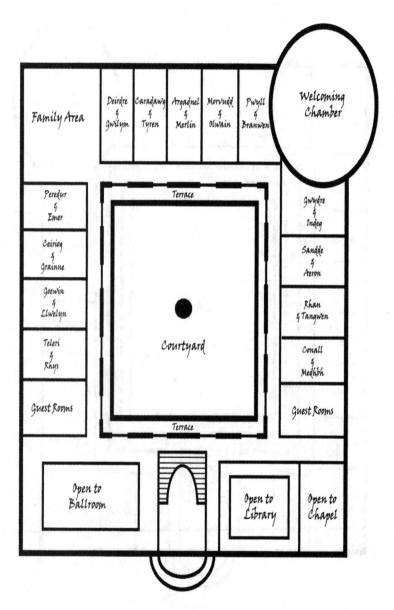

Family Area

Deirdre & Gwilym

Caradawg & Tyren

Arganel & Merlin

Morvudd & Olwain

Pwyll & Branwen

Welcoming Chamber

Peredur & Emer

Gwydre & Indeg

Ceiriog & Grainne

Sandde & Aeron

Goewin & Llwelyn

Rhan & Tangwen

Teleri & Rhys

Conall & Medhbh

Guest Rooms

Guest Rooms

Terrace

Courtyard

Terrace

Open to Ballroom

Open to Library

Open to Chapel

Beltene House - 2nd Floor
Sevyrn Michigan

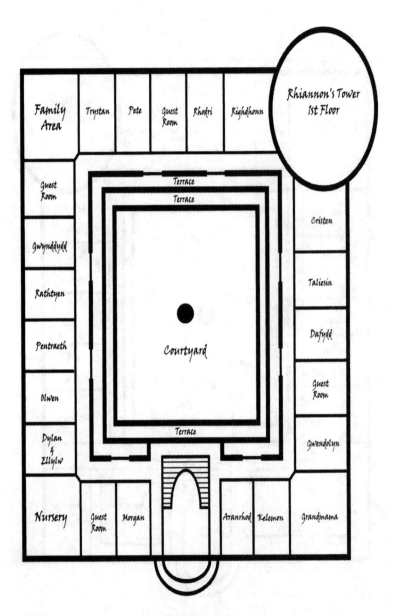

Beltene House - 3rd Floor
Sevyrn Michigan

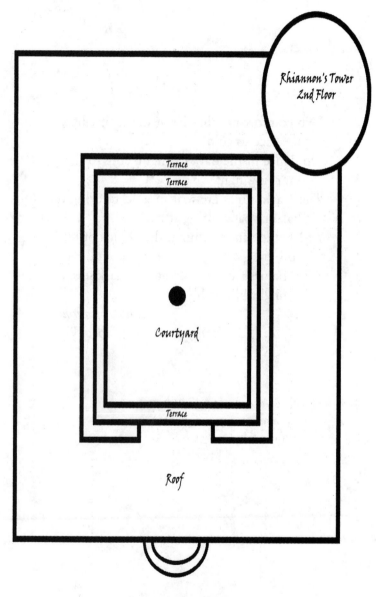

Rhiannon's Tower
2nd Floor

Terrace

Terrace

Courtyard

Terrace

Roof

Beltene House - 4th Floor
Sevyrn Michigan

"No comfort has the fire at night that lights
the face so cold.
Oh dance in the dark of night, sing to the
morning light.
The magic runes are writ in gold to bring the
balance back. Bring it back.
At last the sun is shining, the clouds of blue
roll by.
With flames from the dragon of darkness, the
sunlight blinds his eyes."

—*Battle of Evermore*
—Jimmy Page and Robert Plant

Chapter One

Tuesday, just before midnight

"Brennen County Sheriff's Department. What?" Rachel Conwy's rough voice came across the phone lines with all the sensitivity of a Mack truck at full throttle.

"Rachel, it's Rhiannon ..." I began. The knowledge that was making my stomach roll and the muscles across my back tighten hovered over my shoulder like a perverted guardian angel.

"Good Lord, what the hell do you want?"

I closed my eyes and counted to ten to hold down my anger. I reminded myself that she couldn't possibly know why I was calling and was only behaving in her normal manner.

"Well?" she prodded. "What is it you think we should be doing for you?"

The residents of Brennen County, myself included, call our local sheriff's department only as a last resort. Rachel has been the dispatcher since before I was born and she not only hates to answer the telephone, she feels it's her right to interrogate anyone silly enough to call.

Unfortunately, ever since I inherited my brother's position six months ago, I've been obliged to deal with the office instead of beeping a deputy, like everyone else. This means I am forced to talk to Rachel. I'm not one of her favorite people for a number of reasons, up to and including her inexplicable fondness for my cousin Trystan and my perceived persecution of said cousin.

"I'm calling because—"

"Because you're a nuisance," she interrupted.

"I found a body," I finished, making a concerted effort not to visualize the state of the body I'd found. It was a dismal effort at best and I closed my eyes as a shudder rippled through me.

"Do you know what time it is?" she asked, unfazed.

"It's quarter to twelve." Like it mattered when I called. It could have been high noon instead of midnight and her response would have been the same.

"Too late to be fooling around with any kind of nonsense."

"I found a body," I repeated, hopping up on Sam's checkout counter, prepared to spend a long time getting through to a real member of the police department.

A 911-emergency system was just what Brennen County needed. Provided, of course, that our sheriff chose not to give Rachel any part of it and allowed the State Police in Negaunee to run it.

"A body?" She sounded skeptical. "What kind of body?"

"A dead one."

"I'm not amused, Missy."

"Neither am I. It's cluttering up my woods." The plan was obvious. Our sheriff didn't intend to ever retire Rachel because she kept crank calls to a minimum. Perhaps we could rent her out to other needy police departments.

"And just how did *you* manage to find a dead body?"

I rubbed my eyes and wished we could gloss over this part. "I tripped over it."

"That doesn't surprise me," she snapped. "You walk around with your head in the clouds long enough, you're bound to trip over something."

I ignored the "head in the clouds" crack. "It was under the ferns, except for an arm stuck out into the path. Could you please send someone over?" I asked, trying to ignore Sam, who was enjoying my side of the conversation.

"We could have cornered Bonnie and Clyde in the bait room and it would still take hours to convince her to send someone over," he laughed, not quite *sotto voce*.

"Underbrush?" she questioned.

"Yeah. It's in the woods between the house and Sam's."

"And where are you?"

"Sam's." Sam's Black Abbey was our local I-carry-one-of-everything store. Everything included a soft ice cream machine and an ATM machine, my personal favorites.

"What are you doing at Sam's?"

"I came over for some ice cream." I am quite sure real dispatchers do not discuss trivialities with people trying to report crimes. I'm sure they merely take the information, send the police out and let them handle the interrogation.

"Humph," Rachel sniffed. "As if Indeg wouldn't have ice cream in the house."

"I *know* Indeg has ice cream in the house. She even keeps cartons of Deep Chocolate Fudge Häagen-Dazs in the freezer for me. But she's not installed a soft ice cream machine in the kitchen yet. I wanted a cone," I explained, knowing as I spoke that I'd get a faster response if I went outside and discussed the situation with one of the maple trees.

"Installing one of those machines would serve no purpose other than to spoil an already thoroughly spoiled woman."

I was the thoroughly spoiled woman in question. Doggedly, I continued my quest to have someone official respond to my call. "Anyway, I came over to have a cone and on my way back, I tripped over this thing. I thought it was a branch, but it turned out to be an arm."

"You always were klutzy."

There are definite disadvantages to living in a small town where everyone knows you, I thought.

"Are you sure it's a dead body?" she continued.

"Yes, Rachel, I'm sure he's dead." I shuddered anew as, unbidden, my mind called forth an image of the man lying across the path with a beetle crawling out of his mouth.

"You're not a doctor, you know."

"No, I'm not," I said, seeing a possible way to speed up the inquisition. "Perhaps you should send Doc Hellers over here to check him out."

"Ha! As if I didn't know he was the County Medical Examiner."

Well, one more failed attempt. "Could you please send someone over here? I'm not thrilled at having this body in my woods and I want them to get it out of there."

"Just how did this dead body get into your woods?"

"Am I Sherlock Holmes?" I lost my patience; Sam lost control. "I haven't a clue. That's why I retraced my steps here, to Sam's, to call Brennen County's Finest. That's what you all get paid for. I have every faith and confidence that Lige and the boys will figure it out."

There was no response.

Stunned, I held the phone out and looked at it before shaking it and putting it back to my ear. A low murmur was all I could hear.

"Rachel?"

Nothing.

"Rachel?"

"All right," she snapped, not to me.

"Rachel?"

"Someone will be over." Her tone told me somebody had cut her fun short and I wondered just who'd had the balls to even attempt it. The fact that he'd succeeded was mind boggling. With the exception of certain members of my family, the only people in the county more dangerous than Rachel to cross were the Hathaway sisters. And three more terrifying little old ladies you've never seen.

An abrupt click followed by silence was my only indication that her performance had ended.

"You're a lot of help," I told Sam as he leaned weakly against the ice cream cooler.

"Don't you just love talking to Rachel?" he asked, trying to stop laughing and catch his breath.

"It's one of my favorite pastimes," I grumbled. "She never sleeps, you know. I can call at any hour, she always answers. Do you know she keeps track of how many times I call per day, per week and per month? Like I instigate these incidents just to irritate her. Lord and Lady, there's a bloody dead body out in my woods and she spends the better part of ten minutes interrogating me instead of sending someone over. I think we need to retire her."

"Breathe, Sam." His wife joined us, frowning at her husband as he slid down the cooler to sit on the floor. "I thought you'd already headed back to your tower, Rhi."

"I did," I admitted. "But I ran into a problem."

"It must be quite a problem if you decided to call the sheriff's department. Another demented fan?" Lesley Anne Benedict put her hands on her hips and frowned at her limp husband. She looked over at me as I shook my head. "So what kind of a problem are we talking about?"

"I tripped over a dead body on my way home."

She looked sharply at me. "What?"

I wrapped my arms around myself and nodded. "About three hundred yards into the woods."

"Who is it?"

"I haven't a clue; I've never seen him before."

"Did Rachel finally break down and agree to send someone out?"

"Finally. Although, the gods only know when they'll get here. Sam enjoyed my end of the conversation immensely."

"He is amused by the strangest things," she agreed.

From my vantage point on the counter, I had a clear view of the corner of Llanthony and Black Abbey roads, the direction from which help had to come. I drummed my fingernails on the counter. They couldn't get here soon enough to suit me.

Henry Branton emerged from the bait room of the store and laid his purchases on the counter. Henry works for Superior Deliveries in Marquette and lives in a small cottage down Black Abbey Road. He'd arrived at the store shortly after I had.

Lesley added up his purchases, which ranged from Pepsi to nightcrawlers. "Seven forty-nine, Henry."

"Is there a problem, Rhi?" he asked, passing Lesley a ten.

"I found a body over in the woods. I'm waiting for the posse to arrive."

He frowned. "How did a body get into your woods?"

Shrugging, I said, "Who knows? Cris and Grandmama are the experts, I'll let them figure it out."

"They'll not be happy," Lesley said as she handed Henry his change and bagged his purchases.

"Tell me about it."

Henry patted my shoulder. "But they will figure it out, Rhi."

"I hope so."

"They will. Goodnight, Rhi, Lesley."

"Goodnight, Henry," Lesley answered.

"'Night." I checked my watch as the door wheezed shut behind him. "Where are they?"

"It's late, Rhi. Give them a chance to get out of bed."

"They don't get paid to sleep," I grumbled.

Two Chevrolet Blazers painted in Brennen County's colors, one Chevrolet half-ton pickup, and one plain, ordinary car finally slid into the parking lot, lights flashing and sirens wailing.

All this for the first suspicious death in the county since Old Man Morrison (Lesley's father) shot his wife of forty years at the annual Hathaway family reunion fifteen years ago. She'd given him twelve children and a constant stream of inane chatter. Her death was classified as justifiable homicide and considered a great blessing to him and the children. The Hathaway Sisters rated it the second best reunion to date.

I continued to wait on the counter. The body had been long past needing any assistance, other than transportation out of my woods, when I found it. I didn't like the implications that the appearance of this body brought to mind. I was fairly confident that Lige and the boys would come to the same conclusions and they weren't going to be any happier than I was.

And all of us could most certainly do without the flack this was going to stir up. Although, with any luck, the boys would be able to keep the hubbub over the body down to a low roar and the press, especially the tabloids, would miss the whole thing.

I counted bodies as they approached. Lige, our sheriff; Doc Hellers, local doctor and County Medical Examiner; Detective Sergeant Eric Davidson, the entire forensics department; Officers Tom Dalton and Marilyn Hunter; State Police Investigator Lucas St. John and—

And I didn't know the blond walking beside Luke. I frowned, irritated that I hadn't heard about the newest acquisition of the sheriff's department. News usually travels quite fast around here.

"Les, who's the blond guy?"

Oh Lord, I thought as a look of exasperation came over her face, *I should have opted for Häagen D* *äzs and never left my tower.*

The irascible guardian angel on my shoulder chuckled while my stomach lurched.

"Oh, Rhi," she began, but never finished because the troops were upon us.

"Lige," I greeted our sheriff warily, keeping an eye on the blond.

"Rhiannon." He returned my greeting with a weariness that set my already unsettled nerves on edge.

"There's a dead body in my woods," I complained.

"Is there now?"

"Yes, there is." I folded my arms and waited.

He sighed. "I suppose if anyone in the county was going to find a corpse, it would have to be you."

"Look—" I started, rising to his implied complaint. After all, it isn't my fault Sevyrn seems to be a magnet for every lunatic in the Midwest. Not entirely.

"Tell me about this body," he interrupted before I could get into my usual tirade on the irresponsibility of tabloid journalists.

"Why don't you just go and look at it?" I countered.

"Fine, let's go."

Wonderful, I thought, *I get to give them a guided tour. Here we have the Beltene Haunted Forest, filled with wonderful old trees, wailing spooks, a beautiful view of Lake Superior and, oh by the way, a dead body draped across one of the paths.*

"Well?" He crooked a finger at me. "In this life."

Resigned, I slipped off the counter and started toward the door, only to be halted in midstride as the blond grabbed my shoulder and said, "Wait a minute."

"Excuse me?" I frowned at the hand on my shoulder.

"We need to get some information from you first."

Information?

Fascinated, I watched as he pulled a small notebook from his pocket. "What's your name?"

I leaned back against the counter. "My name?"

"Yes, your name."

New police procedures? Not that I was particularly familiar with the old procedures, but my name? I looked from the blond to Lige, then shook my head slightly and decided the polite thing to do was to comply. "My name is Rhiannon Argadnel Beltene."

"Please spell it."

I obliged, in a speed suitable for my three-year-old god-child.

"Your address?"

"Beltene House. How long have you been in town?"

He ignored me. "The address of Beltene House?"

"You can't miss it. It's the stone mansion on the Superior side of Llanthony Road. You should have passed it on your way here."

He frowned. "You don't know your own street address?"

"Of course I know my street address. I'm just surprised that you don't." As an icy stare bored into me, I relented. "One hundred Llanthony Road."

"Your occupation?"

"Why?" My occupation has been a tender spot for more years than I cared to think about.

"For the records."

"I'm in more than enough records, thank you very much. Can we get on with this?"

"Are you refusing to assist us in this investigation?"

"No, I'm refusing to indulge in small talk while there's a dead body in my woods." I was glad to see the boys had all kicked back to watch me chat with their new brother.

"In *your* woods?" It was a chorus. The blond and I both looked at them.

"Didn't Rachel tell you? It's in the woods about three

hundred yards down the path from here," I explained, sidling away from the blond. "I tripped over it."

"In those woods?" St. John pointed out the window.

"Those are the ones in question," I agreed.

"But, Rhi, how did—" Eric began.

"Hold it!" bellowed the blond.

I turned slowly to face him, putting my hands on my hips. "Who are you?" I inquired, in as polite a tone as I could manage.

"I'm the new sheriff."

I couldn't have missed another election; it wasn't the right time of year for an election. The last one I remembered was the school millage and that was weeks ago.

I peered at Lige. "Are you going somewhere?"

He sighed. "I'm retiring, Rhi."

Lige Williams had been sheriff all of my life. I was amazed that no one had mentioned his retirement—or his replacement.

"You're not waiting until the end of your term?"

"Nope. With Katie Sue feeling the cold the way she does now, after her heart surgery, we decided not to wait it out. There're two years left to my term. Midterm vacancies are filled by appointment."

I narrowed my eyes. "Who makes the appointment?"

"Legally, it's the responsibility of the probate judge, the county clerk and the prosecuting attorney. And, of course, here in Brennan County, we also run their choice past the mayor, the county commissioners and the Beltene."

"Oh." Our new sheriff was tall and blond and a stranger. I couldn't believe that they'd given the job to a perfect stranger.

"Rhiannon?"

I stared blankly at Lige as the full impact of what he'd just said washed over me. "Wait a minute. Are you telling me Morfudd, Conall, Tangwen, Rhan and *my father* hired this man?" The smug looks across the store confirmed my fears.

"That's just about enough," our new sheriff interrupted.

I raised an eyebrow at his tone. "I beg your pardon?"

"It doesn't matter who hired me. You reported a dead body. Correct?"

"That's what I reported."

"Are you sure the victim is dead?"

"Yes."

"You don't believe he died of natural causes, do you?"

"Well, no—"

"Then we have a crime to investigate and we need to get to it."

"That's what I've been trying to tell you."

He turned to Lige. "Do you know the location she's been talking about?"

"More or less."

"Good. Then we needn't subject her to another viewing of the corpse. She can stay here and give a statement to Officer Hunter while we go and look at this body of hers."

"I don't think so," I disagreed.

He stopped me with a look. "Do you want to see the corpse again?"

"Of course not." I shuddered. "It's just—"

"Good. Let's go." He got out the door before realizing no one was behind him.

"Is there a problem?" he asked in an even tone after rejoining us.

"That particular section of forest is commonly held to be haunted."

A blank look glazed his eyes.

"You need to have a Beltene accompany you." I looked around and spread my arms wide. "And I seem to be the only one available."

"You don't expect me to believe that kind of superstitious nonsense, do you?" he asked.

I shrugged. "I suppose not, but do you really want to risk it?"

"Look," Eric tried to explain. "It might all be superstitious nonsense, but weird shit happens to people who wander into those woods without a Beltene."

"Really?" the blond drawled. "Does this mean that you don't intend to investigate this crime unless this young lady accompanies you?"

"I'd prefer someone in the family—"

"Do you enjoy being employed?"

"Now, wait just a minute," I began.

"This does not involve you."

"Perhaps I could be of assistance?" Dylan asked.

Everyone, including our new sheriff and myself, jumped. Dylan's greatest joy is his ability to appear next to someone, scaring them out of several years' growth.

"Who are you?" the new sheriff asked, after catching his breath.

"Dylan Gwynedd Beltene, at your service." His bow was elegant as his shoulder-length dark hair swept forward across his face. "You must be Sheriff Daniel L. Thorpe."

"Yes." Sheriff Thorpe looked relieved to be speaking with someone whom he believed would be able to help him.

"What's the 'L' stand for?" I asked, my curiosity getting the better of me.

"Lincoln," he answered automatically, then frowned at me.

"Daniel Lincoln Thorpe." I considered him for a long moment. "English Saxon," I sniffed.

"Your sister found a dead body in the woods." Sheriff Thorpe came to the conclusion that since Dylan and I both had the same last name and were dark-haired and dark-skinned that we were closely related. "It's necessary for us to get to it. However, there seems to be a popular local myth, which incorporates these woods, ghosts, and a need for a member of your family to escort visitors. It's a grand way to keep trespassers out, but more than just children believe it." His gaze swept over Eric.

Dylan spun to face me. "You found a what?"

"Cousin," I said at our new sheriff. Dylan spends far too much time with Trystan for me to be willing to let that assumption ride.

"What?"

"Dylan's my cousin, not my brother."

"Rhiannon," Dylan said. "You found a what?"

"There's a dead body in the woods, about three hundred yards from the road. I've been trying to light a fire under these police officers to get them out there."

"In *our* woods?"

"You didn't come straight here from the house or else you would've tripped over him. He's sprawled across the path."

"In *our* woods?" Dylan repeated. There were good reasons for his surprise; we don't encourage the haunted theory for nothing.

"Rhiannon," Luke St. John interrupted.

I took several steps closer to the state policeman. "Luke. I didn't expect to see you tonight."

"I was on my way home when I heard the call, so I radioed into the office and volunteered to swing by. Eric's good, but we thought assistance in a murder case was in line."

"*Murder?*" I yelped.

His gaze was serene as he watched me. "You've managed to tell us the body's male, dead, unfamiliar and in your woods. I'm quite proud of you. But none of us really believed you'd have called the sheriff's department for a heart attack."

"Oh."

"Now, we've gotten a bit sidetracked here, so I think you should just take us out to where you found the body and when we get there, you can tell us what's bothering you."

"Oh."

He opened the door and gestured toward the woods. "Come on."

I left Sam's and started across the parking lot. Eric ran into me as I stopped short in response to Lige's shouted command that I was to wait while they collected their equipment.

"Goddamn it, Rhiannon," Eric growled.

"Watch where you're going," I snapped, putting my feet back into my tennis shoes.

"Next time put your brake lights on," muttered one of my lifelong bosom companions.

I made a rude noise and disappeared back into Sam's, returning moments later with my ATM card clutched in my hand.

Lige shook his head. "Are you still carrying that damned thing in your back pocket?"

"Do you see anywhere else I could carry it?"

"She leaves that blasted card all over the county," Lige muttered to Daniel Thorpe.

"I do not."

"Who called last week and wanted to know if their ATM card had been turned in?"

"I called Merlin."

"Did you or did you not lose it?"

"I temporarily misplaced it," I qualified.

"Elise sent Gray over to the bank with it."

"Okay, so I left it at the Gypsy Witch. Shoot me."

"The thought has crossed my mind," Lige grumbled.

I crossed my arms and eyed our sheriff. "Wonderful. Is it at all possible to get this show on the road? I've got things to do, so if you all will just follow me, I'll take you to the body and you can do all the weird ritualistic nonsense that sets your wee little hearts on fire."

Not one of them paid the least bit of attention to me.

Chapter Two

Tuesday, just after midnight

Eric, Luke and Doc took their time gathering the equipment they intended to use. I returned one last time to Sam's for another ice cream cone before he closed for the night.

The woods in question is a small three hundred-acre plot of virgin trees. The family had chosen to keep the forest immediately surrounding Beltene House intact and private, bordering it with a three-foot stone wall. I sat on the wall eating my ice cream while I waited for the deputies to collect their equipment so they could come look at the body.

"Do you know who it is?" Tom asked as he joined me, our new sheriff close behind.

"No." That was really bothering me.

Tom frowned. "What would a perfect stranger be doing in here?"

I shrugged. "I don't know. It's not like we have a great deal of trouble with strangers wandering around on our property."

"The haunted forest," our new sheriff interjected.

I raised a shoulder, then dropped it. There wasn't any way for me to explain our beliefs about this particular section of forest to him.

We waited in not-so-companionable silence for the rest of the officers to join us.

When they did, I waited until everyone, except Marilyn who got sent back to the office for something they'd forgotten, had crossed over before relinquishing my seat. Then I led them into the forest.

The moonlight filtering through the trees reduced the men, either in uniform or dressed in dark colors, to mere moon-dappled shadows, flitting along the path behind me. I, on the other hand, was visible at fifty paces. My Reeboks were hot pink, my Aerosmith T-shirt was a vivid shade of blue and if jeans are valued by the number of holes they contain, then this pair was worth several thousand dollars.

Rhan had pointed out, not two hours earlier, that my attire was inappropriate for someone of my age, position and marital status. I'm thirty-two, I didn't want to be the Beltene and I'm single. None of which pleased Rhan or the rest of my family.

I stopped several yards from the body, waved a hand at it and announced, "It's all yours."

The men circled the body like sharks coming in for the kill. Finally, after setting up portable lights, taking an incredible number of pictures, picking up numerous invisible objects and taking more notes than I'd ever seen any of them write, Lige motioned for Doc to begin his initial examination.

I watched as the troops scrabbled around in the under-brush until Doc looked over his shoulder and muttered some-thing to Luke.

The state policeman squatted next to the body and lis-tened intently to the medical examiner.

I shifted nervously as they both turned to look at me. I should have gotten out while the getting was good instead of hanging around to watch the guys do their thing.

Luke's gaze returned to the body for a moment, then swept over the area before returning to me. With a shake of his head, he stood and waved me over. "Okay, what happened?"

"I was walking along the path and I tripped." I stood with my back to the body and kept my gaze firmly on Luke's hands. I'd already seen more of this body than I cared to and if I was watching Luke take notes, I wasn't looking down at the body trying to figure out just what is lacking in death that made a body look so compressed and lifeless. "I could go home and type this up for you."

"Just answer the question."

"I tripped, fell flat on my face, and ripped my jeans."

"I don't know how you can tell," Luke muttered.

"It's easy." I bent over and fingered a hole in the vicinity of my knee. "It's this hole right here. I think."

"Never mind, continue."

"Well, I hadn't been paying too much attention. I'd just been down the path less than an hour earlier and there hadn't been anything in the way. Nor had there been much wind. I got up and came back, looking for the branch I'd fallen over. But it wasn't a branch, it was his arm, kind of flung across the path. I touched his wrist and he felt cold. Most of his body was back under the ferns—"

"Sweet Jesus, Rhi, you moved him?" Eric yelped.

"Well, of course I moved him."

"She moved him," he muttered to Luke.

"I didn't think—"

"That much is obvious." Sheriff Thorpe's voice came from behind me.

I cursed in Gaelic before spinning to face him, adrenaline racing. "What the bloody hell are you talking about?"

"A little jumpy, Rhi?" Dylan asked as he passed by.

"You said you didn't think," the sheriff answered. "I simply agreed with you."

"I wasn't sure he was dead when I moved him. Lord and Lady, do you think I'd deliberately touch a dead body?"

Sheriff Thorpe picked up the interrogation. "You said his arm was cold."

"It was, but how the bloody hell was I to know he was

dead? I thought he might just be suffering from hypothermia. It is September and we've already had our first frost. I certainly couldn't do anything to help while he was stuffed under the ferns."

"Uh-huh."

"So I pulled him out to look at him."

"Wait a minute." Sheriff Thorpe stopped my explanation. He walked to the body and looked it over carefully. It was male; around six feet tall and had probably led a fairly sedentary life because he was about fifty pounds overweight.

Then he turned and looked me over carefully. I'm female; around five foot eight inches tall and I walk everywhere to keep from being fifty pounds overweight.

"How'd you move him?"

"I pulled him out of the underbrush."

"How?" he persisted.

I frowned. "I pulled him."

"How? He outweighs you by a good hundred pounds."

"Oh. Like this." Without thinking, I reached down, grabbed the body's outflung wrists, braced my feet and leaned backward. The body obligingly moved several inches. "See."

The groan that swept around the forest, if heard, would have added a great deal of fuel to the legend of the haunted Beltene Forest.

"Rhiannon Argadnel Beltene!" Lige yelled.

"What?" Startled, I looked down. Dropping the wrists of the dead man, I took several quick steps back and rubbed my hands on my jeans before sliding them into my pockets. "Oh shit, I'm sorry."

"Sorry? *Sorry?*"

"I don't think it really matters." To my amazement, it was Daniel Thorpe who came to my rescue.

"What?"

"She'd already pulled it out from under the ferns. A few more inches is a moot point."

"I suppose," Lige agreed. Pointing a finger in my direction, he instructed, "You keep your hands in your pockets. Don't touch anything else. Do you understand?"

"Yes." I studied the ground.

Lige has even less patience than I do, so it was only a matter of seconds before he snapped, "I said not to touch anything, I didn't say to quit telling us what happened."

I took a moment to collect my thoughts and remember where I'd been in my story when we'd gotten sidetracked. "I pulled him out onto the path. Once I had him out here, I could tell he was long past any help I could give him. He wasn't breathing, his skin was waxy and . . ." I debated how to continue, opting for as little as possible, "I went back to Sam's and called you."

"About what time would you say you found the body?"

"Eleven-thirtyish. I was talking to Rachel about a quarter 'til twelve."

"And it wasn't here when you went to Sam's?"

"Not draped across the path."

"What time did you get to Sam's?" Sheriff Thorpe asked.

"Which time?"

"The first time."

"About a quarter 'til eleven."

"Was anyone there?"

"Just Sam and Les," I answered. "Well, I'm sure the kids were over in the house, but they were probably asleep."

"No one else?"

"Nope. Just me."

"What did you do?"

"Used the ATM machine and got an ice cream cone."

"The ATM machine?"

Eric laughed. "Sam used to keep a credit account for Rhi, but when Keltia Bank started using ATM machines, he had one installed in the store so he could make Rhi use it. He says it's a hell of a lot less trouble than keeping track of how many ice cream cones she's eaten."

Sheriff Thorpe raised an eyebrow and looked at Luke and Lige.

Luke shook his head. "Anything else, Rhi?"

"I thought it was a joke at first."

Daniel Lincoln Thorpe raised both his eyebrows. "A joke?"

"How was I supposed to know it was a real dead body?" I snapped, angry with myself for sending the conversation in a direction I'd intended to avoid. "We haven't had a violent death in the county since I was sixteen."

"Uh-huh."

"You may have seen a lot of dead bodies in your time, Sheriff Thorpe, but I can assure you, it's an uncommon sight in Brennen County."

"One I would have preferred to remain an uncommon sight, Ms. Beltene," he returned.

"Well, I certainly didn't go out of my way to get you one as a Welcoming gift."

"Rhiannon." Luke's quiet intervention stilled my words. "Let's get back on track. You thought it was a joke." Our new sheriff thoughtfully watched the exchange between Luke and me. "Come on, Rhi. I know you weren't expecting this, so just tell us what we need to know and you can go back to your tower."

Jerkily, I nodded. He was right about my not expecting to find a body. I hadn't expected a dead body for more reasons than our new sheriff could possibly comprehend. "I really did think someone was playing a joke on me. It's been known to happen. Well, not with bodies, but . . ." My voice died off and

I made an effort to quit babbling and bring my end of the conversation back on track. "Once I got him out onto the path, I could see it wasn't a joke and I called in the troops."

"Who would have carried out this kind of joke?"

A question only an outsider would ask.

Trystan, I thought, as I looked askance at Daniel Thorpe and frantically cast about for a suitable answer. Failing to find one, I remained silent.

"I see. Why were you out so late?"

"It's not late."

Sheriff Thorpe looked at his watch. "It's twelve-thirty. Most people consider that late."

"I don't."

"Okay." The sheriff checked his notes. "What did you do for about an hour at Sam's?"

"Ate my ice cream, hassled Sam, chatted up Henry. Normal things."

"Henry, who's Henry? You didn't mention any Henry before."

"Lord and Lady, I forgot all about Henry. Henry Branton. He got to Sam's about quarter after eleven. Stopped to pick up a few things, including nightcrawlers."

Sheriff Thorpe frowned at me and continued, "Did you see him drive up?"

"Yes."

"From which direction?"

"Llanthony Road."

"What does he drive?"

"One of those mini-vans."

"Do you know what kind?"

"It's green."

Luke sighed as Sheriff Thorpe continued his questioning. "Could he have dropped the body off before coming into the store?"

I stared at him for a moment. "Henry?" I managed before starting to laugh.

He waited me out. "Could he?"

"He came directly into the store from his car," I answered, still chuckling.

"Did you see which way he turned off Llanthony Road?"

"From Marquette." I glanced round at the others, who avoided meeting my eyes. "But let's get real here. Henry's a repatriated Gwynn-O'Keefe."

Before I got Sheriff Thorpe side-tracked into a discussion of the Gwynn-O'Keefe's, Lige interjected, "I'll explain about them later, Dan. But I do agree with Rhi, it's unlikely Henry is the killer."

Sheriff Thorpe acknowledged Lige's comment with a nod, then continued, "As the crow flies, how far away is one hundred Llanthony Road?"

I contemplated the concept of distance.

"It's about half a mile," Dylan answered.

"Thank you," Sheriff Thorpe said.

"You know that voodoo doll Jody has that looks just like you?" My question drew a sharp glance from our new sheriff.

"He does not have a voodoo doll that looks like me," my cousin returned.

"He will after I ask him to make one," I said. Then I answered the sheriff's question, "The house is half a mile from Sam's. Is there a purpose to this questioning? Should I be looking for an alibi?"

"I was trying to learn what you were doing out here, in the middle of the night, wandering around in a *haunted forest*," Sheriff Thorpe said. "I do not, at this point, suspect you of anything other than being deliberately obstructive."

"Obstructive? How could I be obstructive? All I did was go out for ice cream."

"At this time of the night?" He looked politely skeptical.

I looked up at the gently moving trees and focused on patience. "Surely I'm not the only person in the world to leave their home in the depths of the night in search of soft ice cream. Lord and Lady, Sam is open later than the Dairy Queen. Okay?"

"While Doc finishes his examination, Rhi, why don't you tell us what it is that's bothering you about this body," Luke said.

"It's dead."

"Besides that."

"It's in my woods."

"Besides that."

"Nothing."

"Rhiannon."

I frowned up at him. "What?"

"Just tell us."

I scuffled my feet in the mulch and counted the eyelets on my Reeboks.

"Spit it out, Rhi."

Taking a deep breath, I said, "When I pulled him out of the ferns, his head sort of tipped to one side and there were these ... marks on his neck."

"What kind of marks?" Sheriff Thorpe took up the prompting as he peered toward the body.

"Well, they were sort of ..." I floundered as the expression on his face darkened.

"What? What were they? Cuts, scratches, what?"

"It looked more like a couple of holes."

"Was there any blood that you could see?"

"There didn't appear to be any," I answered. "In fact, there didn't seem to be any at all."

"Well, since I doubt he was killed here, I don't expect

there'd be much blood lying around. We'll do a thorough check in the morning."

I blinked rapidly at him. He'd completely missed the point. Then, I caught Lige's glare from the corner of my eye. "It's not my fault," I protested.

"I never said it was your fault," he said.

"Why," our new sheriff asked, "would any of this be Ms. Beltene's fault?"

"Do you know what I do for a living?" I asked.

"No, you refused to tell me your occupation earlier, remember?"

"Oh, yeah, I did, didn't I?"

"Does your occupation have some relevance?"

"I wouldn't have brought it up if it didn't."

"Of course not." He sighed. "Well, I don't see what relevance it could possibly have, but why don't you tell me and let me decide for myself."

"I write vampire novels."

Knowing what I was going to say, everyone deserted me for Doc and the body.

"Vampire novels," he repeated.

"Yes."

"And that's supposed to have some sort of bearing in this case?"

"Yes."

"What?"

"I write vampire novels," I explained. "My first couple were under a pseudonym. They sold fairly well for a novice writer. Then, a journalist traced me down and the next thing I knew, my picture, name and address were printed in one of the tabloids. It was too good for the rest of them to pass up and within two weeks, I'd been in every tabloid magazine in the country. I gave up on the pseudonym and published under my own name after that, but I still end up in the tabloids once or twice a year. I haven't a clue what the attraction is." I stopped to breathe.

"That's nice, but—"

"I'm not finished," I said. "We are often visited by budding vampires, vampirettes, vampire hunters and other weirdos. You, as the long arm of the law, are sworn to uphold my right of protection from said weirdos. Normally, it's not too bad, except when I've been in the tabloids. Then I've been known to require your assistance as often as once or twice a week."

"Once or twice a—"

"Of course," I continued, wanting to get it all out in one burst. "It got really bad last year when I spent eight straight months in the tabloids. Every single bloody week for eight months. It was horrible. That's really when I started doing my wandering at night. Most of our visitors had a problem with going outside after dark and I must admit, after the first month or so, I did encourage Trys to be seen flitting about the night in his cape."

I had his undivided attention.

"So, when I found a body which appeared as though a vampire sucked on its neck, I assumed it was a joke."

He turned to look at Lige.

"Rhi and her visitors were on the bottom of my list since it's been fairly quiet recently. I don't think we've taken more than five or six calls from her this year. You could ask Rachel. I'm sure she'd know the exact number of times we've responded to Rhi's calls." Lige's grin did little to sooth his replacement.

"Jesus H. Christ," he muttered.

"Now there's an interesting notion," I said. "One could develop a theory concerning his arousal from the dead that could tie him into being—" Eric covered my mouth.

"This is the wrong time and wrong place for experimental theories, Rhi."

I wrinkled my nose at him. "Spoilsport."

"Usually," he agreed.

"You get used to it," I assured Sheriff Thorpe, patting his arm. "In the meantime, could we get this body out of my woods?"

He pulled himself together. "There are a large number of Beltenes in Brennen County, including the five who hired me. Your woods?"

"Well, yes. I'm the current owner of all the Beltene holdings."

"Why?"

"I'm the Beltene."

"*You're* the Beltene?" The incredulous tone in his voice didn't surprise me. It was merely a reflection of the view voiced around the county about my inheritance of the position.

"Unfortunately."

"Rhiannon!" The voices of the surrounding men merged into a stinging slap that silenced any further comments I might have had regarding my position.

I scowled indiscriminately around the area. "What?"

"Behave yourself," Lige scolded.

"Well, I—"

"That's enough," Dylan's words were soft in my ear. "You must be aware he's not Welcomed."

"Show us where you found the body before you moved it," Luke said.

Silently, I skirted around Daniel Lincoln Thorpe and swept back the ferns, showing them where I found the body.

"Jesus, Rhi," Eric grumbled. "You certainly know how to get into trouble."

"Me? Me? Get into trouble? Whatever would give you the idea I could possibly get into trouble?"

Eric looked up from his position in the underbrush and commented wryly, "All this innocence from the woman who decided we could surf on Lake Superior during a storm because the waves would be high enough?"

I laughed. "I think I'll plead the fifth. Where shall I send the blackmail money?"

"Rhi." Doc joined us.

"Yes?" I watched Sheriff Thorpe quarter the area, one more time, with a flashlight.

"How'd they get a body in here?"

"I haven't a clue. I've got to talk to Cris and Grandmama about it."

Doc shook his head. "I don't like this, Rhi. Not one little bit. You know what it's supposed to look like."

"Care to join me when I tell the rest of the family?"

Doc shuddered and crossed himself. "No, thank you. I'll just stay out here with murderers and corpses. It's safer. Besides, I'm sure everyone in the county will be able to hear Rhan."

"Chicken," I teased.

"I've seen him angry." He paused, darting a glance at our new sheriff. "Rhi, you do understand the purpose of this, don't you?"

"I don't even want to contemplate it."

The others joined us.

"Well?" Sheriff Thorpe asked Doc.

Doc gazed at the body for a long moment before speaking. "If you want the truth, I'd just as soon not speculate on any aspect of this death until after the autopsy."

"Why not?" Oddly enough, Sheriff Thorpe was the only one in the forest who didn't look perplexed or peeved over the medical examiner's reticence.

Doc sighed before grinning wryly. "That's as good as asking me to speculate. Okay, here goes. There isn't an apparent cause of death." He held up a hand to stem the flood of protest. "Incisions on the neck aside, there's no apparent cause of death. No stab wounds, no gunshot wounds. The cause of death will have to be determined in the lab."

"Ms. Beltene seems to think the body's been drained of its blood," Sheriff Thorpe said in a deceptively offhand tone.

"There is a definite lack of blood in the body," Doc agreed.

"Excuse me?"

"That's part of the problem. You'll note the lack of lividity."

"And?"

"And this body's been embalmed."

"Embalmed?" Lige burst out.

"Yep."

"How the hell did he get embalmed?" Tom's voice was hoarse with shock.

Doc shrugged. "That's the tricky part. This could be a body stolen from a funeral home or it could be a murder victim who's been embalmed."

"Are you saying he was alive when the embalming began?" Eric asked, a sick expression moving across his face.

"It's a possibility."

"How possible?" Sheriff Thorpe asked.

Marilyn, who had arrived with the extra equipment only minutes before, bolted into the underbrush and with a presence of mind I doubt I would have had, vomited outside the established crime perimeter.

I covered my mouth with both hands and closed my eyes in horror. Moments later, I opened them, hoping to stop my imagination from showing me what it thought a death by embalming would consist of.

Doc shrugged again.

"The marks on the neck?"

"They're consistent with embalming incisions."

I contemplated the new hole in the knee of my jeans as Daniel Thorpe's gaze fell on me.

"Are they consistent with an attack by a vampire?" There was a good five seconds of silence before he clapped a hand to his forehead and moaned, "Oh God, I can't believe I asked that."

A half smile flitted across Doc's face as he answered. "I've never been privy to a vampire attack, but if Rhi's descriptions are anything to go by, yes, they are consistent with a vampire attack."

"Don't be looking at me like that," I said as Thorpe continued to watch me. "I'm not a vampire. I only write about them."

"Embalmed," he muttered as Doc nodded agreement. "Embalmed. So where's the blood?"

"Generally speaking, after a body's embalmed, it gets flushed down into the sewer system."

"But if this body wasn't embalmed at a funeral home—then where's the blood, where was he embalmed and why would our killer have embalming equipment?"

There was a rush of conversation as a game plan for canvassing all the funeral homes in a 100-mile radius was discussed.

"So," Sheriff Thorpe summarized, "we have a body which is either stolen from a funeral home or murdered and embalmed by persons unknown and very probably all this was done simply to make it look like a vampire attacked it."

"That sums it up fairly well," Lige agreed.

I didn't like any of their conclusions. And I most definitely didn't want to be part of the conversation so, to eliminate any eye contact, I studied the toe of my Reebok. I should have sneaked away while they were engaged in arranging their funeral-home sweep.

"And it would appear, Ms. Beltene, that not only are you the local vampire expert, but you're the catalyst for all this."

I bit my lip and stuffed my hands deep into my pockets. "I will grant you the local vampire expert. That's what I write about. But a catalyst?" I shook my head.

Luke put his hand on my shoulder. "I think Dan's right, Rhi."

I continued to shake my head. "Catalyst for what?"

"We don't know yet," Sheriff Thorpe answered.

For once the forest, usually a place of comfort and peace, seemed to close in on me. "I have to go back to the house."

Lige and our new sheriff exchanged a look.

"Okay, Rhi," Lige said. "Go on back to the house. But you'll need to come down to the office tomorrow morning to sign a statement and we will need you to go over some vampire stuff with us."

"In the morning," I agreed, nodding.

I turned and headed toward my tower. It took every bit of control I had to walk. Every nerve I had was screaming to run. I didn't turn as I heard Dylan catch up with me. Nor did I turn as he left to follow the instructions I gave him.

Much as I wanted to go to my tower and hide until this situation had been resolved, I knew that my first order of business was to apprise the family of what was happening. A fair majority of the family was in Wales, but I could certainly start with those currently in residence. Trystan had been the only other person not in the house when I'd left earlier. Dylan was about the only person who had a chance of finding him at this time of night.

We were in trouble. We were most definitely in trouble.

Chapter Three

Wednesday, around two AM

Instead of entering the house through the tower door, I made the first executive decision of my six-month career as the Beltene and entered via the kitchen. If I was going to call a family meeting, there was a certain amount of etiquette I was required to follow; arranging for food and drink was only part of it. Of course, nothing I intended to do or say at this time of the night was going to endear myself to my family, but at least following tradition was going to get us off on the right foot.

Two of the older members of the household, sprawled comfortably in front of the fire, looked up as I breezed into the kitchen.

"Our beloved leader." Righdhonn saluted me lazily.

I spared a moment to roll my eyes at him.

Cristin frowned. "It's well past time for you to be settling into your position, Rhiannon."

Now was not the time for another debate on my reasons for not wanting to be the Beltene. "Jody," I yelled, looking around the huge room for the master of the kitchen.

In Beltene House, you're on your own for breakfast and lunch. There's always a wide variety of food and drink on hand. The cozy area between the kitchen itself and Jody's office has a fireplace and comfortable seating which encourages the family to gather there.

A long-standing family tradition dictates everyone's appearance at dinner. Buffet style is the only way to cope with a family the size of ours. Weekday dinners are served between six and eight with Sunday dinner being served promptly at two. The tradition provided more grist for Rhan's mill; I manage to join the family for dinner only about three times a week.

Jody appeared in the doorway of his office. "What is it now?"

"I'm calling a family meeting. We're going to meet in the library in half an hour. Could you please send some refreshments over?" Jody, a master chef who could work anywhere, used to play professional football. He's six-six, weighs two-forty and is a babalawo, a high priest of Santeria. And he would make me a voodoo doll of Dylan, if I asked.

Silence met my announcement.

Cris and Jody stared at me thoughtfully, while Righ moved smoothly from his reclined position to his feet in a move that was both sinuous and dangerous.

I shifted from foot to foot under their scrutiny. "I found a dead body in the woods."

Righ's hand strayed unconsciously to the gun he wore in a shoulder holster, loosening it. "Are you all right?"

"I'm fine." I answered automatically, knowing that they could see I wasn't all right.

"You called Lige and Dan?"

"They're out playing detective in the woods."

"Where?"

"They're about three hundred yards this side of Sam's."

"I'll be back," he said on his way out the door.

Cris put an arm around my shoulders and guided me to one of the couches. "Sit for a moment."

"Cris . . ."

"Not now, child. One telling will be enough. Are you sure you're all right?"

"As right as is possible under the circumstances. Lord and Lady, Cris, what am I going to do? I've barely attended family meetings, let alone run one. I can't believe I'm even attempting this."

"You'll do just fine."

"Rhan's bound to be deeply impressed."

"He doesn't bite."

"Hah!"

"Only a little and his bark is much, much worse than his bite." She hugged me. "I know the last six months have been difficult for you—"

"Difficult? Now there's an understatement. My only consolation has been that Rhan was even more shocked than I was by my inheritance and almost as displeased."

"He's very fond of you."

"I know he is." I still haven't figured out what his familial feeling for me had to do with my inheritance of an important community, family, and business position. "I'm quite fond of him, but we don't see eye to eye on how my responsibilities should be handled. He feels my new ones should take precedence over older, longstanding ones." I kissed her cheek. "Face it, Cris, I was the last person anyone expected to become the Beltene. I don't think even Rhodri considered who'd replace him when he laid the scepter down."

"I'm sure he didn't. It was his choice, however, and his time. Rhan will get over his pique and you, my dear, will become the finest protector we've ever had."

I looked askance at her. "Prophecy?"

"Grandmama should be in the library," she said, kissing the top of my head as she stood. "I'll collect everyone already abed."

"Jody?" I leaned on the counter, watching him prepare trays to take to the library.

"Prophecy," he answered. "And a truthful one by my sight."

"Wonderful," I muttered, leaving the kitchen.

Beltene House is huge; a three-story square with a court-yard in the center and a four-story tower gracing the southeast corner. It had been finished in 1796 with not only our large, extended family in mind, but as a fortress for the townspeople if the community came under attack.

I wound my way forlornly through the house to the library, wishing Dad was home instead of visiting Wales. I knew I wasn't up to handling the meeting or the problem.

The library, along with the ballroom and the chapel, occupies the front of the house. Its southwestern exposure provides exceptional light most of the day.

As promised, Grandmama was in the library. I paused in the doorway to study the head of Clan Beltene. Her determined spirit had taken our family into realms of impossibility and, at the same time, managed to keep us shrouded in obscurity.

"Come in, child, and shut the door. There's always been a draft in that hallway."

Smiling, I complied. But after I settled on the stool near her chair, my smile faded.

"What's the problem?" she asked.

"I found a body in the woods." I looked up at her, fear in my eyes. "It was staged to look like a vampire killed it and left for me to find."

She reached out to stroke my hair. "You called the sheriff's office?"

"Yes. Lige came out with the boys and Luke St. John. Righ went out there a few minutes ago."

"Good." She nodded. "Then the technicalities are being taken care of. You said it was made to look like a vampire killed it?"

"Actually, it had been embalmed, but with the blood having been removed and the two incisions on the neck it could be assumed that a vampire attacked it."

She raised an eyebrow. "No blood and incisions on the neck? That does sound as if Count Dracula might have passed by."

"Our new sheriff was less than pleased."

"I can imagine."

"I called a family meeting."

"That was sensible."

"I don't call anything this time of night, sensible." Rhan blew into the room like the thundercloud he resembled.

"She had cause."

The storm subsided under Grandmama's endorsement. "And the purpose in dragging everyone out of their beds?"

"I found a body."

"And this constitutes a reason to awaken the world?" he snapped, his tone acid; harshness being his preferred method of dealing with me over the last six months.

"It was a dead body and it was within the confines of the wall."

"Who was it?" Indeg asked, entering with her husband, Gwydre, and Rhan's wife, Tangwen.

"That's the really weird part. It's a stranger. I've never seen him before."

"How far past the wall?" Gwydre asked.

"Around three hundred yards."

"Impossible," Rhan growled.

"Right," I returned, throwing my hands up in the air. Defensiveness put an edge of sarcasm to my tone, one that I rarely unleashed on my family. "The sheriff's department and the state police have turned out for a dead body, which isn't really there."

"Enough." Grandmama's voice wasn't loud, but it did curtail both Rhan's response and my rebuttal.

"Can I assume you were over at Sam's?" Gwydre inquired.

"Yes."

"So the body is on the path?"

"Actually, only the arm was across the path when I found it. The rest of the body was under the ferns and it wasn't there when I went over to Sam's."

"Interesting," he mused and wandered across the library to the windows.

"How did someone get that far within the confines of the wall?" Rhan asked.

Grandmama shrugged. "We'll need more information before Cris, Gwydre and I can determine how it happened."

Rhan rubbed his chin. "So what's the catch? I agree there's reason for a family meeting, but I've not heard anything yet which makes it imperative we have it in the depths of the night."

I took a deep breath and strength from Grandmama's encouraging look. "A theory has been put forward that the body was deliberately set up to look like a vampire killed it."

"That's the most ridiculous thing I've ever heard," my younger brother, Daffyd, exclaimed as he entered the room with Rhodri, beating Rhan to the punch.

"Do you think I'm not aware of the touches of absurdity inherent here?" I asked, my temper slipping a mite.

"A vampire kill? Come on, Rhi, give me a break."

"I realize that finding a dead body isn't the most normal thing in this neck of the woods, and that finding one without blood is even more unusual. But trust me, I found a dead body which has been made to look like a vampire killed it."

"That's crazy!"

"My thoughts exactly," I snapped.

The remainder of the available family—except for Dylan, who was still tracking down Trystan, and Righ, who was still out with the cops—came in, ending the conversation. By the time Jody and his wife, Erin, brought in the trays he'd prepared, I was past ready to begin.

"When Dylan gets back from running Trys to earth, we can start," I said as Righ entered the room.

"This could be a long wait," my younger brother muttered.

"Let's hope not," Rhan said.

We were all settled in, food and drink in hand, when Dylan finally arrived, Trystan in tow. Trys was clearly unhappy about being dragged away from whatever he'd been up to. I let his glare slide off me as I waited for them to serve themselves before starting the meeting.

I stood as I began, "I think everyone is fairly well apprised of the problem ..."

"Hell, yes," Trystan muttered, slouched petulantly in his chair. "The problem is she's getting cold."

"Trystan Gwilym Beltene!" Rhan thundered.

Trys, obedient to his father as he was to no one else except Grandmama and Cris, straightened in his chair and sipped quietly from his wineglass.

"My apologies, Rhiannon, please continue," Rhan said in a reassuring tone. I was always in much better graces when his son was in the doghouse.

"Thanks." Nervously, I tapped my nails against the wineglass in my hand. "There are two major problems as I see it. The first is how did the murderer get the body past the wall? The second is the new sheriff."

Righdhonn chuckled. "Dan is impressed with you, *cariad*."

"Did they find anything new while you were out there?"

"No." He shook his head. "Nor could I find anything. He wasn't killed in the woods. Someone literally dropped him off and, whether they realized it or not, wall and wards aside, they managed to pick a nearly perfect spot to leave a body.

"The path is well traveled enough not to take footprints, but not enough that he'd have much fear of getting caught.

There weren't any tracks heading off into the woods in any direction off the path. I checked."

"So have they come up with a more realistic motive yet?" I asked.

"No." His tone was gentle. "I think the boys have the motive, such as it is, right."

I covered my eyes and groaned.

"Explain," Grandmama commanded.

"The body was embalmed, bloodless"—he empathized the word "bloodless" with air quotes, "and left on the path so Rhi could find it. It wouldn't take much investigation to find out she takes that path to Sam's almost every evening. They'd simply wait until she'd passed, drop the body and leave. With no one the wiser."

"But how did they manage to negate the wards enough to get three hundred yards in? Lord and Lady, Eric and Pete can't even get in that far." I looked at Cris.

She was shaking her head before I finished speaking. "They probably didn't do anything to the wards. There have always been loopholes in the wards and not much we can do to fix them. Especially in this case."

"The wards are there to protect us by discouraging entry into the woods surrounding the house," Gwydre elaborated.

Discourage? I suppose that was one way of putting it. The warding was established shortly after the 1785 uprising and its purpose is to guard us from attack.

The symptoms range from not wanting to continue any farther into the forest to finding it impossible to move and having severe visual and auditory hallucinations. A Welcomed member of the community generally experiences only mild auditory and/or visual hallucinations, hence the haunted forest myth.

"The problem is that a person whose single-minded purpose doesn't allow him to see anything off his direct path, would be unlikely to be affected by the wards," he finished.

The warding idea both worked and backfired. No one intending to harm us can enter the woods surrounding the house, but we're stuck with the haunted forest myth and the children of the community have spent the last couple of hundred years or so daring each other to cross the wall. They've had such a good time scaring each other that Grandmama refused to allow Cris to adjust the wards.

Of course, the Beltene children are immune to the effects, but that's never stopped us from daring our friends into entering the forest without us. Eric and Pete wouldn't speak to me for a week after I encouraged them to spend the night at our usual campsite without me.

"And this single-minded purpose," Grandmama picked up the thread, "would be focused not on harming us, for the wards would prevent that, but on gifting one of us."

"Meaning Rhiannon," Rhan said, glaring in my direction.

"That would be a reasonable assumption."

"Wonderful," I muttered. "What about the county wards?"

"Inapplicable," Cris said. "They're just a general sort of ward to make incompatible people uncomfortable enough not to spend a lot of time here."

"I hate to bring up more bad news," Righdhonn said, "But, all things considered, none of us see any reason to believe this is going to be a solo performance."

Cris finally voiced the question none of us wanted to ask. "Why?"

Righ sighed. "It's too neat, too specific, aimed too directly at Rhiannon, not to be part of a campaign to attract her attention. If he doesn't get the response he wants, why would he stop at only one? The expectation at the sheriff's department is that there'll be more bodies and each one we find will be more intense, more personal."

The strength seeped out of my legs and I dropped onto the stool next to Grandmama. She laid her hand on my head as I buried my face in my hands. "Lord and Lady."

I let her calmness soothe me before looking up. "This is going to attract the worst of the tabloids," I said, knowing this was the part my family really hated. "They're going to invade full force and if the killing does continue, we're going to have the real press joining them."

I didn't need to hear Rhan's mumbled comment to understand its context.

"I do not have to apologize to this family because some idiot of a journalist discovered my real name and address and decided I was a prime candidate for their cover," I said in an icy tone.

"You had to write," Trystan snarled.

"I appeased the family, Trystan, by using a pseudonym and was already into my third novel before I was unveiled in the tabloids. I seriously doubt the invasion would have ended simply because I quit writing."

"Not right away, but if you hadn't continued to write and given them more fuel for their—"

"People," Grandmama smoothly interrupted the long-standing disagreement. "The horse is out and it's a bit late to be trying to close the stable door. The issue is closed."

"Thank you," I said as Trys mumbled in the background. "Now, can I assume everyone here is aware there's a new sheriff in town?"

The communal sigh, which dusted the nearby books, didn't surprise me.

"Rhi, love," Rhodri said sympathetically, "There has been little else discussed around the county for the last three months."

I frowned. "I've been busy. I have a deadline in three weeks."

"We know, dear," Indeg said gently. "But you have to be keeping up with these things now that you're the Beltene."

"He's not a member of the community," I stated, more confidently than I felt. As the Beltene, I'm almost sure they have to notify me if someone's Welcomed into the community. In fact, I think I have to participate in the ceremony. I looked sternly at the county commissioner and the prosecuting attorney.

Neither Rhan nor Tangwen looked even a little guilty. "There wasn't anyone qualified in the community."

"What about Eric or Luke?"

"Neither one wanted the job."

"So what was the plan? To wait to see if he fit in, then Welcome him? Or what?"

"For the most part, that was the plan. He's been here a couple of weeks without any side effects. Prior to this, we'd figured to give it a couple of months and then Welcome him," Tangwen said.

"After all, no one will say anything until then, so we didn't feel it was that critical," Rhan explained. "Then again, no one expected a corpse to pop up. At least not one that appears to be ravaged by vampires."

"Very funny." Actually, it wasn't. Aside from the fact that someone had been murdered; it was the method in which he'd been killed, the location where he'd been left and the only motive we could attribute to him, which threatened my family's existence more than anything at any time in the last two hundred years.

"Lige has decided to pull Rhi in as a consultant," Righ interjected. "He wants her to bring everyone up to date on vampire lore and see if they can come up with any other motive for the murder. Aside, of course, from the prevalent one."

I studied the floor at my feet. With little effort, I could see my entire world crumbling in ruins. Grandmama's hand rested lightly on my shoulder and I lifted my head to look at the woman whose name I bore.

She finds it amusing when people say she looks good for her age: eighty-nine. Of course, since she fought in Boudica's army against the Romans in the mid-first century, she's quite a ways past eighty-nine. Her marriage to a royal prince, a druid priest, involved her in a barely remembered ritual in an attempt to save some of their Druidic ways. The ritual ended with Brenainn's death and Grandmama's acceptance of a new way of life.

One aspect of the ritual, which has had a long-reaching effect, bestowed an extended lifetime on Grandmama and her heirs. And heirs there would be; for at the time of the ritual, she was carrying Brenainn's son.

It would be several generations, however, before she offered extended life to one of her family. Nowadays, it's an open choice and currently, most of the family is changed. In fact, only Daffyd; Olwen; my younger sister, Aranrhod; and I were not.

One of the more unpopular things I've ever done (and one of the main reasons Rhan was against my appointment as the Beltene) was to refer to the family as vampiric. I thought the word expressed my family's peculiarities perfectly. Everyone else thought I'd lost my mind.

"I can't believe this is happening," I muttered.

"You'll do our new sheriff just fine," Tangwen assured me. I could feel Grandmama's chuckles through her hand on my shoulder.

They were matchmaking again. As the eldest unchanged family member, I am the Beltene, the family protector. In charge of all contact with the outside world, which consists of anyone outside the county and anyone living in the county but not Welcomed. Our new sheriff fell into both categories.

"What did you think of Daniel?" Rhan asked, far too casually.

"He's English," I replied, referring to his blood, not his citizenship. I'd placed his accent from somewhere in the southwest. I was also sure his qualifications had included intelligence, good looks and a lack of marital ties.

My unmarried state at the advanced age of thirty-two is a perpetual disappointment to my family and they amuse themselves by throwing eligible men in my direction. Olwen, still unmarried at twenty-seven, is due to get married on St. David's Day, next March. Daffyd at twenty-two still had plenty of time before they started throwing women at his feet.

"A large, fairly nice looking, ill-tempered, bad-mannered English Saxon," I elaborated. "Who's not Welcomed and might never be."

"He'll be Welcomed," Rhan said confidently.

"And just how is the sheriff's department going to be able to conduct this investigation, in a way that doesn't endanger us, with an Unwelcomed sheriff?" I asked, thinking we'd been in northern Michigan since 1780, survived an uprising in 1785 from among our own people and built a county full of illusionary protection only to lose it at the end of the twentieth century because we had a sheriff who couldn't protect us.

"Now, Rhi, Daniel is an intelligent man—"

"May the gods help us."

"And will be easy for you to work with," Tangwen finished.

"What if push comes to shove and we need him Welcomed?"

"I went to great lengths to recruit someone I thought would fit in, Rhiannon. Daniel has the potential to fit in exceptionally well. He's by no means stupid and he has the vision to accept our Welcoming without being emotionally attached to a member of the community," Rhan said.

"He'll be fine," Cris said from the corner where she and Gwydre were discussing the warding.

"Lord and Lady," I moaned.

"More than fine and Welcomed before his time." She returned to her discussion.

"Are we finished?" Morfudd, our county clerk, asked.

"Well, we haven't found any werewolves or covens in the neighborhood yet, so I suppose we are."

Rhodri gave me a quick hug as he returned to the depths of his laboratory with Pentraeth. Soon, Grandmama, Cris, Righdhonn and I were the only ones left in the library.

"There are a couple more things, Rhi," Righdhonn said.

My sigh wasn't nearly powerful enough to dust any of the books.

"The Gwynn-O'Keefe's."

"Oh, sweet Jesus." I dropped my head into Grandmama's lap. "Diuran doesn't like me."

"Diuran doesn't like anyone," he returned.

"I suppose it is necessary for someone to check on them."

"It is."

"Anything else?"

"If this is going to get as nasty as I think it is, I don't think the sheriff's department is going to want to try to keep track of all their information by hand. They're going to be needing a computer and I know the courthouse, hospital and the Metalworks don't have any free."

The Metalworks, more formally known as Beltene Woodcarving and Metalworking, is the family business.

"And I do?"

"You're their next best bet. There are a number of computers in the house."

"And who would they send over to run them and amass this information?"

He appraised me silently, then changed the subject before I could protest. "What do you think of Dan?"

"I think this family has marriage on the brain. He's tall, blond and green-eyed with a nice ass." Grandmama choked and Righ chuckled. "Other than that ..." I shrugged.

"Sounds like love at first sight," Grandmama teased.

It was a lost cause. Quickly kissing her on the cheek, I signified defeat by exiting the library on the crystalline shards of their laughter.

Chapter Four

Wednesday, just before seven AM

Not even the specter of my three-week deadline could motivate me into working after I reached my rooms. Of course, sleep eluded me just as much as anything. Dawn was just beginning to color the horizon when I finally drifted off.

The telephone woke me an hour later. Without emerging from beneath my blankets, I slid a hand out and grabbed the offending object.

"What?" Maybe I did know why Rachel answered the phone the way she did.

"Rise and shine, *cariad.*"

My brain shifted gears slowly. "Righdhonn?"

"Now who else would be calling at this hour?"

"What time is it?"

"Not quite seven a.m."

I opened an eye and looked at the phone. "Excuse me?"

"It's a little before seven. Drag yourself out of bed; I'll be there in a few minutes. I'll even bring coffee."

I sat up, shivering in the early morning chill. "What's wrong?"

"I'll give you ten minutes."

"You'd better bring a lot of coffee," I warned him as I flung the covers to the end of the bed and swung my feet to the side. His laughter was my only response as I dropped the phone into its cradle.

It took me about fifteen minutes to get showered and dressed. As I descended to the lower level of my rooms, I was not surprised to find my mercenary cousin sprawled in the window seat.

He silently waved at the cup of steaming coffee on the end of my desk. Neither of us spoke until after I'd finished the first cup and had gotten a refill from the nearby carafe.

I leaned back in my office chair, propped my feet on the desk and sipped my coffee. "Okay, why did you want me up?"

"Did you hear the phone ring at all this morning?"

"I answered it, didn't I?"

"Lige tried to call you."

I wasn't fully awake and it was habit—I quickly ran through a list of my recent activities, trying to decide what I'd done that would involve the services of the sheriff's department. At the end of the list, I blanched and looked at Righ.

"No, *cariad*," he was quick to assure me. "There's not been another body."

I heaved a sigh of relief. "What did he want?" I asked, trying to forget that Lige had requested my presence in his office.

"You," he answered blandly. "There have been some new developments that have a direct bearing on the case and when he couldn't get you on the phone, he called me. He requested that I get you out of bed and bring you over to the sheriff's department. That's not a direct quote, by the way. He was a bit more graphic."

I caught myself before I asked a stupid question and studied my cousin as I considered what might have such a bearing on last night's body that Lige would want me at the sheriff's department this early *and* with an escort. I hadn't missed the fact that Lige had sent Righdhonn instead of Cris or Grandmama. I finished my coffee. "Well, let's not keep the boys waiting."

I didn't even ask how he'd gotten into my rooms. Righdhonn's ability to appear inside of locked rooms was the stuff of legends. He watched with a grin as I locked the door behind us. Of course, he could have merely picked the locks, he could have a key or, all things considered, he could have just turned into smoke and drifted through the cracks.

He burst into laughter as we headed down the stairs and continued to chuckle as he guided me through the kitchen (I snagged a biscuit on my way through) and out to his Blazer.

"It's not like the sheriff's department is an excessive distance from here," I commented as I climbed into the truck.

"Orders, *cariad*."

I had just finished rolling my eyes when he stopped in front of a two-story stone building that, like most of our municipal buildings, was old enough to have a centennial plaque on the wall next to the Brennen County Sheriff's Department and Jail sign.

"You're not coming in?" I asked, as he made no move to shut off his vehicle.

"Nope, I have a couple things I need to check for Lige. I'll see you back at the house."

"All right." I opened the door and slid to the ground. "Take it easy."

"Always, *cariad*."

He waited until I'd opened the door to the sheriff's office and had stepped inside before putting his Blazer into gear and leaving. It was a point of courtesy, but since the sheriff's department is open twenty-four hours a day, the door would hardly be locked.

Lige was leaning back in a chair, feet resting on a desk near the woodstove that was blasting the chill off the fall morning.

"Son of a bitch," was his only comment as I allowed the wind to sweep several leaves in with me.

The heat from the woodstove hit me as soon as I closed the door. Luckily I'd dressed in layers. I pulled off my sweater as I crossed the room to drop into the chair next to him, leaving a tank top as my concession to decency.

"How the hell do you breathe in here?"

"We breathe just fine," Rachel snapped. "Put your clothes back on."

"I have clothes on, Rachel."

She sniffed and returned to her paperwork.

Lige leered at me. "I'm practicing for Florida. All the ladies start taking off their clothes when they get in here."

"Humph," Rachel snorted as she buttoned up her cardigan.

"You're a terrible old man," I said affectionately.

Lige dropped a foot to the floor and nudged a pile of papers toward me. "Recognize any of this?"

The pile materialized into a tabloid newspaper as I studied it.

"No."

He leaned over and grabbed it, dropping it neatly into my lap before I could move. "Look closer."

I held it up between two fingers and looked at him. "It's a tabloid."

"Look at the front cover," he instructed patiently.

Obediently, I turned the front toward me and immediately dropped the paper on the floor. "Lord and Lady."

"Take a good look at it."

I didn't need to lean over to read the two-inch-high headline, VAMPIRE KILLS IN NORTHERN MICHIGAN. Or, in slightly smaller letters, its sub-headline, BLOODLESS CORPSE FOUND IN BRENNEN COUNTY. Taking up the remaining portion of the paper was a picture of a corpse, allegedly ravaged by a vampire. I thanked all the gods that it wasn't actually a picture of our body. If I'd tripped over their conception of our John Doe, I'd never have gotten to sleep and I would've had nightmares for the remainder of my life.

I pushed it closer to the woodstove. "Fire is a wonderful cleanser."

"Do you know anything about that story?" The voice came from behind me.

I twisted around to look at our new sheriff. "It was only a matter of time, although I didn't expect they'd have it so soon— Wait a minute, I found that body not eight hours ago. How did they manage to get that into the stores already? I'm assuming you found it in a store—is it a special edition?"

"No, it's not. Which means they had the information at least forty-eight hours ago." Thorpe sighed and watched as I scooted the paper closer to the woodstove. "Just for the record, did you call and divulge this information to the tabloids?"

I stared at him. "Have you lost your mind?"

"Not yet."

"Forty-eight hours ago—was he killed that long ago?" I asked slowly, very sure I didn't like where I was heading.

"No."

"Then, only the—"

"Only the killer could have called the tabloid."

"But that's stupid, you could trace him."

"First Amendment rights," Lige interjected.

"But now that's it actually a murder, couldn't you call ..." my voice died off as I realized just how ridiculous my suggestion was. It was as if I thought that a tabloid would actually divulge their sources. Coming from a family consisting of several attorneys and judges (some for extended lengths of time), I tend to look at the First Amendment a bit differently than the average journalist. I kicked the paper under the woodstove.

"Now, Rhiannon, it'll catch fire under there," Lige chided.

"Good."

Daniel leaned between us and pulled the tabloid to safety. "You need to sign your statement."

"Okay."

"And we need some insight into vampires."

"First of all, vampires are a myth."

"I know that and you know that and it's even quite possible that the killer knows that, but he obviously wants us to look in that direction."

"Couldn't it be a red herring?"

He shrugged. "Could be, but we still have to check it out as well as funeral homes and try to nag tabloids into giving us some information. And it is possible that in the mountain of superstition surrounding vampires is his motive."

I raised an eyebrow and looked skeptical. "Where do you want to start?"

"Your statement."

Rachel suddenly appeared with paper and pen. She slapped them down on the desk beside Lige's feet and retreated to her desk.

"*Voila.*" Lige waved a hand at the papers.

The statement I'd given Luke earlier was neatly typed. Rachel refused to use anything other than her 1941 Olivetti. It might be an antique, but it did work and woe be to the person who messed with it or suggested she use something slightly more modern.

"Sign away, madam."

"Can I read it?"

"Don't you trust me?" a new voice asked.

I looked up to find Luke St. John lounging against an inner doorway. "Don't you have a day job?"

"Until this is settled, I've been reassigned."

I picked up the papers. "From what I told you last night?"

"Yes, ma'am."

Just to assert my right to read it, I skimmed it before I signed and dated it. "There. Now, can we get on with this?

We've been graced with a miracle since the tabloid journalists haven't arrived yet and we should take advantage of it."

"True," Lige agreed.

"Don't expect this to last," I said to Sheriff Thorpe.

"I know," he said wearily. "They'll be here soon, expecting everyone to spill their guts."

"They know you?"

"Not directly. But they have covered some cases I've been involved with."

"So you're familiar with their *modus operandi?*"

"Unfortunately."

"What sort of front line defenses are you planning?"

"It's a crying shame the amount of work she makes for us." Rachel raised her voice above the chatter of the radio.

Daniel Thorpe was the only one of us who turned around to acknowledge her contribution. She beamed approvingly at him.

"What are the results of all the tests?" I asked.

"All the tests, she says, all the tests," he muttered, looking at Rachel.

Lige answered my question. "None of the tests are back yet, Rhi. I don't expect any results until tomorrow at the absolute earliest. Doc is doing the autopsy later this morning, but when I talked to him a few minutes ago, he didn't have anything to add to what he told us last night.

"About the only thing we have going for us is that the equipment and materials needed to embalm someone are re-stricted items. You need to be a registered mortician or facility to purchase it. That does limit where we need to look.

"Unfortunately, there was next to no evidence at the site where you found the body to indicate how it got there or who left it there."

"No evidence?" I questioned. "What happened to the six and a half billion things you picked up last night?"

"Realistically speaking, most of what we gathered will have no bearing on the case. But, just in case we got lucky, Luke took it all over to Negaunee to send down to the lab in Lansing." He frowned as I chuckled.

"It's an excellent lab," Luke snapped.

"It certainly is," I agreed. "And Brennen County's first murder in fifteen years is going to be right at the top of their list of things to do."

Luke flashed a look of censure at me. "It will be. I put a rush on it."

"Brennen County Sheriff's Department. What?"

I am always relieved to notice that I'm not the only one subject to Rachel's ire.

"And if our suspicions are correct and we end up with a spree killer, they'll pop us to the top of the list." Lige dropped his feet to the floor and studied me.

"Spree killer?" I asked. Righdhonn's assertions from several hours ago had led to thoughts of a serial killer like Gacy. I wasn't sure what Lige meant by spree killer.

"We have to consider the possibility," Luke said. "None of us expect this to end with just one body. It's too clean. No evidence to speak of. It's geared toward a specific person and we don't know why. This is a detective's nightmare. Yes, ma'am, we have all the makings of a spree."

"Oh, dear God." I leaned on the desk.

"And you, my dear," Lige took hold of the conversation, "you, we need to keep under wraps. That's why I had Righ bring you over here this morning. It's not out of the realm of possibility that you could become his eventual target. Especially if you don't respond to his overtures in the manner he thinks you should. So, no more late-night forays. And you're not to leave Beltene House alone."

"You've got to be joking," I said, lifting my head to stare at him.

"Not even a little bit. And I don't want any arguments out of you."

I closed my eyes, taking a deep breath and letting it out slowly.

"As Rhi pointed out a mite earlier," Luke spoke into the charged silence. "We're about to be invaded."

A guilty silence occupied the room, punctuated by Rachel's "Harumph."

"Your first order of business is to visit the Gwynn-O'Keefe's before the press gets here. I don't even want to contemplate the consequences of the press invading their commune," Lige instructed.

"Oh, sweet Jesus," I muttered and closed my eyes, wondering if I could emigrate to Siberia.

"The Gwynn-O'Keefe's?" Obviously, no one had bothered to explain them to our new sheriff.

A wicked chuckle emanated from the dispatcher's area.

"Rhi?"

I ignored Lige.

"Rhiannon!"

Leaning back, I put my feet up near his and stated clearly, "They make my skin crawl."

"That's a hell of an attitude for the Beltene to take."

"I never wanted the bloody job," I flared.

"There were others better qualified," came a bodiless voice from the Teletype room. (Not that I actually believe they have a Teletype machine in that room, but that's what it's always been called. I have suggested it would make a perfect computer room.)

And as badly as I didn't want to be the Beltene, I shuddered to think of Trystan having the job.

Lige sighed. "Don't you think it's time you quit bitching about it?"

I grumbled under my breath.

"Could I please have an explanation?"

Rachel materialized next to Sheriff Thorpe. "The Gwynn-O'Keefe's are our dark side, locked away to keep us safe. You visit them at your own risk. Many have visited and never returned." She paused, looking thoughtful as her gaze fell on me. "Even with the dubious company of our current Beltene, you risk much." She returned to her desk.

Thorpe wiped the sweat from his forehead and glared at Lige. "A nice quiet northern community where nothing ever happens."

Lige shrugged. "Most of the time."

"Perhaps the Beltenes' keep the Gwynne-O'Keefes' for breeding," Rachel intoned.

Luke left the room and choking sounds were heard from a rear office.

"Okay, okay," I dropped my feet to the floor and stood, putting my sweater back on. "I'll get Righ to go out there with me, but I have real serious reservations about the need."

"I doubt that you'll find anyone responsible for this particular crime out there," Lige agreed. "But I'm thinking Niall will need rescuing about now."

Niall was the latest Gwynn-O'Keefe to spend more of his time in town than at home. For him to move permanently to town, we were required to indulge in an archaic little ceremony officiated by the Beltene.

I grit my teeth and smiled. "Anything else?"

"I think that covers it."

"Wonderful."

Luke rejoined us, still chuckling. "I've got to run over to Sam's. I'll drop Rhi off at the house."

"I can walk." Frowns appeared in quick succession around me and somewhat belatedly, I remembered my new restriction. I sighed. "All right."

Sheriff Thorpe moved to stand beside me. "Perhaps I should accompany Ms. Beltene out to see these people."

Hiding out in my tower in no way prepared me for my initial response to our new sheriff's innocent question. The explanation crowding my throat was impossible for me to express. Wildly, I looked from Lige to Luke.

"Nah," Lige drawled. "You and I have some things we need to take care of before the press arrives. Righ will suit our Beltene just fine for this trip."

My deep sigh of relief brought an unsmiling look of contemplation from Daniel Thorpe. I didn't care—I was just grateful I wasn't the one who had to come up with a creative way to explain the Gwynn-O'Keefes and besides, I couldn't think of a safer person to accompany me out into the swamps than Righ. No one ever messes with him.

"Call when you return, Ms. Beltene," the sheriff said into my relief. "We still need to have that chat about vampires."

Luke hustled me out the door before I could do more than nod my head. "She will," he assured Daniel. "She will."

Chapter Five

Wednesday, around nine AM

Luke dropped me off at the front door of Beltene House with an admonition to behave myself, to find Righ and to get myself out to the Gwynn-O'Keefe's within the next millennium.

I entered the house, gave a fleeting thought to going back to bed, but resigned myself to being mature and responsible and started toward the kitchen to find Righ. I stopped at the junction of the hallways and stared out into the courtyard, chewing on the inside of my cheek as I thought about the last twelve hours.

Nodding decisively, I headed away from the kitchen and into the Beltene's office. I avoided this part of the house, except on Monday mornings, when I was forced to attend to my duties as the Beltene. Grandmama, Cris and either Rhan or my father normally escorted me in. I did exactly what they required of me and escaped as soon as humanly possible. This was the first time in thirty-two years that I entered this office of my own free will.

Eula, the Beltene's secretary, the one I suspected truly ran things, looked up expectantly as I entered. "Good morning, Rhiannon."

Ah, the mark of a perfect secretary; she didn't turn a hair in surprise or pass out from shock at my entrance without the prison guards.

"Morning," I returned, my eyes darting everywhere in the room but at Eula. "I ... um, I ... need to use the phone."

"Of course," she answered smoothly. "Is there anything I can do to assist you?"

"I don't think so." I backed into the sanctum of the Beltene.

I leaned against the door and looked around the office. I had decided more than once, during our Monday meetings, that if I had to be the Beltene, I really did need to redecorate this office. I'd been called on the carpet too many times to be truly comfortable in here.

Sitting down behind the desk, I reached for the phone and made the first of several calls.

As usual, I found Righ in the kitchen.

"And where, my lady, have you been? I expected you about forty-five minutes ago."

I waved a hand. "The Beltene had things to do. And she won't be able to do anything more unless she gets food." I tried to look pitiful and wasted, like those starving children on TV.

Jody shook his head and passed me a plate.

"Jody, my love, you are a saint. Are you sure you won't be divorcing Erin to marry me?"

"Get away with you. You've better things to be doing than teasing the likes of my husband," Erin scolded from behind me.

"Ah, but Erin," I said, smiling as I gave her a one-armed hug, "what better man for me to be teasing than the likes of your husband?"

"Eat your breakfast and get about your business."

"Yes, ma'am."

I sat next to Righ on the couch, putting my feet on the table.

"Where have you been?"

"Can I gather from the impatience in your voice that the Powers That Be have already contacted you in regard to our upcoming visit to see Diuran?"

"It's a good thing I'm fond of you, *cariad*, or I might have called the sheriff's department and reported you missing."

"I wasn't missing. I was merely conducting business within the sanctity of my office."

"You weren't in the tower. I checked."

"My office, Righ. Not my tower." Smiling, I watched the expressions across the kitchen change from censure to amazement.

"Your office?"

I dropped the empty plate onto the coffee table and buffed my nails across my shirt. "Yep."

"Without an armed escort?"

"Are you ready to go see Diuran?"

He shook his head and smiled. "Ooh, my lady, you are playing with fire."

I opened my eyes wide and tried to look innocent. "Maybe it's time."

He laughed. "Come along, *cariad*, let's go aggravate Diuran."

"You go get the Blazer while I run up to the tower and get the torc."

"Well, at least you remembered it this time."

The commune came into sight. It had taken us the better part of an hour to cover the equivalent of six miles as the crow flies. I slept most of the way, although Righ had awakened me when we started up the cow path. It was my duty to wear the torc, for identification—like Diuran really couldn't remember from one visit to another who I was. I had been forced to come out here twice before in my short career as the Beltene. Once to introduce myself and once because Cris needed to come out. I really didn't think she needed to have my presence. I think she was trying to involve me in my new role. As an encouraging factor, it was a dismal failure. Diuran scares the shit out of me.

The common appeared deserted except for a young man in his early twenties sitting on a suitcase in the middle of the green.

"Is that Niall?" I asked, sure Righ would know.

He deftly parked the truck off to one side. "It surely is," he answered.

I let the rumble of the engine fade into the surrounding forest before getting out of the Blazer. In the oppressive silence, I moved to join the waiting boy.

"Niall?" I hoped Diuran wasn't going to insist on formal attire for this farce, because I hadn't dressed for a visit.

"My Lady Protector." He bowed his head.

Silently, I vowed to smack him if he attempted to pull his forelock. "Put your things in the Blazer," I said.

"Yes, my Lady."

Rolling my eyes, I shooed him toward Righ.

"Stay here," I told them.

Taking a deep breath, I walked to the middle of the green. Switching to Welsh, I invoked the power of my office and said, "Diuran Senan O'Keefe. Rhiannon Argadnel Beltene, Lady Protector and Head of Clan Beltene calls you to join her."

Then we waited. Since they were the exiled portion of our clan they were not obligated to respond immediately. They did have to greet me, but it could take a while. I stood motionless, my torc gleaming in the sunlight as it filtered through the trees. The quiet murmur of the river was perfect accompaniment for my vigil.

Thirty-five minutes later, the encampment came to life as Diuran, dressed in his formal best, materialized in the doorway of one of the houses. He paused, allowing me time to admire his finery before striding forward to fall on one knee in front of me, head bowed.

Lord and Lady, we really do need to come into the twentieth century, I thought as I laid a hand on Diuran's head for the traditional blessing. Continuing in Welsh, I bade him rise.

"And to what do we owe the honor of your presence, my Lady Protector?" he asked as he came to his feet.

"Two reasons," I answered. "First, we believe there is a member of this community who wishes to rejoin the greater part of the clan."

"This is true," he agreed.

"Second, a crime has been committed on Beltene land and while we do not believe any of our clan guilty, it is still necessary for us to question everyone." This was the dicey part. Diuran, just as likely as not, would shoot me for even obliquely insinuating that his people might have been involved.

"It is the right of my Lady Protector to ask any questions of us that she chooses. Ask and I shall answer as best I can." Diuran looked interested.

"Last night, a body was left within the confines of the wall, near the road to Black Abbey Point. Do you or any of your people have knowledge of this act?"

"A moment, my Lady Protector." After bowing again, he turned and joined the people grouped behind him.

I might shoot *him* if he didn't stop calling me his Lady Protector. It still amazed me, as illiterate as they appeared to be, (and neither my dad nor I were totally convinced they were as ignorant as they seemed) that their spoken language, in Welsh anyway, was as smooth and fluent as ours was.

It might well be that one day soon, the Beltene was going to have to investigate just how backward this part of her clan was—and do something about it.

I waited, not as patiently as before.

Sooner than I expected, he returned. "My Lady Protector, we cannot find anyone within our scope of influence who has knowledge of this crime."

"Very well."

"If I may ask a question, my Lady Protector?"

"You may ask," I answered.

"We fervently hope that none of our Lady Protector's family was the injured person?"

At last, a chance to wipe that smirk from his face. "No, Diuran Senan O'Keefe, the injured man was from outside Clan Beltene."

He bowed his head. "For that we are pleased."

Sure you are, I thought. "Now, to the matter of the person who chooses to rejoin the majority of the clan."

"Yes." This time Diuran looked genuinely saddened. No one from his immediate family had chosen to leave in three generations. I imagined Niall had been subject to a fair amount of abuse before we arrived. "Niall Conall O'Keefe."

"Very well." Regally, I swept the assembled crowd with my eyes. "Niall Conall O'Keefe, Rhiannon Argadnel Beltene, Lady Protector and head of Clan Beltene calls you to join her."

Niall was on his knees before me before I finished speaking. "I am Niall, my Lady Protector."

"We will hear your request," I said after bidding him rise. I was grateful our new sheriff didn't accompany me on this visit. Explaining my use of the royal 'we' would tax even my imagination.

"I would request to be released from the shackles which bind me here and ask sanctuary from my Lady Protector as is my right as a member of Clan Beltene, albeit in exile."

"Do you understand the consequences of your request?" I asked gently.

"Aye, my Lady Protector, I understand. I understand that I will be allowed to leave here and never be forced to return. I will be allowed to move amidst the people of my clan who do not reside here. I will be taught and succored in my time of need until I no longer have need. I will be required to renounce the ties which bind me here and to pledge my allegiance to the majority of the clan." Niall said the entire speech in one breath.

"We can see that you have truly considered the consequences of your request." Once again I scanned the crowd. "Is there any here who dispute Niall Conall O'Keefe's right to renounce the ties which bind him here?"

There was silence. I held the silence for the prescribed fifteen-minute count.

"Diuran Senan O'Keefe, as patriarch of these people, do you dispute Niall Conall O'Keefe's right to renounce the ties which bind him here?" I asked, trying to pretend I wasn't asking a father to give up his son.

"I do not dispute his right, my Lady Protector."

"I, Rhiannon Argadnel Beltene, Lady Protector and Head of Clan Beltene, do hereby sever the ties which bind Niall Conall O'Keefe to this exiled portion of Clan Beltene, headed by Diuran Senan O'Keefe. From this day forth, he is a member of the majority of Clan Beltene and heir to all the rights and privileges therein."

As I uttered the last word, a low keening began and rose both in volume and tone. Niall stood dumbfounded, staring at a woman on her knees, mourning the loss of her child. When he started to move toward her, I grabbed his arm and pushed him toward Righdhonn. "Get in the truck, " I hissed. "Now."

Holding out my hand to Diuran, I said in Welsh, "You have the sympathy of Clan Beltene on the loss of your son, Diuran Senan O'Keefe."

Taking my hand and bending over it, Diuran replied, "And you have the Gwynn-O'Keefe's congratulations on my Lady Protector's acquirement of a new son. May you have many more." His part in this farce done, Diuran turned and rejoined the crowd. My last view of him, as I climbed into the Blazer, was as he dropped to his knees and gathered the grieving woman into his arms to comfort her.

"Shit!" I muttered as Righ turned the Blazer around and headed back toward the road. I hadn't considered the ramifications of bringing Niall home and no one had seen fit to remind me.

Traditionally, a rescued Gwynn-O'Keefe becomes a member of the Beltene's immediate family. As Diuran had said, I'd just acquired a son.

Righdhonn didn't say anything while he navigated us out of the swamp. Niall sat silently in the back, radiating misery. For all that he had finally accomplished what he wanted, the shock of watching his mother go into mourning for him appeared to be more than he'd planned. And I considered what in the world I was going to do with a son.

"Back to the house, *cariad*?" Righ interrupted my contemplation with his quiet question.

I looked around to find we were on the outskirts of Sevyrn. "Yeah, I need to talk to Erin."

"She and Jody are a good pair to foster the lad with," he said. "You're going to have your hands full enough the next few days without worrying about Niall."

Righ boldly drove straight through town, ignoring my suggestion that we take the back way into Beltene House. There was a small eddy of journalists outside the sheriff's office. I wondered what front-line defenses they had finally chosen. For my money, I'd empty the front room of everyone but Rachel.

Cris and Sheriff Thorpe were sitting in front of the fire when I burst through the kitchen door a good fifty feet in front of Righ and Niall. I skidded to stop.

"What the bloody hell are you doing here?" I asked, gasping as I tried to catch my breath and ignored Cris' look of censure. My use of the word *bloody* usually irritates most of the older members of my family. Here in the states it seems to be an innocent curse; however, in Britain, it's a curse of the highest order.

"Waiting for you," he answered in a much more polite tone than I would have used had someone asked me the same question in that particular tone of voice.

"Oh." I stared at him for a moment before remembering why I'd come in the back door. "Jody?"

"Yes, Rhiannon?"

"Jody," I pleaded, as Righ and Niall came through the door. "Please, please, please, tell me you know where Erin is."

He looked from Niall to me for a moment before a huge grin split his face. Niall, on the other hand, stood in the doorway and stared at Jody in a mixture of amazement and horror. "Try the dining room."

"You stay here," I commanded, trying not to run for the dining room.

"Erin?" I called as I barreled down the hall.

"Here, Rhi." Jody's wife had been born Erin Arianne Gwynn and had come to live in Beltene House twenty-six years ago. My paternal great-grandmother had been in charge of the kitchen at the time and Erin had preferred being in the kitchen with her to anywhere else.

"Erin, I, ah ..." What was the proper method of asking someone to baby-sit a newly repatriated Gwynn-O'Keefe?

"Did you bring Niall back?" she asked, taking pity on me.

"Yes, he's in the kitchen."

She hugged me. "And you're not quite sure what you'll be doing with him now?"

"I forgot what was going to happen until I was done with the ceremony and had given Diuran my condolences. He congratulated me on my new son and wished many more on me.

I think it was the high point of his morning." I slumped against the wall.

"Jody and I have talked about it; he's welcome with us."

"But aren't I supposed to, um ..."

She laughed. "Rhi, honey, no one expects you to personally care for him. You're unmarried for one thing, and it wouldn't be proper, him being over twenty. You have to provide for him until he can provide for himself, but it's not necessary for you to personally do the nurturing."

"Thank the gods."

"Come along," she laughed, "I've yet to meet this young relative of mine."

Niall was still staring at Jody as we entered the kitchen. I had to repeat his name three times before I got his attention.

"Yes, my Lady."

"This is Erin, Niall. She, like yourself, is a repatriated Gwynn-O'Keefe. For now, you'll live here with Erin and her husband, Jody. Erin can help you get settled, here in town."

"You look like my moth ... Arianne Mary O'Keefe," Niall blurted out.

A shadow passed over Erin's face. "Arianne was my baby sister."

Niall's face lit up. "You're my kin?"

"Yes, Niall, I'm your aunt."

He turned to me. "I'd be liking these arrangements just fine, my Lady."

"Great. Get him whatever he needs and have him run through the testing. We can decide where to go once we get the results," I said to Erin.

She patted my shoulder. "You're doing just fine, Rhi."

I turned to the trio by the fireplace as Erin collected her nephew and his baggage. I hadn't expected to find our new sheriff waiting for me.

"Good morning, Sheriff Thorpe."

"Dan or Daniel. I have a feeling we're going to be working together quite a bit in the next few days and we might as well get rid of the formality."

I didn't know what he'd been told about the Gwynn-O'Keefes or about Niall or even what he thought about what he'd heard here in the kitchen, but he seemed disinclined to question it—for which I was thankful. "I suppose you're ready to discuss vampires?"

"More than ready," he said.

"Okay, come on." I headed for the doorway. "No, wait a minute."

"What?" He looked perplexed.

"I want to get a tray, it's almost lunch time."

"Rhi," Jody injected, shaking his head, "I'll fix a tray and bring it up shortly. Scat." He shooed us out of the kitchen.

I noticed Righ was still with us as we started up the tower stairs. "Just what are the two of you going to do up here?" he asked, looking curiously from Daniel to me.

"Rhiannon's going to educate me in the legends and superstitious nonsense I'm about to be deluged in. Perhaps if I know what's coming, I can defuse it before it gets too messy and maybe, just maybe, in the process, we can figure out how and why we ended up with a corpse."

"Rhi's definitely your best bet," Righ said as the two men stood several steps below me while I unlocked my door. "She knows more superstitious nonsense than almost anyone else I know."

I opened the door and looked down at our new sheriff. "One thing you have to understand, Dan, is that while there's an incredible amount of written lore, most people only know what they've seen on TV, in the movies, on the Net or in virtual reality games. All of which run the gamut from traditional to sensual to comic."

"People actually buy this shit." It wasn't a question.

I raised an eyebrow and sighed. "Yes. They not only purchase these items as books, movies, comic books and any other medium you can think of, but many of them do believe in the reality of vampires. Then there are the people who are into role-playing—either live or on-line. None of which is going to make your job any easier." I paused, jingling my keys.

"My novels, which by the way, are not classified as shit, sell by the hundreds of thousands, in at least eight languages. The one I'm working on right now is due to the publisher in three weeks. They already have orders for about thirty thousand copies and it's not due out until April."

I moved into the living room and stood back to allow the men to enter. Dan was shaking his head.

"Vampires are big business, Daniel. Very big business. If you look in the horror and fantasy sections at any bookstore, you will find dozens of books, which deal one way or another with vampires. Go to a computer or hobby shop and you'll find entire sections devoted to vampires."

"I've always managed to miss those sections," Dan commented, watching me lock the door.

"Rhi always was a bit warped. Even as a child, she'd watch *The Wizard of Oz*, terrified of the wicked witch, peeking out at her from between her fingers. But she wouldn't leave. If you forcibly removed her from the room, she'd throw a temper tantrum." Righdhonn ran his fingers over my videotapes and CDs, checking to see if I'd acquired any new ones since his last visit.

"Thank you, Righdhonn," I said frostily, locking the door.

"Any time, *cariad*."

Ignoring my cousin, I turned back to our new sheriff. "What brings you over here for your class on vampires?"

Dan shrugged. "Lige sent me over. He thought it would be better if we talked over here."

"Well, considering that the press has declared open season on your office I think he's right. Here, we can always pull up the drawbridge, let the piranha loose in the moat and threaten to drop boiling oil on top of their siege ladders."

"You've been watching *Masada* again," Righ accused.

"I adore Peter Strauss," I returned.

"My God," Dan breathed, looking around.

My rooms take up the top two floors of our tower. The first floor contains the Ritual Chamber and the second, the Welcoming Chamber. Rhodri's lab resides in the dungeon beneath the tower.

The tower rooms are forty-five feet in diameter with twelve-foot ceilings. The upper floor is a half circle open to the floor below; a stairway following the contour of the wall is the only egress to the upper floor and the roof.

The first floor is my office/living area. My office, dominated by a huge, custom-made monstrosity of a desk, takes up about a third of the space. It houses my computers, printers and assorted other sundries that a computer-literate person considers vitally important.

Right off the office, just past the window seat (set into the six-foot-thick walls at the bottom of the stairway) and tucked beneath the stairway, is a small kitchen area. It contains a compact refrigerator, a microwave and a coffeepot. It's a long way to the kitchen.

A huge fireplace, which more often than not has a fire in it, is directly across from the window seat. The remainder of the floor is filled with bookshelves, comfortable furniture to lounge on and my stereo, twenty-nine inch television, VCR and controls for one of the satellite dishes that decorate the southern end of the roof.

My bedroom and bathroom are on the second floor with a smaller entertainment center, a papa-san chair and another window seat.

To get to my rooms via the front door, you have to travel half the length of the house, the depth of the house, climb two flights of circular stone stairs and convince me that I really do want to allow you access.

Looking at it through the eyes of a stranger, it probably looked rather impressive. I raised an eyebrow at our new sheriff.

He moved his gaze back to my three-hundred-year-old carved oak door. "Sevyrn has the lowest crime rate of any place I've ever seen. I understand locking the house doors, but that's an awful lot of lock for an interior door," he said.

"True," I agreed.

He looked around. "And the purpose is?"

"Trystan."

"Trystan?"

"He's one of my cousins. Privacy is a concept he fails to understand."

"You lock the door against your cousin?" His tone indicated his disbelief, but then, he had yet to meet Trys.

"Yes."

"Okay."

"Trystan is a pain in the ass," I explained from the bookshelves where I was selecting a variety of books for him to read. "He just can't keep his hands off anything mechanical. He loves to tinker, but unfortunately, he's unable to fix anything. He can't put something back together in the same shape it was before he tore it apart."

"And," Righdhonn said, as he circled the room, "he's always amazed when it never works again. I once had an antique pistol—"

I choked back a burst of laughter.

"I was quite upset, Rhiannon."

"Upset? I don't think upset is an appropriate term,

Righdhonn," I returned. "It was worse than when he played with my computer. I didn't see hide nor hair of him for weeks."

"That's because Rhan sent him to Wales to herd sheep for two months," he explained.

"Really? And here I thought he'd just found a good hiding place—either that, or you chained him in the dungeon. I was jealous, you know."

"Well, my Lady, I didn't announce to the world at large that I wished to incarcerate him in the dungeon and torture him for days on end," he said as he started up the stairs.

"I wasn't planning on killing him or anything, I just wanted to damage him a little." I turned from the shelves, my arms full of books.

"A little? I heard what was on your agenda, Rhiannon Argadnel."

"Pfft." I waved an arm in dismissal as I dropped the books on the couch. "There," I said to Dan.

"What do you want me to do with these?" He sat gingerly next to the books.

"Research." Dan jumped as the trapdoor hit the roof. "Don't worry, it's just Righ."

Dan raised an eyebrow. "Doing what?"

"He went up on the roof."

"Maybe I don't want to meet your cousin, Trystan." He riffled his fingers through the books.

"No one does."

"He carries a gun," Dan commented, holding one book at arms' length between two fingers. It had a particularly lurid cover.

"Rhan would never permit it," I said, startled by his comment.

"He doesn't appear to be the type to ask Rhan's permission."

I frowned. "Who are you talking about?"

"Righdhonn."

"Oh, well, that's different. He has a permit. I thought you were talking about Trys."

Once again, I was on the receiving end of one of his scowls. "I know he has a permit. What I can't figure out is why he needs one and why he carries his gun around all the time."

"Well ..."

"I hope you don't play poker with that face."

Righ leaned down into the open trapdoor. "I love playing poker with her. Someday I'll manage to convince her to play for more than just pretzels. I'm going downstairs."

"'Bye," I called, waiting until the sound of the trapdoor closing faded away before looking at Dan. "He's a mercenary."

He dropped the book. "He's a what?"

"Mercenary."

Dan closed his eyes. "Good Lord."

"He's a very good mercenary."

"I don't doubt it," he said, sitting up and collecting the book from the floor. "Tell me again, what do you want me to do with these?"

"Skim through them," I said. "It shouldn't take too long, then we can discuss the high points. I'll be over at my desk trying to get some work done. Let me know when you're finished."

"Yes, ma'am."

I spent the time wisely and chapter twelve was definitely the better for it. I'd just finished when there was a knock on the door.

Jody brought us an incredible lunch. Fresh baked wheat bread and roast beef sandwiches with mayonnaise. Macaroni salad and deviled eggs. A plate of huge rounds of molasses and sugar cookies still warm from the oven, a pitcher of milk and two bowls of chocolate mousse.

"Jody, you're a saint."

"It'll hold you until dinner."

"Maybe."

"No maybe about it," he rumbled. "You're going to be too busy to be raiding the kitchen."

I glanced at Daniel, who was so engrossed in the last book that he still hadn't noticed Jody. "I suppose. Has Erin got Niall settled in?"

"She's working on it."

"I don't know how to thank the two of you for taking him," I said, nibbling on the roast beef.

"Erin's tickled to death to have her nephew in the house. Don't you be worrying your head about it. He'll be just fine." Jody closed the door behind him. I locked it and turned to find Daniel watching me.

"Finished?"

"Overwhelmed." He rubbed his eyes slowly. "Now what?"

"Now we take this tray and go upstairs."

"Upstairs?"

"To the roof." I thrust the tray into his hands. "We can monitor the invasion from there."

And having lunch on the roof would keep our new sheriff out of the way while the result of my calls from the Beltene's office arrived.

Chapter Six

Wednesday, lunchtime

I adore the roof of the tower. The battlement is six feet thick and ranges in height from three to five feet. With the exception of the stairs, which lead over one section and down into the courtyard, there is a wide seat in front of each three-foot section. I chose the one that gave us the best view of the front yard and town.

"Listen," I said, standing motionless. With both of us silent, you could hear the rumble of the press eddying in front of the sheriff's office. "Aren't you glad you're here?"

"I suppose I would rather be here than in the office, faced with that crowd. But don't you kind of feel sorry for them?"

"Sorry for them? Why? Their sole purpose in being here is to make our lives a living hell."

"True, but consider this. I have no doubt that Lige is safely ensconced in his office and guess who he left to guard the front door?"

"Rachel." I laughed. "They'll never know what hit them."

"Does she always argue with callers like she did with you last night?"

"Were you the one who stopped her inquisition?" I stared at him with new respect.

"Yes."

"Damn. I didn't think anyone less than one of the Hathaway girls could slow Rachel down. I'm impressed, Daniel."

"Shouldn't she be retired?"

"I don't think you should start something you can't finish."

"She's got to be of retirement age."

"She is. Long past it, in fact. But no one's had the balls to mention it to her yet. Everyone just figures she's going to be dispatcher until she gets so angry with someone she just keels over. That way she'll die happy."

"You aren't serious."

"I most certainly am. But if you insist on trying, I'll see to it you have a wonderful funeral and a prime plot at St. David's."

"Rhiannon."

"Really, Uncle Morgan will do a High Mass for you and everyone in town will come. We'll put up a magnificent monument and there'll be flowers on your grave for years to come, as your bravery becomes legend. It'll be wonderful."

"All right, I won't delve into why she hasn't been retired."

"Of course, the other possibility is she's probably the only person who knows where all the bodies are hidden."

"I don't even want to touch that one. Rachel's job is safe. Do you think it would be all right for me to ask her to be a little more polite on the phone?"

"You can ask."

"You don't sound hopeful."

"I'm not." I motioned for Dan to set the tray on the wall as I sat down.

"Cushions would be nice," he commented, gazing down at the smooth stone seats.

"I seldom remember to bring them up and if I do, I invariably forget to take them back down and they get soaking wet. So I usually don't bother."

Dan lowered himself to the cool stone with a sigh and picked up a sandwich. "Shall we discuss your vampires now?"

"Certainly. How do you want to start?"

"I'll go down the list of main points I got out of your research library and you can give me an explanation for each one."

"No problem." I picked up a sandwich, poured a glass of milk and settled myself comfortably into the seat. "Shoot."

Dan pulled a notebook from his pocket and opened it to a page of neatly printed notes I hadn't even noticed he'd taken. "Okay, these are what I found to be a vampire's main characteristics:

"One: they need to drink blood to maintain their lives and it seems to be necessary for them to terrorize their victims as much as possible before they feed.

"Two: to become a vampire you have to be bitten by another vampire, usually three times, and exchange blood with them, after which you die and then rise from your grave as a vampire.

"Three: they can only be up and about between sunset and sunrise. If they're caught out in sunlight, they disintegrate into dust or explode, generally in a graphic sort of way.

"Four: they have to sleep in a coffin with bits of their native earth beneath them.

"Five: they can't enter a building without permission.

"Six: they don't appear in mirrors or photographs.

"Seven: they can turn into vapor and other non-human forms, most notably a bat.

"Eight: crosses and garlic send them screaming into the night, holy water burns them and they aren't able to enter sanctified ground.

"Nine: last, but not least, they aren't capable of physical sex, although I did notice that several of the newer books ignored that particular theory."

He took a bite of his sandwich and contemplated his notes. "I think that about covers it."

"I hope so. I don't outline an entire novel that well," I said, leaning over to peer at his notebook. "Did you actually write it all down as neatly as you recited it?"

Dan closed his eyes. "It's habit. I write everything down."

I eyed his notebook as I finished my sandwich and wondered just how much of the last twenty-four hours I shouldn't read. Swallowing, I pushed temptation away and said, "Okay, let's see if I can make some sense out of this for you.

"First, the consumption of blood. You're right, an overwhelming majority of them use terror side-by-side with the feeding. It's kind of like having icing on your cake. Taking the blood from a live victim is a constant thread throughout most of the myths, legends and stories.

"And like you said, some of the newer ones are modifying the myths to suit themselves. The movie *Love at First Bite* has its vampire drinking blood from the blood bank. Most of the legends concede the vampire is capable of drinking and maintaining on non-human blood, although it's not nearly as satisfying."

I carefully chose a molasses cookie. "I've never found a concrete source which states why the blood needs to be fresh. My own personal guess is that it became part of the legends because, until this century, there wasn't any way to store blood. I imagine trying to drink congealed blood would be a fairly fruitless, not to mention rather disgusting, task.

"Then too, there's the notion that the drinking of blood is sacred. A number of religions advocate blood as a sacrament, up to and including Christianity." *And Druidism*, I added silently.

Dan set his second sandwich down and gazed out across town. "I'm really having a difficult time with this."

With more perception than my family credits me with, I asked, "With vampires or with me?"

"With you. I don't like having civilians dumped into my lap during an investigation."

"I have been deputized, you know."

"What?" Surprised, he turned to look at me.

"Ah, I can see that the Powers That Be never bothered to explain why they've tossed me into your lap."

"No, I don't recall anyone mentioning you were a deputy, nor do I remember seeing you on the payroll."

"Payroll," I chortled. "That would be the day. Do you really think they'd pay me money?"

"Please explain why a novelist, a vampire novelist, no less, would become an unpaid deputy?"

"That's easy. They made me."

"Made you?" Dan was pretty good himself at raising one eyebrow.

"I'm the Beltene, remember. The Beltene's always deputized."

"Why is the Beltene always deputized?"

Good question, I thought, *and just how in the bloody hell do I explain it to him?* Failing to come up with anything concrete, I shrugged and answered the question he hadn't asked. "Civilian deputies are our answer to a manpower and specialty shortage which is directly attributable to our isolation and the size of our sheriff's department. It's not an uncommon solution; at least, not around here. Under normal conditions our police force is more than adequate for what we need. But there's always an expert you need or a few extra people to help search a park." I flung a piece of beef over the wall and watched as one of Gwenddydd's peregrine falcons caught it on the fly.

"Is that supposed to make me feel better?" Dan asked, rising to pace off some of his frustration.

"No, it's to try to explain how we came to have a number of volunteer deputies. We can expect a certain amount of help from the state police, but only as much as we request and as much as they can afford to spare. They've assigned Luke here for the duration and they'll let us use their facilities when we need them. But they're in Negaunee and quite often the things we need are things they're already using. So, we decided to deputize a number of community members to take up the slack."

Dan's eyes grew wary. "And who can I expect to be popping up, volunteering to help and already deputized?"

"There aren't that many of us," I said. "Rhodri and Pentraeth, they do a fair amount of lab work for you; me; Dad, 'cause he's the Mayor and between the Metalworks and Beltene House we have the best computers in the county. You really do need to pull your department into the twentieth century, Dan. Righdhonn, I think," I confided, "they deputized him because he's the best shot in the county and the best armed. He has quite a collection."

I paused as our new sheriff made an inarticulate noise. I waited to see if there was any comment forthcoming, but when he dropped his head into his hands and leaned against the battlement, I continued, "Then there's Norm Cole, in case we need big equipment; Jody, he's great when you need to intimidate someone, not to mention that he has a masters in psychology; Old Man Morrison and his son, Ed, because most of the posse keep their horses at the farm. And it goes without saying that they're all good in the woods, excellent shots and good on horseback."

"Horseback?"

"For the posse. A fair amount of your work is finding people lost in the woods. Tourists are forever wandering off in the state parks and losing themselves. When necessary, we go into nearby counties and help with searches and when we need them, they come here."

He shook his head.

"Oh and I forgot, Trys is also a deputy."

"Your infamous cousin?"

"That's the one," I agreed. "He is an excellent skulker, which is why he's the best tracker in the county. Even better than Righdhonn. The state police and the Marquette County boys use him from time to time."

"So basically I have the Keystone Kops at my beck and call."

"We're not that bad."

He turned around and studied me, "And all these people have gun permits?"

"Lord and Lady, no. Most of them just have rifles and shotguns. Righdhonn's the only one with a gun permit." I shuddered at the mere suggestion that Trys be allowed to run around armed. "And now, back to your original question. I don't know that I can give you a reason why the Beltene's always deputized, other than the importance of the position in our community. I'm sure if Rhan had had his way, I wouldn't have been. But, even though I've never had my deputization hauled out of the mothballs before, and even without official notification, I did assume I'd been called to active duty."

"Actually your being deputized makes me even more uncomfortable with your involvement."

"It's not a very big involvement."

His level gaze pinned me to my seat. "Not a very big involvement? You were involved in this before you even called us last night. Every minute that passes drags you in deeper. You are his motivation. You are his beginning and his end."

I crossed my arms and frowned at him. Did he think I hadn't been paying attention?

"Rhan swore to me this was a nice quiet northern community," he muttered, staring out across the bay.

"Sometimes that's all it is."

After several minutes, Dan returned to his seat and a sugar cookie. "Let's get back to the vampires." He absent-mindedly nibbled the edges off his cookie as he studied his list.

"Anything you say."

He sent a dark frown in my direction. "I think becoming a vampire is next. The prevalent theory seems to be that you have to get bitten at least once and usually three times. And a transfer of blood from the vampire to the victim seems to be necessary. Then when you die, you rise on the next nightfall as a vampire, or something along those lines. How do they get around embalming?"

"The author is omnipotent," I answered, considering the depth of superstitious twaddle we were about to embark on.

"Meaning you can do any damn thing you want with your characters?"

"Heavens, no. Characters have their own set personalities and whatever you do must be within the scope of their reality."

"You're not serious."

"Of course I am. I usually know my main characters, the beginning, the end and some semblance of what I want the middle to look like. After that, I just need to control the characters when they get out of hand." I hoped he really didn't want to get into a discussion about my rather slap-dash method of writing.

"Good Lord."

Taking pity on him, I returned to the point. "Mostly, they get around embalming by having the vampire killed in a spot where he won't be found or have the vampire rise before the embalming begins—having the body disappear in the morgue is always an excellent technique—or they just mention that it takes longer for the vampire's body to reconstruct itself after the embalming so it can arise. I haven't a clue why it was decided vampirism could be transmitted with a bite and a transfer of fluids." I stopped and looked thoughtfully over the forest.

"Of course, since the normal vampire isn't capable of having sex, I suppose it would make sense to have the transfer in blood. It's definitely better than making it a pneumatic transfer, less chance of a plague."

Dan shuddered. "A plague of vampires? No, thank you."

"The three bites," I continued dreamily; the idea, which had been flitting about the outskirts of my mind since the night before starting to come together, "could tie into the three days between the crucifixion and the resurrection, which leads us into a really fascinating area."

My mind raced with the possibilities as I sat staring off into the distance. I returned to my immediate surroundings when I noticed Dan waving a hand in front of my face.

"Damn." I appropriated his notebook and speedily put a brief precis of my next novel on paper. "What a stroke of bloody genius. This is going to give Kate heart palpitations."

"Do I want to know what you're talking about?" Dan asked, sounding plaintive.

"Just the glimmer of genius," I said.

"Uh-huh." He decided to ignore my outburst. "Another constant thread is their inability to be out in the sun. During the daylight hours they're in some sort of coma and have to be in hiding. Well, at least in a closed area with no trace of the sun. There's usually someone who knows where they are. And if sunlight does touch them, they disintegrate into dust, implode, explode and are generally gross."

"Ah, yes. The Creature of the Night Syndrome." I looked down and watched my brothers standing in the middle of the front yard watching the press who were still milling about in front of the sheriff's office.

Bouncing to my knees, I leaned on the battlement. "I think the sunlight disintegration theory, and all that accompanies it, came about because vampires are supposed to be evil. The night has always been the playground of evil. Turning to dust in the sunlight is just another example of good conquering evil."

"I really didn't think it was possible to come up with logical-sounding explanations for these absurdities." Dan leaned back and studied the toes of his boots. "Next on the list is their habit of having to sleep in their coffin with bits of their native earth beneath them."

I refrained from rolling my eyes. "My guess is the native earth has to do with our natural ties to the land. And since the vampire is dead, the coffin would be the most comfortable place for them to rest."

I tried to imagine Rhodri as one of the undead, forced to spend his daylight hours in a coffin. We'd have to find a quiet, large, padded room for him to spend the remainder of his days. He's not only a firm believer of rise with the sun, to bed with the sun, he's claustrophobic. Big time claustrophobic.

Generally, we blame Mom for this particular problem. She's a tiny little thing; barely five feet tall and a hundred pounds dripping wet. Rhodri, at birth, was a strapping ten pounds, fourteen ounces. Mom spent the last three months of her pregnancy flat on her back and refused to become pregnant again for four years. I was a normal-sized baby, not quite six pounds.

His inability to tolerate small places culminated in the largest closet in the house; it runs the length of his bedroom and is ten feet wide.

"You didn't give me any of your books to read," Dan said into the silence.

"No, I didn't," I agreed.

"Why not?"

"I, like a number of the newer authors, don't always subscribe to traditional views. You wanted to look at the norms for vampires. I gave them to you. My vampires aren't usually the bad guy."

"Tsk, tsk. Do they tar and feather you for these unorthodox notions?"

"Not yet, although my next one may set a new record for the number of people offended. That'll make my agent go into raptures." I shook my head. "But then, the more radical I get, the better Kate loves it."

"Who is Kate?"

"My agent."

"What happens when one of your books offends someone?" Dan asked with a peculiar look on his face.

"I usually get into the tabloids, the reviewers pan the book and the loonies start coming out of the woodwork. My mail increases dramatically and sales skyrocket."

"Good Lord."

"It's all right. The one I'm working on now is quite tame as far as radical ideas are concerned and it'll be over a year before the radical one comes out. We'll have plenty of time to prepare," I consoled him.

"You can predict when things like this are going to happen?" Amazement was not the most predominant emotion in his voice.

"What?"

"I don't believe this," he raged, springing to his feet again. "You know things like this are going to happen."

I rose to face him. "Now, you just wait a minute. Things like this have never happened before. I never intended that things like this would happen. I can't pull my books from the shelves and I can't be responsible for people who think that everything they read is true. I'm a novelist and a damn good one. I do not incite people to break laws. I provide them with a bit of fantasy to enjoy. That's it."

"I didn't mean to imply you started out with the notion of inciting people, I'm just saying that you're consciously aware that people come here and cause trouble because of your books."

"Look, by the time anyone actually came to Sevyrn I had

established a perfectly good career. Neither I, nor anyone else, saw any reason to cease said career simply because we had an occasional brain-dead person wandering about. They, usually without any assistance, wander right back out again. The tabloids create more trouble than anything or anyone else."

"The current problem isn't going to go away."

I crossed my arms and glared at him, unable to refute his statement.

"Let's finish up this charade," he sighed, returning to his seat.

Making a number of vulgar sounds discreetly under my breath, I leaned on the battlement.

Daniel picked up his notebook and scanned his list. "Vampires aren't allowed to enter a building without permission."

I paused just long enough before answering for my displeasure to be evident. "It falls in with willing sacrifices and the peasantry's habit, centuries ago, of battening their houses down at night. And I've always thought there was a certain amount of good manners involved."

"Good manners?"

"Sure, it's not proper to eat before your host sits down at the table. It's not proper, once your victim has ensconced himself in his home, his personal sanctuary, to enter without first having been invited in. You know, 'a man's home is his castle.'"

"Good Lord." Dan looked skeptical. "They don't appear in mirrors or photographs and they can change their shapes, most notably into a bat."

"I've always maintained that Christianity had a hand in the lack of a reflection. Outside of Jesus of Nazareth, if you've died and have risen from the dead, you no longer have a soul. Mirrors are a reflection of the soul, so if you don't have one, by way of being one of the Undead, then you don't have a reflection.

"Being able to shapechange. Since the legends worked to make the vampire a fearsome creature, unusual powers made them even more frightening to the common man. It also allowed them to get into places a normal human would be unable to go." This one took the cake for nonsense. Trystan was the only person I knew who wished he could change into a bat. I just thanked the gods that he couldn't because it would only make him even more impossible than he already is. "Next."

"Holy relics send them screaming into the night and-slash-or burn them. Crosses and holy water come to mind. Garlic keeps them away and they aren't able to enter sanctified ground." Dan marked off the points as he recited them.

"I haven't the foggiest idea why they picked garlic, except it's pungent and was used in the middle ages as both a spice and a medicine. Perhaps they figured if it was capable of driving a cold away, it would keep a vampire away." I traced the mortar and continued my explanation without looking at Daniel. "Crosses, holy water and sanctified ground takes us back to good conquering evil and having no soul."

"And my last point?" Dan prompted.

"Ah, yes. That they're incapable of physical sex. Well, I suppose if you're dead, you shouldn't be able to have sex. Although considering the role blood plays in the act itself and the rapture a vampire induces in his victim, and himself, while feeding, I would think that physical sex shouldn't be a problem. It is becoming more common with authors for their vampires to use seduction instead of terror, at least for the good guys."

"Okay," he said, after mulling over my explanations. "The sixty-four thousand dollar question is—do you believe a vampire killed that man?"

"Do I look like the cheese has slid off my cracker?"

"Why not?"

"Please. Vampires, as blood-sucking monsters of the night, do not exist outside of literature and the depths of one's imagination."

"Exactly."

I quirked an eyebrow.

"The depths of one's imagination. Picture, if you please, someone whose cheese *has* slipped who also believes that he's a vampire."

I ran my hands through my hair, feeling a bit frazzled. Daniel's statement had been a nearly perfect description of Trystan or at least a nearly perfect replica of my normal description of Trystan.

"Why leave the body out where it could be readily found?" I asked, as I listened to footsteps climbing the stairs from the courtyard.

"So you would find it, *cariad*," Righdhonn said as he and Dylan joined us.

"Thank you."

"I think it's a fairly undisputed fact, Rhiannon, that the body was deliberately placed for you to find it."

Only the gods know, I thought, *how much I'd give if they'd just quit telling me that someone left an embalmed body lying about for my approval.*

"The question is just how far into vampirism this person has sunk and how long it's going to take to run him to ground," Dan commented.

Trystan? My computer? The Metalworks? Lake Superior? My soul?

"And how long it's going to take before the killer completely snaps because Rhi's not reacting the way he wants her to," Dylan contributed. "And, of course, what he'll do after he snaps."

I really do not want to know all this. I stared icily at Dylan and wondered how many times he'd bounce if I flung him over the battlement.

"Now, *cariad*, it's not proper to be tossing family members about like they were crockery," Righdhonn admonished, correctly reading the look in my eyes.

"Back to the issue at hand," Dan interjected. "I can't see any reason to assume the killer will stop with just one body. Is there anything in your library which tells us how often a vampire must feed?"

Stricken, I stared at him. "Every night. They can go several nights without if they have to, or if they've had an exceptionally large amount of blood, but the norm is every night. Sweet Jesus."

Dan and Righdhonn shared a glance, then they both nodded. "I think we can expect a body per day," Dan said. "From all you've told me, I don't know if it would be logical to expect any less."

I buried my face in my hands.

"Now, just to reiterate what Lige said this morning, we don't want you going anywhere outside of this house without an escort."

"Okay." I raised my head to look toward the slowly growing group of journalists by the sheriff's department.

"Good. Now what about the press?"

I looked askance at him. "What about them?"

"Who'll talk to them?"

"Not anyone from town. Of course, they could very easily get someone from Marquette to talk to them. There are people there who think we're more than a bit clannish," Righdhonn answered as I watched Olwen, one of my cousins, walking down the driveway.

She walks even more than I do. I walk wherever I need to go, but Olwen goes out just to walk. A bizarre concept.

I stood as I noticed her attention being drawn by something in a group of bushes near the end of the drive. She stopped, parted them and peered inside. Even at this distance, I could see the perplexed, then frightened look on her face. She disappeared into the bushes, reappearing moments later with the object of her scrutiny dangling from her hand. She looked first at the house, then at the sheriff's office.

She stood, indecisive for a moment, then started toward the sheriff's office. When she caught sight of the press, she turned and resolutely headed for the house.

Recognizing the object and hoping against hope that I was wrong about its contents, I was halfway down the courtyard steps before the men noticed my departure.

Chapter Seven
Wednesday, late afternoon

I skidded to a stop next to Olwen in the front hall. She, Trystan and Rhan were clustered about the object. They looked relieved as Dylan, Righdhonn and Daniel burst into view behind me.

"I didn't realize you were here," Rhan said to the sheriff. "Thank the gods, you are. This is not something I'd be wanting to haul through that crowd to show you."

"Righ and I went to have a chat with Diuran; Sheriff Thorpe was here waiting for me when we got back," I said, a chill passing over me as I looked down.

At my feet sat a medium-sized Coleman cooler. A white body and green lid with black-and-gold stick-on letters spelling out SUSTENANCE on it.

"Where was it and how did it get in here?" Daniel asked.

"I was going for a walk," Olwen said. "As I was going past the shrubbery out front, it caught my eye. It was in about three feet and with that white color, I couldn't miss it. When I got closer I could see what it said. I was going to take it over to the sheriff's department, but there were all those people over there. So I brought it in the house. I figured I could call your office from here. I only touched the handle." Dan's pained look and sigh made her wince. "Sorry."

"Don't worry about it. I don't think we're going to find any prints on it anyway," he said. After studying the cooler for a moment, he looked up. "I need a phone."

"This way," I said, heading for my office and hoping Eula wouldn't pass out from seeing me twice in one day.

I leaned against the wall, watching the shadows of the trees dance on the lawn while our new sheriff made arrangements with his staff to join him. I turned when I heard the phone drop into its cradle. His expression didn't encourage conversation, so our trip back to the front hall was silent.

Rhodri and Dafydd joined us just before Eric arrived via the back door, his forensics field kit clutched in one hand and Luke trailing along behind him. We moved back as he circled the cooler, then looked at his new boss.

"I carried it into the house," Olwen told him.

"Did you touch anything other than the handle?" Eric asked.

She shook her head wordlessly.

Daniel's gaze skirted restlessly around the foyer and I had the feeling that he wanted to dismiss us all, but was quite sure we wouldn't leave.

"I doubt there're any prints on this pebbled surface," Eric said as he dusted the exterior of the cooler.

"I'd be very surprised if you found any prints on it at all," Dan muttered.

"*Uffern Dan!*" The curse was a sigh that wafted around the hall as Eric carefully lifted the lid. Inside the cooler, snuggled along the sides by blue ice, were bags of blood.

Daniel let out his breath in a long sigh. "Either Count Dracula knocked over the local blood bank or we've found the blood from last night's body."

Eric prodded the blood with a gloved finger. "Well, I haven't seen Renfield wandering around town nor has the hospital been screaming that their blood supply has gone missing, so I imagine after we get it typed and matched, we'll find it's from our corpse. I don't see any ... unless it's not human. In that case, it could have come from Morrison's slaughterhouse."

The doorbell boomed.

Desperate for something to do, I answered it.

"Hi, Henry." I smiled at the small man standing on the doorstep, a box sitting by his feet.

"Rhiannon." He nodded a greeting. "That's quite a mess in town. The vultures have come in for the kill. Over last night?"

"Unfortunately. Freedom of the press and all that," I answered absently. "Is that the package I've been waiting for?"

"Yes, ma'am. If you'll sign here." He held out his clipboard.

I signed on the indicated line and leaned around the door. "Rhodri."

My brother looked through the open door, then walked over. Shaking his head, he pulled out his wallet and dropped a five in my outstretched hand.

"Thanks."

"No problem," he said, returning to where Eric was fingerprinting the top edge of the open cooler.

"I thought you were going fishing today?" I asked, making idle conversation.

"I was, but one of our trucks got hit by a semi this morning and they called me in to help pick up the slack," he explained. "I was punching out when the boss told me your package had come in and I volunteered to drop it off on my way home. We know how patient you've been, waiting for it."

He was being tactful. I'd been calling twice a day for the last week to see if it had arrived yet. For some reason, the company I'd purchased it from had chosen to send it by mule train instead of Fed Ex like I'd requested.

"I appreciate it." I handed him the clipboard with the five

tucked under the clip. "Thanks again."

"Would you like me to take it in for you?" he asked, hesitating on the steps.

"That's all right, I'll get it for her," Daniel said, startling me. "Henry Branton, right?"

"Yes, sir."

"I'm Dan Thorpe, the new sheriff." They shook hands.

"Pleased to meet you, sir."

Dan leaned against the wall. "You were at Sam's Black Abbey last night when Rhiannon found the body?"

"Yes, I'd stopped to pick up some Pepsi and nightcrawlers so I could go fishing this morning, but unfortunately, I got called into work." Henry tucked the clipboard under one arm.

"Did you see anyone entering or leaving or even near the store?" Dan continued.

"Not unless you want to count the three deer that crossed in front of me a quarter of a mile down Black Abbey Road."

Dan smiled. "No, I was thinking about something a little more dangerous than a deer."

"Ha!" I snorted. "You've never been in close contact with some of our deer."

"Sometime in the next day or so, I'll send a deputy over to take your statement, so we can have it on file," Dan continued, ignoring me.

"Any time," Henry said. "I'm usually home in the evenings."

"Thank you, Henry."

"You're welcome, Sheriff. See you later, Rhiannon."

"'Bye, Henry." I waited until his van turned onto Llanthony Road before gracing Daniel with a glare. "Is my front step the appropriate place for an interrogation?"

"That wasn't an interrogation," Dan said, bending over to pick up the box.

"Well, if that wasn't an interrogation, I'd hate to see it when you finally get around to having one," I grumbled, following him and my package back into the foyer.

"Jesus, this is heavier than it looks. What the hell's in it?" he asked, bouncing it onto the floor.

"Medieval manuscripts," I answered, frowning as I watched the box settle into one spot and thanked every god I could think of that the manuscripts were always incredibly well padded and packaged. Otherwise the next tabloid headline the world saw would read "Vampire Novelist Kills Sheriff Over Broken Manuscript."

"Manuscripts?"

"Medieval illuminated manuscripts," I said shortly, not particularly caring to explain my passion for reference materials. Nor did I mention their topic. As soon as I had perused the delicate manuscripts, they'd be stored in the library with the other manuscripts the family had collected over the last couple of millenniums.

"Right," he agreed, eyeing me warily, before turning to rejoin Luke and Eric.

Rhan joined me. "I think we need to have the family home, Rhiannon."

"Agreed. Dylan, Daffyd, Olwen." I waited until they'd gathered around us before continuing. "I need you three to coordinate your efforts and notify everyone of this latest development. Also, call Wales and have everyone come home. Help them with reservations and whatever else they need. I want them home Friday morning, at the latest."

"No problem," my brother said, walking off with Olwen on his arm. Dylan disappeared into the shadows without a word.

"I'll call Morgan in Marquette and tell him to get his ass home," Rhan said. "We need him more than the Bishop does."

"Thank you, Rhan."

He frowned at me. "Hopefully, this will show you—Trystan, leave that alone," he bellowed.

Once again, I was saved from a long, boring lecture on the responsibilities of the Beltene because of Trystan. Daniel, Luke, Righ, Eric and Rhodri had been huddled together with their backs to the cooler, as had I. We all turned to find Trys hovering over the cooler.

"Can I keep it?" he asked eagerly.

Daniel looked expressionlessly at him.

"Go with Dylan," Rhan ordered.

"But, I—"

"Now, Trystan."

Trys went. He sulked, but he went.

I buried my face in my hands. "Wonderful."

"Trys will behave."

I gave a mirthless chuckle. "Sure he will, and what do we have to threaten him with this week?"

"It is not necessary to threaten him in order to get him to behave," Rhan said stiffly.

"Really? It's always been my best tactic."

"This could be—" Rhan cut himself short. "This is neither the time nor the place to be discussing this." Without another word, he turned and joined the men.

Rhodri put his arm around me as I moved to stand next to him. "Are you okay?" he asked softly.

"I'm just spiffy." I laid my head on his shoulder.

"Shall I take your new toys up to the tower for you?"

"You're going to be busy. I can take it up."

"There's a lab here, in the house?" Daniel asked, in surprise, responding to a comment of Eric's I hadn't heard.

"In the dungeon," I offered around Rhodri's shoulder.

"In the dungeon?"

"Under the tower."

"You have a dungeon under the tower." He shook his head. "You live in a tower, so I suppose it shouldn't surprise me that there's a dungeon beneath it. Where else would it be?"

"We generally refer to it as the basement," Rhan said, flashing a repressing look my way.

"I've always preferred dungeon," I muttered *sotto voce* at Rhodri.

"Behave yourself," he murmured back at me.

"Why do you have a lab here in the house?" Dan asked.

AIDS, I thought.

"Rhodri and Pentraeth are both doctors," Rhan explained. "Along with their work at the hospital, they do a lot of research. They also like to do this research at odd hours, therefore, they have a lab in the basement."

All of which was true, as far as it went. He just neglected to mention that their main research, in the lab in the dungeon, was the family's extended lifetimes. They're determined to find a nice, solid scientific reason for it. Grandmama finds their research a source of great amusement.

On Beltain Eve and Samhain Eve, all the changed members of the family are required to participate in Druidic ceremonies with Grandmama. It's both an affirmation of the continuation of their lives and a celebration for the man who made it possible. Part of the ceremony is the symbolic drinking of Brenainn's blood. There's a rotating schedule of volunteers from the Clan who donate blood for the ceremonies.

The suggestion had been broached, not by me, that it was time the ceremony became more symbolic and that we dispense with the actual drinking of blood. After all, even the Catholic Church uses wine. It was not well received and was accompanied by an excessively long lecture on why real blood was necessary. No one's mentioned it since.

Modern technology being what it is, we're now able to test blood for impurities and diseases. No one wants to risk introducing a killer virus into the family if we can avoid it.

Part of their research is centered on why some people don't survive their Ritual of Change. Mom gave them one of their latest theories. She had a terrible time during her Ritual; we almost lost her until Rhodri happened to discover she's allergic to type O blood, both positive and negative. It makes her violently ill.

Then, of course, there's Trys. Even though they prefer he not haunt the lab, they do a lot of research into the differences in him. Trys is the only one in the family born of changed parents and the sole reason a person is now required to get sterilized before beginning the Ritual of Change.

One of his weirder notions is playing vampire with his favorite ladies. Garlic, crosses, being bitten on the neck, Van Helsing—they act out the whole sordid script.

Personally, I think they should chain Trys in the dungeon until they figure out just what it is that makes him tick. We were going to have to keep Trys away from Dan. His eccentricities were only going to lead Dan away from his investigation and that could endanger us even more.

"We're going down to the lab," Rhodri said. "Are you sure you don't want me to take that upstairs for you?"

I shook my head. "I can take it. It's not that heavy."

"Are you sure?"

"I think I can manage it."

Eric picked up the cooler and headed for the tower. Rhodri started to follow, then turned and studied me.

I raised an eyebrow. "Yes?"

"Are you going to tell me what you're up to?"

"*Moi?*" I laid a hand on my chest and did my best to look innocent. "I'm up to about five-eight."

"Oh my God," he muttered. "I'm going to go hide in my

lab. Call me after the battle is won, okay?"

"You don't want to hear my St. Crispin's Day speech?"

He shook a finger at me. "Too much Shakespeare."

"There is no such thing as too much Shakespeare."

"Never mind, I'll be in my lab if you need help raising the drawbridge."

Smiling, I watched as he walked away down the hall muttering to himself. When I couldn't hear him any longer, I turned in the opposite direction and headed for the kitchen.

Jody, thankfully, (since I had been banned from the kitchen for the remainder of the day) was nowhere to be seen as I slunk into the freezer and appropriated three pints of Häagen-Dazs. I snagged a six pack of Diet Coke on my way out and was on my way up the tower stairs when I heard Jody repeatedly asking who'd been in his kitchen.

The main reasons that I had chosen to juggle a good-sized box, a six pack and three pints of ice cream up the tower stairs were sprawled across my couch as I entered my rooms.

"Well, if it isn't the Beltene," Roseanne Davidson drawled.

"Shut up," I said rudely, sliding the Diet Coke and the Häagen Dazs off the box into her lap.

"Ow," she yelped as she caught the six-pack. The ice cream bounced off her knees and onto the floor. "Shit, Rhi, how the hell am I going to explain these bruises to Eric?"

"That's easy, just tell him Rhi did it," Elaine Dalton advised. "No further explanations will be necessary."

"It's a damn good thing you're pregnant." I stared at Elaine as she smiled complacently back at me and patted her bulging abdomen. "How far along are you?"

"How many times have you asked that question?"

"Recently? Every time I see you."

"Do you have some sort of maternal mental block which prevents you from remembering this information?"

"Well?"

"Twins."

"We knew that three months ago when you took on the dimensions of the Goodyear Blimp. I would've expected you were up to quadruplets by now. What's the latest due date?"

"The first of November."

"Maybe I shouldn't volunteer you."

"I'll be fine. You're not planning that I should do any lifting, moving any furniture, calisthenics?" She continued as I shook my head, "Then I'll be fine."

"You probably should be home in bed."

"Nonsense, I feel fine."

I shook a finger at Roseanne. "You're the nurse. If she goes into labor, you're responsible and I'm leaving."

"She's just fine. Quit fussing, Rhi." Roseanne stood, put three of the Diet Cokes in the fridge, got spoons and then handed out the pop and ice cream.

"Okay," she said as she settled herself back on the couch. "Jessie had all the stuff you wanted ready when we got there; we retrieved your spare key from Eula and the shipping guys from the Metalworks hauled it all up here. You want to explain what the hell's going on?"

I dropped onto the couch across from them and propped my feet on the coffee table. "You know about the body I found last night?"

Roseanne looked pityingly at me. "Breakfast conversation, Rhi. Normally it would have been pillow talk, but you kept them out all night."

"Then you're aware of all the circumstances surrounding it and the fact that it looked like a vampire kill? And that everyone is sure it was left there for me to find?"

At their nods, I continued, "They still don't have any computers over at the sheriff's department—and let me tell you, that is a problem I intend to resolve in the very near future, whether they like it or not. Righ mentioned last night that Lige intends to have me take care of the computer stuff for this crime wave of ours. Particularly since they don't think last night's body will be the last. So, I've decided to get a jump on things and get rolling before they ask. To that end, I recruited the two of you to assist me.

"In those boxes we now have two more computer systems, Pentium II's complete with CD-ROM, MS Office Pro, modems and printers. We're—less Elaine, of course, who's not going to pick up any more than a sheet of paper at a time— going to rearrange my desk, set those puppies up, set up an area for incoming shit from the sheriff's department, and we're going to be ready to roll whenever they get around to mentioning it."

Elaine was shaking her head as I finished.

"What?"

"Who knows you've started this?"

"Us. Well, Rhodri suspects something's going on, but I doubt anyone else has. Except maybe Taliesin, since I sent him over to run the photography studio while you're here. And Jessie, since I badgered the systems out of him and away from their intended owners."

Elaine grinned at Roseanne, "We get to have ringside seats when the word gets out."

"Amazing, isn't it?"

Sometimes it's best not to say anything.

It took Roseanne and I the rest of the afternoon to rearrange my desk and set up the new computers. Roseanne and Elaine fiddled around with their new systems while I straightened my end of the desk.

Dinnertime was upon us when we finished. I stretched the kinks out of my back as I looked down at my friends. "So, do you want to be brave and have dinner downstairs or do you want to leave and see if your spouses have found their way home?"

Elaine groaned and pressed a hand against the side of her abdomen. "Home," she voted.

Roseanne nodded, "Home. I'm not up to Trystan tonight."

I looked at her. "Are we ever up for Trystan?"

"Well, there was that one memorable time when I actually went out with him."

"Temporary insanity."

"He can be extremely charming when he wants to be."

I rubbed a hand across my eyes. "Yeah, when he wants something."

"Now, Rhi, in a family of very attractive men, he stands out in the crowd," Elaine said. "And don't give me that put-upon sigh. Trystan and Dylan are probably the best looking men in your family, with Rhodri and Righ not very far behind."

"You've been deprived of sex for too long," I informed her.

"Nonsense," she returned. "Where there's a will, there's a way."

"Please don't give me any details. I don't think I could stand it."

Laughing, Roseanne held out a hand to help Elaine out of her chair. "We're out of here, my lady Beltene. We'll see you in the morning."

"What time do you plan on starting, Rhi?" Elaine asked, picking up her sweater and purse.

"Oh, hell, we might as well start at the break of dawn. Eight?"

"Eight it is," Roseanne agreed. She dangled a key in the air and looked inquiringly at me.

"Keep it," I said. "Chances are you'll get here before I get up anyway."

She nodded. "We probably will. See you in the morning,

Rhi."

"'Night, ladies."

I was deep in the middle of reading one of my new manuscripts, subject vampires, when someone tapped me on the shoulder. The manuscript, which I'd thankfully not been holding, slid across my desk as I came several inches out of my chair. I had obviously forgotten to lock the door behind Elaine and Roseanne.

I took a moment to collect myself and return the manuscript to its original position before turning to find our new sheriff standing several feet away. "Don't sneak up on me!"

"I didn't sneak. Can I turn that down?"

That was my CD player. My standard practice is to load it with seven CDs and press random. Then I have hours of unrepeated music. This evening's choices were Aerosmith's "Nine Lives"; Led Zeppelin's "BBC Sessions"; Wynton Marsalis' "Tune in Tomorrow" soundtrack; Seal, Page & Plant's "Walking into Clarksdale"; and George Michael's "Older." Daniel seemed to think the volume was too loud.

I raised an eyebrow and shrugged. "I suppose," I said ungraciously, not bothering to point out that the windows weren't rattling.

"I didn't sneak," he repeated after turning down the volume. "The entire United States Cavalry could have come up those stairs and you wouldn't have heard them."

"Did you come up here just to scare the bejesus out of me or did you have a reason?"

"Shit," Dan muttered, dropping onto the nearest couch and leaning his head back.

"Well?"

Without lifting his head, he said, "There's another body."

"Oh," I said in a small, guilty voice.

Daniel sat up and looked at me.

"The same as last night's?" I asked. So much for my fervent hope that we wouldn't find any more bodies.

"Not quite. This time he left the cooler sitting next to the body. Otherwise it was identical."

"Where was this one?" *Hiding out in my tower has definite advantages*, I thought, *provided I get a deadbolt for my door, one without a keyhole on the outside. At least that way I wouldn't hear about or find any more bodies.*

"Across town, at the edge of a corn field on Llywelyn Road. Lars Morrison's place. Laid out on its back, hands folded on the chest with the cooler sitting by its feet. Morrison's youngest boy found it about four this afternoon."

Dear God. I'd rather find the bodies myself than subject the Clan's children to the experience. "How is he?"

"Dead."

"*Philip?*" I shrieked, surging to my feet and flipping my chair over in the process.

"Excuse me?" Dan frowned.

"Philip Morrison? Old Man Morrison's youngest boy? The sixteen-year-old who found the body? He's dead?" I questioned, sure as soon as I spoke that the sheriff and I were talking about two different people.

"Oh." He took a deep breath. "No, he's fine. Better than most of us, actually."

"Thank the gods." I picked up my chair and sank heavily into it.

"He thought it was rather exciting. His dad didn't seem nearly as pleased."

"I miss all the good stuff," I grumbled. "Did he have the shotgun out?"

"Yes, as a matter of fact, I did see a shotgun."

"It's the one he shot his wife with," I confided.

"What?"

"In the arbor."

"Mr. Morrison shot his wife in the arbor?"

"Yep."

"When?"

"Well," I shrugged, "it was fifteen years ago."

"Fifteen years—"

"The Hathaway sisters consider it to be the climax of one of the finest Hathaway reunions ever held."

"He shot his wife at a family reunion?"

"He certainly did."

"Do they have these gatherings often?"

"Every year on the first Sunday in October. Attendance for family members is mandatory."

Dan closed his eyes for a moment.

"When did he get out of prison?"

"Who?"

"Lars Morrison."

"He never went to prison."

"Probation?"

"He wasn't charged. It was justifiable homicide."

"Why ... No, I'm not even going to get into it. Could we please keep to recent murders?"

"Okay. You're sure Phil is all right?"

"He's fine. He went off with your cousin Trystan for something or other. Does your cousin always exhibit bizarre behavior?"

Always. "Of course he does; I've been telling you that for days."

"Days?" Dan raised an eyebrow.

"All right, so it hasn't been days. It certainly seems like it." *Lord and Lady,* I thought, *if Phil has started hanging out with Trys, I might be forced to intercede. Phil is too young for Trys' shenanigans and the gods help us all if his dad decides to take matters into his own hands.* "What did Trys do that you found particularly strange?" I inquired, looking at him from under my lashes. Grandmama was fast becoming the person at the top of my list of people to talk to.

"He wanted to keep the blood. Both the blood in the first cooler and the new blood. He got pissed off when I refused to let him have it."

I didn't answer. Obviously, we were going to have to keep a tighter rein on Trys until this crisis was over. It was one thing for everyone in the clan to know about him and overlook his strangeness, but Daniel didn't know, and Trys catching his attention could only lead to trouble. I was definitely going to have a chat with Rhan about his son.

"What did he intend to do with the blood if I'd let him have it?" he persisted.

The spectrum was limitless, and I knew I didn't really want to know what he planned to do with the blood. Hell, I didn't even want to speculate on what he *might* want to do with it. "Trys is a warped idiot," I answered.

Daniel's silent scrutiny only lasted until I couldn't take the stress any longer. Silence has always been one of those things guaranteed to drive me screaming into the streets. I changed the subject.

"Was the new one ... embalmed, too?"

"Yes."

I was relieved that he let my change of subject pass without comment. Not that I thought for a moment that he wouldn't return to the subject sooner or later. And then an explanation would be required. Hopefully, we could postpone the question until after he was Welcomed, because I wasn't sure there was any way for me to explain Trystan to an Unwelcomed person. "Was it someone from the county?"

"No."

"That's a relief."

"I suppose that's one way of looking at it."

My look was intended to chill his bones.

"It's difficult to find a motive or find a killer when you don't know who the victims are," he explained, not looking the least bit chilled.

"I hadn't thought about it that way."

"I noticed."

"I've been more concerned about how this is ..." My words died off as I realized there was no way for me to discuss my concerns with Dan while he was Unwelcomed. This was fast becoming a real pain in the ass. I could see we were going to have to remedy this problem soon.

"What time is it?" I asked, noticing the deepening shadows.

"Quarter to eight," he answered, as he kindly refrained from pointing out that I was wearing a watch.

Horrified, I stared at him. "You're kidding."

He waved at the window.

"I missed dinner." Again. This was not going to put me in good graces. I hadn't made it down to dinner since Sunday. "Well, shit."

"I need to talk to you."

A huge yawn caught me before I could get an answer out of my mouth. "Now?" I managed.

"I suppose it can wait until the morning."

"Good. What time in the morning?"

"Eight o'clock."

"Lord and Lady." This was not good. Roseanne and Elaine planned to be here at eight. "This fixation you have with early morning hours does not bode well for our working relationship, Sheriff Thorpe. Go away."

"Eight o'clock is not early," he returned.

"It's earlier than I prefer it to be." With a minimum of respect, I herded him toward the door and into the stairwell. "Good night, Daniel."

I closed and locked the door on his response. All I wanted to do was find something to eat and fall into bed. The crack of dawn and everyone accompanying it were going to come all too soon.

Chapter Eight
Thursday, far too early in the morning

My first indication that the crack of dawn had arrived was the smell of freshly brewed coffee. While I don't cope well in the morning without drinking large amounts of it, part of my morning ritual is hovering over the coffeepot while it perks, inhaling the aroma. It was a pleasant change to lie in bed and inhale it.

A brisk pounding on the door dispelled the illusion of a quiet morning.

"Good morning, Sheriff Thorpe," Roseanne said after flinging my door open.

"Mrs. Davidson." His wary tone was the final blow to my illusion.

"Don't you dare go up there and wake her," Roseanne said firmly over the sound of footsteps crossing the room below me.

"She knew I was going to be here at eight," he responded, stopping by the window seat.

Elaine giggled. "You expected her to be up?"

The charged silence below catapulted me out of bed. I really did need to go rescue our new sheriff. He didn't have a chance if he got into a battle of wits with my two cohorts.

The silence had disintegrated into an armed truce by the time I joined them. The ladies were sprawled on one of the couches and Daniel was sitting stiffly in the window seat.

"Good morning," I said in the most disgustingly cheerful voice I could manage.

No one answered as I filled my cup with coffee, snagged a piece of the coffeecake Roseanne had obviously gotten from the kitchen and settled into my chair behind the desk. A glance around the room curtailed my urge to do Sister Mary Elephant impressions.

"Are introductions in order?" I inquired, knowing full well they weren't, then continued on without waiting for a response, "Elaine Dalton, Roseanne Davidson, Daniel Thorpe." There was a quiet murmur of hellos from the three of them. "There, now that we all know each other, would you like a cup of coffee, Daniel?"

"No, thank you." *A verbal response, things are looking up.* "I was under the impression that we had a meeting scheduled for eight o'clock this morning."

"We did."

"It's eight-thirty."

"I'm running a little late."

"We have an audience."

"I don't think I would refer to them as an audience. They're up here to assist me."

"In what?"

"You're not up here to commandeer my computer?"

His quick frown darkened the room. "Why do you think I might be here to commandeer your computer?"

"Really, Dan, you're in a small town now. The Brennen County Osmosis Line is much more efficient than Ma Bell— if there was a Ma Bell."

"Who told you?"

"There's not a single computer at the sheriff's department."

"I noticed."

"It's an oversight in your budget."

"For once, we agree."

"So?"

"So why do you think I need your computer?" His gaze touched on the two shining new computers sitting at the end of my desk.

"Come on, Danny m'boy, let's just agree that computers are in the near future for you and the boys, but in the meantime, you're going to be collecting an amazing amount of hopefully useful, but probably useless, information and you need a clearing house. One out of the way and already trained. Here we are."

He rubbed his jaw and studied the tapestry on the wall behind me. Through his unintelligible mutter, I heard something about rabbit holes.

I braced my feet on the back of my desk and balanced my office chair on two wheels. "I resent the implication that I make you feel like you've fallen into Wonderland."

His stare moved down to me.

I dropped my chair to the floor and smiled. If looks could kill, I would've died where I sat.

"Tell you what," Roseanne said, standing and holding out a hand to help Elaine off the couch, "we'll waddle off downstairs and visit Grandmama for a bit, then we'll come back. That'll give you a bit of privacy."

I wasn't sure I wanted a bit of privacy with an unhappy sheriff.

"Thank you." He graced them with a smile.

I waited until they were out the door before turning back to face him. The smile had disappeared.

"I've been assured that the only computers I have a chance of using are here at Beltene House and that you really are a deputy. And that you're more than capable of setting up a system to deal with the information that we've already started receiving."

"So I have been volunteered."

"*You*, Ms. Beltene. *You* have been volunteered."

"And just who are you sending over to assist me? Some computer whiz-kid you've been hiding in the basement of the jail for just this sort of project? Some hacker you've locked away for a rainy day?"

His uncomfortable silence was my answer.

"I didn't think so. I will take care of your information and as the Beltene, I intend to conscript a certain amount of labor to assist me." I held up a hand to stop his protest. "If you delegate this mess to me, you have to accept the fact that I'll have Elaine and Roseanne helping me."

"This will be classified information—"

"They're the wives of two of your deputies."

"It's still classified—"

"Lord and Lady, they're not going to be out selling it on street corners as soon as it comes in."

"I'm sure they're quite trustworthy, but—"

I crossed my arms and stared at him until he stopped speaking. "Sheriff Thorpe, their presence here is not up for negotiation."

He contemplated my tapestries again. While he was deciding whether or not to accept my terms, I flipped all the appropriate switches and turned on my computer.

"Will we give them the lobotomies before or after communion?" The question boomed into our silence and raced wildly around the room.

Daniel jumped and looked around for the owner of the snarl. I bit my lip and turned my speakers down.

"What the hell was that?"

"Taliesin, quoting Tom Gilcrist."

"Who?"

"Taliesin is one of my cousins and he's quoting Tom Gilcrist, a character in *The Father, Son and Liam Kennedy*." His silence prompted me to add, "It's a book."

If he continued to glare at me at five-minute intervals, I was going to become immune to the sobering effect.

"Actually, I've replaced most of the common Windows sounds with WAV files. My computer talks back quite a bit."

"Do you normally have the volume set loud enough for everyone in the house to hear?"

I shrugged. "I forgot to turn the sound down last night when I was done playing."

"Playing what?"

"Vampire chess."

"Vampire chess?"

"Pete invented it for Trys. It's cool. Count Dracula is the black king and Van Helsing the white king. It's three-D and the sound affects are amazing."

"Do you get fan mail?" He changed the subject rather abruptly.

"Fan mail?"

"Yes, do you get any fan mail?"

"You're not serious."

"Trust me, I'm serious. Do you?"

"Tons."

"Are any of them threatening?"

I raised my eyebrows and chuckled humorlessly. "Yes."

"How many?"

"Better than half of them."

"What?"

I shrugged. "I write horror novels about vampires for a living. My novels draw weird and strange individuals. Perhaps because I don't always subscribe to the traditional. Or perhaps because I write exclusively about vampires. I don't know.

And it certainly doesn't help when the tabloids publish my name and address a couple of times a year. Some of the mail goes to my publisher, but most of it comes here. A sack or so a week is normal."

Horrified, Dan stared at me.

"I usually get more just after a new book or edition comes out and after the tabloids have played fast and loose."

"And better than half of them are threatening?"

"In one manner or another."

"What's been done about them?"

"Done?" *What did he want me to do with them*, I thought, *frame them?* "Nothing's been done. I just throw them away."

"You throw them away?"

"Yes."

"You take letters which threaten you and throw them away, like there's nothing wrong." His eyes sparked angrily. "Do you realize the killer has more than likely written to you?"

"That's ridiculous."

"No, it isn't. With the way this case is falling out, my guess is that he's written you several times, detailing what he intended to do."

"That's stupid."

"He's looking for your admiration, your awe and your gratitude for what he's doing for you."

I scowled at him.

"You throw them away," he muttered.

"I only keep the good letters," I explained. "And then only long enough to read. I sort them and ship them to the service in Marquette that answers them for me. I don't know what they do with them. My best guess is that they have an entire room devoted to file cabinets full of the letters and their responses. Hell, they could scan them and store them on disk for all I know."

His face took on martyred proportions as I continued. "I'm sorry. I don't keep the nasty ones. How was I supposed to know that you were going to need them? I don't read most of them. Besides a lot of them are more bizarre than threatening, anyway."

"How are they bizarre?" I recognized the tone in his voice. It's the one hounds get when they pick up the scent.

"Well, a lot of religious fundamentalists send me letters. I'm going to burn in hell because I write for Satan and try to lure unsuspecting readers into his clutches." I would be forever grateful that none of those fanatics would ever know about the family Druidism and the side effects it has given us. The thought of the witch-hunts that would follow the release of that information made me nauseous.

"Most of them carry on in that vein. They usually deteriorate dramatically by the end of the letter. These are, of course, the same people who play records and tapes backward so they can claim they heard Satanic messages in them.

"There's a series of letters from a fundamentalist congregation somewhere in Alabama which swears I have a satanic code encrypted into my books and I'm turning my readers into Satanists. They never have explained how I manage it. They have, however, banned my books in their town. There's a fine of five thousand dollars and a jail term of ninety days if you're caught with one of them. My books carry the same punishment as Stephen King's. Don't you just love censorship? Is that bizarre enough for you?"

"Keep going."

Obviously, the man was warped. Maybe he would fit in around here. I racked my mind for a moment, trying to visualize letters I tried not to read. "There are generally really weird letters from California. Nothing particularly threatening, just strange. There's a reason why people say California is like a bowl of granola. Fruits, nuts and flakes."

"You have such subtle viewpoints."

"Dan, I live in the back of beyond. Who's going to hear them?"

"I suppose there's a point in there somewhere. Is that all you can remember?"

I frowned. "Keep in mind, these are letters that I don't like to read. I generally discard them as soon as I see which way the wind is blowing."

"Yes," he said. "Anything else?"

"Just the letters from the vampire hunters. They seem to think I've got Count Dracula stashed in the dungeon. And, of course, you've got the ones who want to be initiated into vampirism."

Dan was shaking his head as I paused. "Unbelievable."

"Believe it. Oh, you should run through your files. Lige keeps records on all of my visitors, even if he doesn't charge them with anything. It's rather pathetic. They come armed with wooden stakes, garlic and holy water. The really sad ones come with silver bullets. They're terribly stricken when you tell them silver bullets are only good for werewolves." I shook my head. "The number of people who can't tell the difference between fact and fiction boggles my mind."

"It doesn't surprise me in the least. Lige already has Rachel sorting through the files. Do you remember any lett— Shit, it's a moot point, you pitched them."

"I'm sorry. The only ones I've kept are the series from Alabama. I get a few every couple of months. It's a testimonial to how stupid and irrational people can get. It's unbelievable."

"Not really."

"In my little corner of the world it is."

"A Cleaver household. Wonderful."

"Well, I don't know if I'd go that far," I complained, closing my eyes and shuddering at the idea of a Druidic-Catholic Cleaver household containing Trystan.

"I do. Now, you'll have to give permission for your letters to be released to us for examination," Daniel said.

I opened my eyes as papers rustled. "What are those?"

"The first of the reports that Rachel has sorted out of the files."

"Put them there." I pointed at the lateral file cabinet next to him. "I'll call this morning and have the service package up the letters. Henry can pick them up and bring them back here."

"Henry Branton?" Daniel stacked the files neatly on the cabinet.

"Yes, Henry Branton. You know, the gentleman you in-terrogated on my doorstep yesterday just before you bounced my manuscripts. He works for Superior Deliveries. He's quite good about picking up and dropping off stuff on his way there or back."

"I remember, but I'd prefer we pick them up ourselves. I don't want to trust them to anyone."

"Whatever turns your crank."

"What kind of phone lines do you have running up here?"

I raised an eyebrow. "Phone lines?"

"Are you going to need any additional lines?"

"I have two lines coming up here. A regular one and one for the fax and computer. There's also an intercom which con-nects me with my office downstairs where there are several lines."

"So there is a way to screen the calls that will be coming in?"

"Sure, we can have Eula take them."

"Eula?"

"The Beltene's secretary."

"You say that like you're not the Beltene."

Open mouth, insert foot. "Eula's been the Beltene's secre-tary through several Beltenes. I guess I tend to think of her more of a fixture than my secretary."

"If she can handle the calls, then we won't need to run a local line over from the sheriff's department."

"She can handle them," I assured him.

"Are you sure?"

"Think of a polite, dignified version of Rachel."

"Got it. The lines you have up here are unlisted numbers, aren't they?"

"I haven't totally lost my mind. Of course they're unlisted."

"Good, then I don't need to worry about you getting any calls up here. We'll filter them all through either our office or yours. If they need to fax or modem anything over, we'll give them the number then, otherwise all the information will be taken down and delivered to you. I don't want you exposed to either the killer or the mobs."

"Mobs? There are mobs in Sevyrn?"

"The media invaded full force last night once the second murder was picked up on the national news. CNN, WXYZ and the local Marquette stations are here, the papers have arrived and, of course, the ever-present tabloids."

"Yuck."

"To say the least. I want you to stay inside as much as possible. If you need something, we'll get it and bring it here for you."

Grabbing my binoculars, I ran up to the roof and peered toward town. Downtown was clogged with news vans, satellite equipment and people. "No problem, Danny m'boy," I assured him as I returned. "I'll keep my travels to a minimum."

"I'm leaving now. I'll be back around lunch time."

"We won't have much done by then. It'll take all morning and most of the afternoon to get everything arranged. And I have to get something to eat before I do anything."

"I understand perfectly," he muttered. "Goodbye."

"Dan?"

I heard his sigh from the stairway. "What?"

"If you really are coming back at lunch time, bring food with you."

"Anything in particular?"

"Nope, just so long as it's not slimy."

"Not slimy," he repeated. "Nothing slimy. Right."

I grinned as I grabbed the phone to locate my partners in crime.

Chapter Nine
Thursday, throughout the morning

I suppose if the truth were told, I would have to admit that Roseanne and Elaine set up the programs for the sheriff's department that morning. After Daniel's departure, I located them in Grandmama's office and we had breakfast before we returned to my tower. Knowing my two friends were as fully computer-literate as anyone in the county, with the possible exception of Trystan, Jessie and Pete, I left the implementation of the sheriff's programs in their hands.

With my extra-curricular duties delegated, I managed to get a couple of chapters edited before we were invaded. Since I had to leave the door open for Eula and the messenger from the sheriff's department—who, to no one's surprise, turned out to be Tom Dalton—it had taken less than an hour for my household to realize that this meant there was free and unlimited access to my rooms and they took it upon themselves to stroll up for a visit. Some, most prominently Cris and Tangwen, stayed.

It's difficult to edit with a half dozen people carrying on several different conversations around you. It only took about forty-five minutes before I gave up and decided to go Web-surfing. If I was going to be interrupted, I might as well be doing something that interrupting wouldn't hurt. Besides, I could always claim that I was doing research for the sheriff's department if anyone objected. Then again, perhaps I could just invoke the power of my office and tell them to get stuffed. Maybe there is something to being the Beltene.

Almost everyone in Brennen County uses ojibway.net. Jessie

Blackthorne, who happens to be a full-blooded Ojibway, is my brother Rhodri's best friend, has been since they were kids. They were practically inseparable until college. Rhodri went to Michigan and Jessie went to Michigan State. Just don't try to talk to either of them on the Saturday of the Michigan/Michigan State football game.

Jessie discovered computers while at college and returned home just in time to become, as I usually put it, our chief teckie nerd. He's installed every major network in the county; the Metalworks, Beltene House, the courthouse, library, schools, bank and the hospital. He, at Pete and Trystan's repeated request, also became one of the first ISPs in northern Michigan.

Rhodri, Dylan and I weren't far behind Pete and Trystan, and the five of us, with Jessie, still remain the foremost users in the county.

With a click, I dialed out. Everyone in the room looked up as my modem blitzed the room with the dial tone and connection squeals.

"Rhiannon?" Tangwen asked, her tone more impossible to ignore than the implicit question in my name. There is a reason why she's Brennen County's prosecuting attorney.

"Okay." I didn't even bother to lie. "So I'm going to play out on the Web."

She and Cris shared a look with Elaine and Roseanne, then they all returned to their previous occupations.

I was wandering happily from one site to another—I love hot links—when it occurred to me that I might actually be able to do some research for our sheriff.

Not that I thought I would find anything of major significance, but I was aware that there are tons of vampire sites out on the Net—I've checked out most of them over the years and from time to time run a search and look at the newest additions. And I was sure I'd seen something, somewhere, on embalming.

Of course, I'd been so wrapped up in my latest novel that I'd done little on-line except check my mail and the occasional reference in months. So, I clicked onto my favorite search engine and typed in "embalming." I was a little surprised at the amount of information available, but I printed off reams of stuff for the sheriff's department to read before moving on to vampires.

The results of my search and my lunch arrived at the same time. I hit PAGE DOWN as Daniel laid a pizza box in front of me. I peeked inside and smiled up at the sheriff. "Bacon, mushrooms and double cheese. Who've you been talking to?"

"Your brother. 'Nothing slimy' wasn't really helpful."

"Of course it was. It means no okra, liver or oysters."

"She has no taste." Trys drifted into the room and the conversation. "Raw oysters are a riveting, sensual experience."

Tangwen choked on her tea.

He flashed a quick, apologetic grin at his mother.

The rest of us managed to ignore him and Dan changed the subject. "Is the messenger system working out all right?"

"It's working fine. Tom's having a high old time running from your office to Eula's to here and back again."

"He volunteered."

"I'm sure he did," I said dryly as Tom's wife chuckled quietly.

"Rachel seems to think that your phone line isn't functioning properly."

"It's functioning just fine."

"Are you sure?"

"I'm positive." His skeptical look prompted me to continue. "Lige has called three times, Eric has called twice, Luke has called twice and Rachel has called at least once every fifteen minutes since nine o'clock. To make sure I'm not slacking off, she says." I rolled my eyes. "Slacking off? Lord and

Lady, will you look at this mess? Slacking off? The last time she called, I told her that we'd get a hell of a lot more done if she'd quit harassing us—"

Daniel made an inarticulate noise.

I raised my eyebrows, grinned and added, "She might be a tad upset when you get back to your office. I didn't let her get a word in edgewise and then I hung up on her." I checked my watch. "And it's been eighteen minutes since she last called."

"She has a wicked tongue when she puts her mind to it," Tangwen commented.

"Thank you," Dan managed.

"You're welcome."

His eyes darted around the room as he cast about for a safer topic. "Shall we have lunch?"

Roseanne retrieved the paper plates, Cris found the Coke and Diet Coke and I slid the pizza onto the plates. We all ignored Trystan. He hates pizza.

"There's enough for your cousin," Dan said, settling one hip on the edge of my desk.

"He doesn't like pizza," I answered shortly, sending a firm look in Trys' direction to make sure he didn't announce what he would rather have for lunch.

None of us had taken more that a couple of bites of pizza when I looked over at my screen. Shakily, I reached out and ran a finger over the impossible words boldly displayed. My mind raced as I thanked every god I could think of that Daniel was chatting with Tangwen and not paying any attention to me. I slid my finger down the face of the monitor, dropped my hand to the mouse and clicked the IE screen down to the taskbar, leaving only the Windows 95 desktop visible.

Slowly, with my rising anger tightly in hand, I rose and walked over to my cousin. "Come with me."

Everyone looked at me. I could feel their confusion, but I didn't move my eyes away from Trys.

"What are you talking about?"

"Come with me, now."

"Why?" He crossed his arms and glowered at me.

Taking him by the arm, I dragged him to the open doorway. "I'll be right back," I said over my shoulder, as I resisted an urge to not only push Trys out the door, but down the stairs as well.

Tangwen and Cris were close behind us as we reached the bottom of the stairs. I waited until they had gotten out into the hallway before flinging the tower door shut. Then, still without saying a word, I dragged Trys down the hall and past Eula into the Beltene's office. I pushed him into a chair and then shut my office door.

"You are a bloody idiot!" I snapped, finally allowing my temper full rein.

"I don't know what you're talking about," he returned.

"Rhiannon," Tangwen began.

"Do you know what this idiot has done?"

She took a deep breath and bit her lip. "No."

"We have a website."

"Rhi, we've had a website for months."

"No, no, no, you don't understand. I'm not talking about the regular website for the Metalworks and the county. I'm talking about the new Beltene House website that comes up on the first page when you run a search on vampires."

Tangwen sat down. "Oh, Trystan."

"It's a lovely website. Pete and I worked very hard on it." Trys recrossed his arms and resumed glowering at me.

"How the bloody hell did you manage—"

"I didn't put anything out there that would endanger the family."

"It comes up under vampires."

"It comes up under a lot of different searches."

"Vampires? Why did it have to come up under vampires?"

"Because of you."

I froze. For all my wandering on the Web, I do not have a personal website, nor can my e-mail address be in any way attributed to Rhiannon Beltene, author. "Because of me?"

"You're the vampire novelist. You've gotten tons of e-mail and the site's only been on-line a couple of weeks."

"I've gotten e-mail?" My voice, which was torn between screaming at him at the top of my lungs and whispering in shock, attempted a compromise and got the words out in a hoarse croak.

"Tons."

He sounded so damned pleased with himself. After taking several deep breaths to calm myself, I turned and sat behind my desk. I looked at Tangwen and Cris, who were still looking at Trystan with indefinable expressions on their faces, then reached for the telephone.

"Come to my office," I ordered without bothering with any pleasantries, like identifying myself.

"Rhiannon?"

"I need to see you in my office," I repeated.

"Is this like, official?" Pete teased.

"Yes."

There was silence as he obviously considered what had prompted such a bald response. "You found the Beltene House website."

"Yes."

"Shit, I told him not to put your tower in there."

"My tower?" This time I opted for loud.

"Be right there." Pete hung up before I could say anything else.

As I sat there, waiting for Pete and glaring at Trystan, who was exuding as much innocence as he could, I decided that I wasn't really surprised that my tower was hidden somewhere in the depths of Trystan's website. After all, how else could I get tons of e-mail—Lord and Lady, if I was getting e-mail, that meant he also set up an e-mail address for me. The dungeon wasn't going to be adequate for the punishments I had in mind for the two of them.

The squawk of the intercom—something I've never had occasion to use—made everyone in the room start and look at the innocuous-looking box on my desk.

"Yes?" I said after figuring out which button to press.

"Sheriff Thorpe is here, Rhiannon. Do you have time to see him?"

"I'll be right out."

"Certainly."

"Don't let this, this ... don't let him out of your sight or out of this room," I ordered.

"Go take care of Daniel," Cris said. "We'll all be here waiting for you after you've talked to the sheriff."

The sheriff didn't look at all pleased to be seen in the secretary's office. Not that he objected to Eula; no, he wanted to see Trystan. But whether he wanted to see him to make sure I hadn't done anything physically damaging to him or whether he thought he'd figured something else out, I wasn't sure. Either way, I intended to make sure he saw very little of my idiot cousin over the next few days; even if I had to gag him and lock him inside his coffin. Tyrstan, that is.

"Yes, Daniel?"

"What's the problem?"

"Problem?" The quickly appearing scowl on his face convinced me of the uselessness of trying to pretend that I hadn't gone flying out of my own room with Trystan in tow, murder raging in my heart. "Trys is an idiot."

"So everyone keeps telling me. You want to give me a reason for your disappearing act?"

"Not really." His head came up and I hurried to intercept his protest. "It's family business."

His scrutiny as he considered the finality in my voice made me shift nervously from foot to foot. "Is it possible that it could become my business?"

"No." I didn't even try to misunderstand his question.

"You're sure your cousin isn't going to become the business of the sheriff's department?" Dan clarified his question just in case I had misunderstood. He looked over at Pete, who had just arrived and was leaning against the hall door with a distinct lack of color in his face.

"I'm sure."

"Are you?"

I lifted my eyes to meet his. "Yes, I'm sure. Trys is a royal pain in the ass, but he's never been a legal pain in the ass. He's not about to start now. Okay?" I offered up thanks to the gods that Trystan's record over at the sheriff's office was for his first persona and there wasn't any way for Daniel to trace it to him. Trystan, in his younger days as Trystan Brenainn Beltene had managed to get into a fair amount of official trouble. Rumor has it that a wee chat with Grandmama and Cris and a decade of sheepherding cured him of such nonsense. Personally I was beginning to doubt it.

He spread his hands and backed off, figuratively as well as physically. "Okay."

I slid onto the lateral file cabinet I'd been leaning against and wondered if obliterating the human male from the face of the earth wouldn't be the simplest solution. I jerked my head at Pete and sent him off into my office.

"Do you have any plans for this evening?"

Oh, hell no, I thought, *I've only got to keep Trys in line, figure out just what in the bloody hell he's pasted all over the Internet, pro-grams for the sheriff's department to supervise and a novel to edit. Not a single plan in sight.* "Not anything that can't be rearranged," I answered, "provided, of course, that I don't intend to sleep anytime in the next three weeks." Now, anyone who knew me, knew what a feeble bitch that was. I *always* get my sleep.

He looked guilty as he considered my sarcasm. "Oh."

"I was teasing, Dan." Well, sort of. I ran a hand through my hair. "What do you have in mind?"

"I have to run over to the State Police Post in Negaunee about five this evening and I thought perhaps you could ride over with me. We could go over some points I have questions about and maybe get a bite to eat after we pick up the stuff in Negaunee."

I would've loved to know who suggested this agenda. "I see."

"Is there a problem?"

They—most likely, in this case, Lige, Luke and Rhan—man-aged to conveniently twist this around so it couldn't be con-strued as a date and therefore I couldn't accuse them of matchmaking. Much as I didn't want to concede this battle, I was backed into a corner because of my promise to aid as much as I could in this investigation. "No, there's no prob-lem. You want to leave about five?"

"If that's all right."

"Five's fine."

"See you then." I stared at the empty, open doorway for a long moment after his departure.

"Damn," I muttered as I slid off the cabinet and headed back to my office to deal with the most immediate problem.

Chapter Ten
Thursday, the afternoon

My most immediate problem was sulking when I reentered my office; he sulked through my entire lecture and he was still sulking when I sent him off with Cris to have a long chat with Grandmama, since I obviously couldn't do anything with him. And I never did get a full description of what the hell he'd put out on the Internet. Pete, on the other hand, just kept laughing and assuring me that there wasn't anything dangerous out there—after all, just how the hell did I think they were going to skirt the compulsion and put anything confidential on the Net.

That's when I gave up, sent Pete to his room, Trystan out for a lecture and stomped back up to my room to see just what they'd put out on the Net.

Roseanne and Elaine, quite thankfully, had already gotten the scoop from the Beltene Osmosis Line and looked quietly busy as I stalked past them and dropped into my chair.

Elaine leaned around her monitor and watched me for a moment before speaking. "Rhi?"

I balanced my chair on two wheels and returned her glance pensively. "Umm?"

"Where is Trys?"

"Hopefully, Grandmama is turning him into a toadstool as we speak."

Roseanne chuckled. "Is the site that bad?"

I shook my head. "I haven't a clue. We couldn't get either one to spit up an accurate description of what the hell they threw out there. It comes up on the first page when you do a search for vampires. Isn't that bad enough?"

Elaine frowned. "I know Trys is into vampires, but why would he set up the key words like that?"

"Probably because the little shit has put my tower into it somewhere and given me a e-mail address so every wacko in the world can send me mail. Aren't we excited?"

"He gave you a public e-mail address?" Roseanne looked a little pained.

"Yep, and proud of it."

"You didn't kill him?"

"They wouldn't let me. Besides, Daniel came wandering down. I think he would've found it deeply suspicious if Trystan disappeared right after I dragged his ass down the stairs." I dropped my chair on to all four wheels. "I could just wring his little neck."

"We sent Sheriff Thorpe down. He was getting restless and I didn't think you really wanted him messing around with your computer."

I rolled my eyes. "Oh, that's all I would've needed, our sheriff getting a good look at what Trystan thinks is the coolest site out on the Web. He's says they've already picked up a couple of awards."

"You still on-line?"

"Yeah." With a click I brought IE back up on the screen. It looked exactly the same as it had before I hauled Trys out of my tower.

"Come on, Rhi, let's look at this." Roseanne reached around me and clicked on the Beltene House website.

Elaine came around the end of my desk, dragging her chair and Roseanne's. They scooted in close and we peered simultaneously at a beautiful Celtic knot wallpaper in pale mauve with a picture of the wrought-iron gate in front of

Beltene House gracing the center. After a moment, Trys' voice informed us that we were about to enter the domain of the Beltene family.

Clicking on the gate latch changed the picture to the massive front doors of Beltene House. This time, Trys warned us that we had entered the domain of the Beltene family of our own free will and were responsible for the consequences of our actions. Clicking on the doorknob zapped us into a full screen picture of the foyer.

"Oh, shit," I muttered, staring at the eleven animated icons scattered around my screen.

"Oh my," Elaine breathed, mesmerized by the animation.

"Sheepherding, perhaps," Roseanne commented, patting me consolingly on the shoulder.

Over all of us, Trys informed us that we had reached the foyer of Beltene House, home to Count Trystan Beltene (he really does have a title of sorts, but it is certainly not Count) and Rhiannon Beltene, noted vampire novelist. He offered us our choice of the icons and thankfully shut up.

"Where shall we start?" I asked, trying to identify what each icon represented, since Trys hadn't felt a need to label them.

"Why didn't he put a description on the icons?" Elaine asked.

"Because he's an irritating, insufferable twit."

"Maybe they're like story problems," Roseanne interjected.

In unison, we all crossed our fingers and hissed. Story problems had never been our strong point. "Okay, lets figure this out." I pushed paper at Elaine. "You keep track."

"This one has to be the ballroom," she said, tapping a nail against the screen. The icon she pointed out was of a couple waltzing, with an arrow that zipped through the icon on a regular basis.

"The Library. This has got to be the library." This icon

was a circular stairway with books tumbling down the stairs in a continual stream.

"I think we should track him down and if Grandmama hasn't turned him into a toadstool, we should do something really nasty to him," Roseanne said. "I think the fountain is probably the courtyard." The fountain icon was fairly sedate.

"How nasty?"

"Really nasty—let's go spike his coffin with garlic, holy water and crosses. The Surfboard's Lake Superior." The person on the surfboard kept falling off and there was a lightning storm behind him.

"Lake Superior?" Elaine frowned at Roseanne.

"Yeah, remember Rhi trying to convince us that we really could surf on Lake Superior, if we only chose the right time?"

It's amazing how sometimes people just won't let things go.

Elaine laughed. "I'd forgotten about that."

"Dracula has to be Trystan and the Iron Maiden is the dungeon," I said. Dracula kept changing from a human to a wolf to a bat to smoke and back to a human. The Iron Maiden creaked open and dripped blood. "The Cuisinart must be Jody—no, the kitchen. The voodoo doll has to be Jody, or maybe just voodoo. Lord and Lady, but I hate guessing games." The Cuisinart appeared to be perpetually spinning and the voodoo doll was randomly stuck with pins.

"The Celtic cross?" Elaine asked. The only animation on this icon was the rainbow colors that slid across the surface of the cross.

I sighed and looked at Roseanne. "St. David's?"

She bopped me on top of the head. "In the house, dummy. Has to be the chapel."

"Okay, then what is the cherub?" There was no doubt of Trystan's hand in this one. The cherub hanging off the monument in the icon was naked and making lewd gestures.

There was silence for a moment, then I shook my head

and laughed. "He took that one out of the house. St. David's Cemetery. Remember the cherubs on the Beltene monument?"

"And The Tower is you." Elaine finished her list with a flourish and looked up. "Where do we want to start?" The tower stayed motionless, but there were a ridiculous number of bats and wolves and vampires that appeared and disappeared around it.

"Not with the tower," I said. "I want to save the worst for last. That way I can work my way up to a glorious rage."

"Let's start with the cross," Roseanne leaned over and stole my mouse again.

We were back to the Celtic knot wallpaper and the quiet and beautiful interior of our chapel was the picture that appeared on the screen. It had obviously been taken when the sun was low in the west because the room was flooded with color from the stained glass windows in the southern and western walls. Sitting along the bottom of the screen were four icons. He actually labeled these and thankfully, they weren't moving. There was one for THE VATICAN, one for STONEHENGE, one for CELTIC MYTHS and, the gods help us, one for the DIVINE CIRCLE OF THE SACRED GROVE.

"Nothing too dangerous there," Elaine said, making a check by the Celtic cross on her list.

I wrestled the mouse away from Roseanne and clicked back to the foyer. "Now where?"

"The surfboard." Elaine was busily numbering her list in the order she thought we should follow.

I clicked on the surfboard. I had to give it to Trys; he'd gone to a great deal of trouble to get absolutely perfect pictures. This one was Lake Superior at sunset. Absolutely gorgeous. I've never figured out why anyone would want to live anywhere else. (Okay, so we get large amounts of snow—every place has its drawbacks.) The icons sitting on the beach were for MARITIME MUSEUMS, THE EDMOND FITZGERALD and MAINLY MARQUETTE. These were animated. THE EDMOND FITZGERALD kept sinking and MAINLY MARQUETTE was an active lighthouse.

"Safe enough," I muttered, clicking back to the foyer. "What's next?"

"The fountain."

With a look at Elaine, I clicked on the fountain and we found ourselves in the sun-dappled courtyard of Beltene House. The fountain, which is actually part of an artesian well, was in the foreground. Four unanimated icons decorated the screen, one in each corner.

Roseanne chuckled. "Versailles, Tripoli, Trafalgar Square and Piccadilly Circus. Jesus, I didn't even know some of these places had websites."

I clicked back to the foyer. "Next."

Elaine tapped a finger on the cherub and I sent us to, as expected, St. David's Cemetery. The Beltene family monument, with Trystan's lewd cherubs, basked in the summer sunshine. Funny, you'd have thought someone would have noticed Trys wandering around with a camera in hand. The cherub's quartet consisted of the TOWER OF LONDON, FUNERAL HOMES, MONUMENTS and the PÈRE LACHAISE CEMETERY. These were animated.

THE TOWER OF LONDON was a suitably bloody beheading; MONUMENTS was a block of marble with the words *Count Trystan Beltene* being perpetually chiseled into it and FUNERAL HOMES was merely a coffin that creaked open and shut.

The icon for Père Lachaise Cemetery gave Roseanne and Elaine the giggles. Jim Morrison stood looking at us for a moment, almost long enough that I decided it wasn't an animated icon, and then he dropped his pants. Shaking my head, I went back to the foyer.

"Maybe I'll just confiscate his coffin," I grumbled as Elaine pointed to the Cuisinart.

It was most definitely Jody's kitchen and the hot links were

French Wines, Cordon Bleu, Dining Etiquette and Recipes. We waited for a minute to see if any the icons intended to move.

"I surely do hope those aren't Jody's recipes," Elaine said.

Obviously, they weren't going to move. I clicked back to the foyer. "I don't even want to know. At least, not yet. Next."

"The dancer."

The ballroom, half of it filled with archery targets and the other half with dancers, appeared with four more of Trys' frolicking icons.

"Does Righdhonn have his targets in the ballroom again?" I burst out, having no trouble translating the weird mixture on my screen. Two Robin Hood links (one with a target and arrows, the other with what appeared to be a traveler getting mugged in a forest). A ballroom dancing link (a repeat of the opening icon sans the arrow) and a Rudolf Nureyev link (I couldn't tell if it was Nureyev, but it was definitely a male dancer) made perfect sense, in a twisted sort of way.

"Not when I came through this morning," Roseanne assured me.

"Thank the gods. Indeg threatened him with all sorts of physical abuse if he set them up in there again. I have more than enough things going on without an internal family spat." I bounced us back to the foyer.

"Here." Elaine touched the voodoo doll.

"Jody might let him live over the recipes, but if he was screwing around with Santeria in here ..." My voice died as a particularly vivid and bloody picture of a decapitated rooster appeared on screen. There was a number of what I hoped were nonsensical drawings surrounding it and four unmoving icons in a vertical row down the left side.

Elaine bolted from her chair and raced for the stairs.

"He certainly is a perverted little shit, isn't he?" Roseanne commented as I flipped back to the foyer. "He covered the bases, too. The Caribbean, Cuba, Miami and New Orleans. Are you going to talk to Jody?"

I looked at her.

"Oh, now don't be giving me that 'I'm the Beltene and I'm going to kick ass' look."

"Yes, I'm going to talk to Jody. If the gods are with us, Trys cleared all this first and there's nothing dangerous in it. If not, I'll let Jody take care of it."

Elaine came slowly down the stairs, stopping to get a Coke out of my refrigerator.

"You okay?" I asked as she settled back into her seat.

She nodded. "I just didn't expect that."

"Neither did we."

She smiled wanly. "Library."

He'd caught the library at about the same time as the chapel picture. It was flooded with late afternoon sun and looked naked without Grandmama sitting next to the fireplace. The links, sitting quietly on the steps of one of the spiral staircases, were WALES, IRELAND, CATHOLICISM and VIRTUAL POSTCARDS.

We looked at each other and shrugged as I clicked us back to the foyer.

"Now?"

"The dungeon."

I paused, ready to click on the IRON MAIDEN. "No, I think we should go into my tower first."

"I thought you wanted to hold that for last."

"I did, but somehow I think we should save Dracula for last." Clicking on my tower brought up an excellent picture of my three-hundred-year-old carved oak door. And we discovered that Trys could count higher than four. By my count there were eight icons scattered around the screen, most of which were constantly in motion.

"Welcome to the lair of renowned author, Rhiannon Beltene," Trystan's voice informed us. "She's rather reclusive, so I cannot allow you to go farther into her world of vampires, but if you click on the key, you can send her an e-mail message in homage." The key kept dissolving into a letter, which folded itself up into a envelope, which then dissolved again into a key.

"Lair?" I sputtered as Elaine and Roseanne burst into laughter. "Homage?"

The remainder of the icons were fairly innocuous. GODIVA (a truffle which some invisible soul was munching on), HÄAGEN DAZS (another invisible person was eating directly out of the pint), DIET COKE (merely a Diet Coke can spinning eternally on an axis), and both Stratfords. LED ZEPPELIN and AEROSMITH finished his collection of icons for my tower. These were both merely hover buttons with the bands' names on them. Considering the icon he'd come up with for Jim Morrison, I was rather relieved. The gods only knew what he might have come up with for Steven Tyler and Robert Plant.

I bopped back to the foyer and into the dungeon. It was my turn to start the laughter. He had hot links for TORTURE CHAMBERS (this time it was an active rack), SHEEPHERDING IN WALES (a cute little lamb bouncing up and down) and an ESCAPE TUNNEL, which did absolutely nothing.

"I have to see what Trys considers an escape tunnel," Roseanne said, stealing my mouse and clicking on the tunnel. Silence descended quickly as we realized what we'd just seen.

"Mother of God," I whispered as I flipped us back into the dungeon to look at his escape tunnel one more time. It hadn't changed. We landed in the BELTENE HAUNTED FOREST— we knew it was the haunted forest because there were two signposts on either side of the picture, one of which welcomed us to the Beltene Haunted Forest. The other had a lot of small printing on it and I leaned close to read the disclaimer. "Can you believe this?"

"Was that what I think it was?" Elaine asked, not being an aficionado of Shakespeare in it's many forms.

"Oh, yes, I rather think it was."

"Keanu Reeves." She identified the actor.

"Don John," I corrected absently, identifying the character—one of Trystan's favorites—as I flipped back to the dungeon and into the escape tunnel again. Trys had taken a film clip and somehow spliced it between the dungeon and the haunted forest. Kenneth Branagh's version of *Much Ado About Nothing* was nothing less than spectacular and Trys had cheerfully lifted the entire escape tunnel scene right out of the movie. His disclaimer gave full credit to Branagh, Reeves and Renaissance Films, along with a little note, which essentially said that his great friend Ken had graciously allowed him to use the film clip.

"His great friend Ken is not going to keep him from getting killed," I sputtered. "This is too much."

"Does he actually know Kenneth Branagh?" Elaine asked. I gazed levelly at her. "I have no idea."

"Oh."

"I don't think I have the strength to look at Trystan's room," I said, dropping my head on the desk. "Besides, I have to go to Negaunee with Daniel at five."

"Really," Roseanne purred. "And why is that?"

I turned my head and fixed her with the best evil eye I could muster. "He has questions."

"Uh-huh."

"Get stuffed," I told her as I bounced us all the way back to the foyer and clicked on DRACULA. I winced as Trys' room appeared.

"That looks fairly normal," Elaine commented. "Although it's a rather eclectic collection of icons."

We have obviously been overexposed to Trystan. Our concept of fairly normal where he's concerned is definitely twisted. The walls were hung with tapestries depicting witch-hunts, beheadings and vampires. Lots and lots of vampires. In the center of all this gore was Trystan's pride and joy, his coffin, with its lid tightly closed. Starkly black, with a scarlet satin interior, rumor has it he's had carnal knowledge of an indecent number of ladies in it.

His collection of icons were MADAME TOUSSAUD'S (unmoving—it must have challenged even Trystan to try to animate a wax museum) and BELTENE WOODCARVING & METALWORKS (one of Trys' sculptures, rotating so you could see it from all views). INTERACTIVE VAMPIRE CHESS (Van Helsing and Dracula with swords), VAMPIRES (a repeat) and DISNEY (the Disney logo, unmoving).

"Give me back that mouse," I snarled as Roseanne stole it again.

"I want to see what he's got under vampires."

"Lord and Lady." Here he had ELIZABETH BATHOY, VLAD DRACUL, BRAM STOKER, Trystan's bedtime stories and vampire porn icons. Luckily, considering the history and content of these icons, none were animated.

"Bedtime stories?" Elaine questioned.

Roseanne clicked on the icon. None of us really wanted to go look at the vampire porn.

I stared at the screen, sure I was about to hyperventilate. Roseanne grabbed my shoulders and jerked me around. "Take a deep breath. Again." I took a deep shuddering breath and looked over my shoulder at the screen.

"That's it. I'm not going to kill him, I'm not even going to send him to Wales, I'm merely not going to allow him to have his hundredth birthday party," I said in a quiet, even tone after scrolling through his index of bedtime stories. "Pete, I'm going to kill."

"Now, Rhi ..."

"There is only one thing that might actually save the two of them and that's that Daniel asked me about these this morning. And, silly me, I told him I threw them all away. How could I not have guessed that Trystan would rummage about in the trash so he could collect all my hate mail and throw it out on the Net for everyone in the bloody world to read." My voice was into the higher registers by the time I finished speaking. Roseanne and Elaine had both moved their chairs away from me.

The telephone rang.

"What?" I snarled into the receiver.

"There is no need to get snippy with me, young lady."

I sighed. The last thing I needed right now was Rachel. "Can I help you?"

"I'm canceling your trip to Negaunee."

My eyebrows rose. "Why?"

"Sheriff Thorpe is otherwise occupied."

"Fine."

Rachel hung up without saying goodbye or asking if I was working diligently on the sheriff's projects. Obviously, she was still pissed about me hanging up on her earlier.

As I laid the telephone down, I looked at my friends. "Just what would supersede our sheriff's trip to Negaunee?" I answered my own question. "Shit, they've found another body."

Chapter Eleven
Thursday, after dinner

There was another body. Tom called to inform Elaine and Roseanne that he and Eric would be working late. He refused to give us any details and in a wee huff, I sent Roseanne and Elaine home for the evening and went looking for Grandmama. She wasn't in the library and it certainly did look naked without her.

I eventually found Grandmama with Cris and Gwydre. They were huddled in Gwydre's office studying something strange and esoteric on his worktable.

"Did you turn Trystan into a toadstool?" I asked, eyeing the object with apprehension and hope.

Grandmama straightened and smiled at me. "It's an interesting thought. Some days that boy is worse than the itch."

I thought she was understating the issue. "He'd make an attractive toadstool."

"We just talked some sense into him," Gwydre said.

"Can I assume you're referring to my son?" Rhan asked as he joined us.

"As ever," I said. "Have you heard about his latest transgression?"

His grunt was the only affirmation I was going to get as he eyed my clothing. "Are you ever going to learn how to dress properly?"

I was dressed for going out into the night and was wearing jeans (a relatively hole-less pair), a vintage '73 Zeppelin tour T-shirt (Righ brought it back from the show for me), a jean jacket and my Reeboks. "I think, under the circumstances, that a discussion of my attire is inappropriate."

Grandmama smoothly interrupted what looked to be an explosion worthy of Chernobyl. "Were you looking for us, *cariad*?"

"I wanted to know how your talk with Trystan went."

Gwydre shook his head. "Trystan is not particularly fond of you at this moment. He has also taken quite a dislike to Daniel."

"I noticed. What did the little twerp have to say about his new website?"

"He insists it's harmless." Grandmama said. "And, to a point, he's correct. The compulsion will not allow him to endanger us, no matter what the medium."

"Harmless? Do you know what he's done?"

"Besides adding your tower and awarding you an e-mail address?"

"Yes."

"No, *cariad*," she said, smiling. "That was the limit of his confession."

"He's been rummaging around in the trash and recycling my hate mail out onto the Net."

"What?" Rhan bellowed.

"It's under his room. He refers to them as his bedtime stories."

Cris' laughter stopped both of us in our tracks.

"What?" I asked.

"Rhiannon, he's been collecting your hate mail for years."

"Years?"

"Years," she confirmed. "Pete must have almost a dozen four-drawer file cabinets in his room. Surely you've seen them."

"Of course I've seen them," I admitted. "But it never occurred to me that they were storing all my hate mail in them."

She spread her hands.

"Okay, fine." I conceded defeat. "It's probably just as well because Dan seems to think I could have gotten letters from the killer, detailing his plans." I stopped and smiled suddenly. "And I'll let the two of them sort the letters."

"Delegation. The trademark of every great leader."

I stopped myself before I told her to get stuffed. Although, from the twinkle in her eyes, I think she knew what I'd very nearly said.

"Is he going to behave around Dan?"

"He's going to behave," Cris said. "I guarantee it."

I narrowed my eyes. "What did you do to him?"

"We simply had a talk with him. He has seen the error of his ways."

I withheld judgement. Personally, I had serious reservations about Trystan seeing the error of any of his ways.

"Trystan aside, Rhiannon," Cris said. "What are you going to do about Daniel?"

Sighing, I sat down and stared thoughtfully at them. After the silence and disapproving looks threatened to become a permanent addition to my life, I relented. "He's going to have to be Welcomed. Soon."

"Do you think he's ready?" Grandmama asked.

"No. And even if he were, it'd still be a difficult Welcoming, with this vampire-obsessed idiot running about. The trick, of course, is going to be presenting the information to him in a manner he'll believe." Hell and damnation—it almost sounded like I knew what I was talking about.

"Will he believe it?" Grandmama directed the question to Rhan.

"I don't know. He's capable of accepting it, but whether he'll be able to so early, I don't know."

I shrugged. "As far as I can see, it's a moot point. He needs the information to combat these murders effectively and he hasn't run screaming from the county yet. Which is a positive sign."

"I never thought he would," Rhan said smugly.

"I don't know what you were thinking about. An Unwelcomed sheriff," I scolded.

"If you were attending to the business of being the Beltene as well as you do for your writing, you'd have known," he snapped.

"I'm aware of that and my views on being the Beltene are equally well known," I replied tightly.

"Rhiannon is quite correct. Daniel needs to be Welcomed. As soon as possible," Grandmama said into the charged silence.

"Do we have the proper numbers to Welcome him?" Gwydre asked.

I relaxed. "I think so. I'll take a formal vote in the morning."

"Your parents need to be here," Cris said over Rhan's *sotto voce* grumbling about my inexperience.

"When are they due in?"

"Tomorrow morning, with the conference set for noon. This fiasco needs to be ended," Grandmama answered.

"I agree. I assume you want to talk to Mom and Dad about Daniel before the meeting?"

"They have to see Daniel before it begins," Cris said.

I looked askance at her. "I expect they've both already seen him. After all, Dad did help hire him."

"True," Cris answered. "But they need to see him tomorrow morning."

I didn't ask. I should have, but I didn't.

"We'll gather with your parents in my room tomorrow morning at ten," Grandmama said. "Then they can meet with Daniel."

"Actually," Cris said, "they'll meet him before ten."

I sighed, decided to ignore her and rested my chin on my hands. "I wish Dad or Rhodri was handling this."

"You're doing just fine," Grandmama assured me.

I sighed again.

"You're just feeling sorry for yourself," Rhan admonished.

"I've been up at the crack of dawn two days running. There's a lunatic out there somewhere embalming people and storing their blood in Baggies for me. My rooms have been invaded. Your son is being a pain in the ass. I'm entitled to feel sorry for myself," I returned.

Daffyd skidded around the corner and into the office. We all turned to look at his breathless figure with a certain amount of trepidation. "Man, am I glad I found you," he blurted out.

"Daffyd, there are five people in this room, all of whom you could conceivably be looking for—which one of us did you want?"

"You, my lady Beltene," he answered with a low courtly bow. Either he'd been hanging out with Dylan and Trystan too much or his Druidic training included more than just magic.

"What now?"

"If I hadn't found you, like, in the next five minutes, we were going to gather up a posse to look for you."

"Excuse me?"

"Where have you been?"

I stared at him for a long moment, before trusting myself to answer his question. "Here."

"You have to keep us posted on your whereabouts."

"Who is us?" I asked after unclenching my teeth.

"The sheriff's department and those of us in the house who are keeping an eye on you."

I added both the sheriffs to my hit list. "So who was looking for me?"

"How did you know it wasn't just me looking for you?"

"Daffyd. Credit me with a little intelligence. If you'd been looking for me and I wasn't there, it wouldn't have been any big deal. You would have run across me sooner or later. You wouldn't have been systematically searching the house. So someone else was looking for me and discovered I wasn't there and put you on alert. Who is it and what do they want?"

"Daniel was looking for you."

"Wonderful, what does Daniel want?"

"He needs something explained."

Cris and I exchanged a look. "Explained? What does he need explained?"

"He didn't say. He just said I needed to find you."

"Am I supposed to meet him somewhere?"

"He didn't say."

Exasperated, I turned and grabbed Gwydre's telephone, dialed Eric's beeper number and entered Gwydre's direct line number after the tone. If there was a new body, I was confident that Sheriff Thorpe was somewhere close to Eric. I picked up the phone before the first ring ended.

"Eric?"

"Jeez, Rhi, where the hell have you been?"

"I'm in Gwydre's office."

"Ms. Beltene." The voice on the phone was becoming as familiar to me as the irritation in his tone.

"Sheriff Thorpe."

"Where are you?"

"I'm in Gwydre's office." I answered with as much patience as I could muster.

"In Beltene House?"

"Where the bloody hell else do you think Gwydre might have an office?" Rhan's disapproval of my language was palpable. I was either going to have to ignore my family's censure or be more careful; Daniel, I was sure, was totally unaware of the seriousness of my crime.

"You need to keep us informed—"

"If you think I'm going to call in every time I leave my rooms for a moment, you're sadly mistaken, Sheriff Thorpe."

"Perhaps a better idea would be to give you a pager."

"A beeper?" I questioned incredulously.

"Yes, I'll bring one with me when I come over with this note."

"And what note is that?"

"I have something that needs to be explained. Eric said, and Lige agreed, that you or your grandmother would be the most logical people to decipher it's meaning. I'd rather not bother your grandmother, if you don't mind."

"Of course not. Where are you?"

"Glyndwr River Park."

"In the park?" I was outraged. "This lunatic left a body in our park? Children play in that park."

"The body's in the courtyard of the community center, near the river."

"In the park," I muttered. "Who found it?"

"Your brother, Rhodri."

"When?"

"Almost two hours ago."

"No, I mean when do you want your note translated? Do you want me to come over there?"

"No!" His tone was sharp and immediate. He brought it down to a manageable level and continued, "No, I don't want you to leave Beltene House tonight. I'll be over when I finish up here, but it will be late—or early, depending on how you look at it."

"Sheriff Thorpe, under normal circumstances, I much

prefer to go to bed with the rising sun instead of getting up with it."

He chuckled. "So I understand."

"Call before you come and I'll meet you at the door."

I could almost see him nodding his agreement. "Thank you, Rhiannon."

"You're welcome."

Chapter Twelve
Three-thirty AM

I decided, all things considered, that I probably wasn't going to see Daniel much before two or three in the morning and made my plans accordingly. Cris, Grandmama and I had a quiet dinner together and tried to figure out what Daniel could have that needed translating. And why Eric figured Grandmama or I would be best at translating whatever it was they'd found. Grandmama, I could understand, but me? I have very specific ranges of information I can be considered an expert on—none of them related to each other. After we finally gave up, I went straight to my tower, locked my door securely and went to bed with the telephone right next to me.

It took several rings before I realized that the phone was the object making all that noise. I punched the appropriate buttons and tried to sound wide-awake. "Hello."

"It's Dan."

My clock said three-thirty. "Good morning."

"Ready?"

"I am, but you sound beat. Are you sure you want your explanation at this time of the morning?"

He sighed. "I'd love to say no, but there's too much we need to do tomorrow and if I can get this taken care of tonight, it's one less thing we need to worry about."

"No problem. Come to the kitchen door."

"Thanks. Give me ten minutes."

"Okay. Dan?" I caught him before he hung up.

"Yes?"

"Coffee?"

"I would be forever in your debt. See you in a few minutes."

I got dressed, made coffee and beat Daniel to the back door. Righdhonn, whom I firmly believe only needs to sleep about once every six months, was lying on the couch watching the fire. I settled into the chair across from him.

"Were you over at the park?"

He nodded, the shadows of the fire transforming him from the affectionate cousin I loved to someone dangerous and angry, someone who has followed his dark sword into battle after battle in search of justice.

I shook off my fanciful thoughts. "What's the matter, Righ?"

He sat up slowly and looked seriously at me. "He's getting weirder, Rhi. And everything he does is aimed directly at you. I'm very fond of you, *cariad*. I do not want you becoming a statistic."

Before I could think of a response to his concern, someone knocked on the door. Righ beat me to it, gun drawn, standing to one side of the doorway. He motioned for me to stand away from the door.

"Righ?" Surprise made my voice come out in a husky whisper.

"Hush," he commanded softly. Then, in a louder voice, asked, "Who is it?"

"Daniel."

The sheriff didn't seem to be at all surprised to be met at the door by my cousin and a drawn weapon. After making sure Dan was alone, and locking the door securely, Righ slid his gun back into its holster.

"Guys?"

"No, Rhi, we're not being too cautious." Righ answered.

He put a finger under my chin and tilted my worried gaze up to meet his. "There's no predicting this killer. Right now, you're not in danger. But if he decides you should be the audience for his next performance or if he decides you've somehow betrayed him—I'd rather be overly cautious than let you get hurt."

Dan's confirming nod did nothing to settle my shaky nerves. That I could be in danger had, to this point, seemed like something silly the men were fussing about. That the danger might seek me out within the confines of Beltene House had never even crossed my mind, until now.

"The coffee should be ready," I said. "Want some, Righ?"

"Maybe later," he said, lying back on the couch.

Guard duty? I wondered.

Shaking my head, I turned and headed for the tower, with Daniel close behind. Once securely locked in my rooms, I poured us both a cup of coffee and then settled into the window seat to study the exhausted man sprawled in Roseanne's office chair. "Was this one like the others?"

He nodded. "With one difference."

"Whatever it is that you need to have deciphered."

"Yep." He stood and came over to the window seat, pulling a 3 x 5 card encased in plastic from his pocket. "This was rubber-banded to the body's left wrist." He frowned as I made no move to touch it. "It's been fingerprinted."

I shook my head. There wasn't any way to explain the sense of terror and dread that came over me just reading the card. I certainly wasn't going to touch it. And I knew now why Eric sent Daniel to me. There were only three other members of the family who could have explained this as well as me; one was in Wales, one was babysitting a photography studio and I really didn't want Grandmama to have to deal with this.

"I don't understand this—message." He turned the card around to look at it. "Nor do I understand anyone's response to it. Eric and Righdhonn both swore in several languages. Rhodri couldn't believe it had been left, but seemed puzzled over the content. And no one wanted to explain the damned thing to me. All they wanted to do was send me over here with it. Can you really explain what it means?"

"Yes."

Shaking his head, he read the message aloud. "'A sacrifice for Our Lady of the Night, beloved of the God of Death.' What the hell is that supposed to mean?"

I dropped my head into my hands and said a quick prayer to any listening god for strength. I could hear Dan as he paced up and down the room. Finally he stopped and dragged Roseanne's chair over to sit in front of me.

"Rhiannon?" he prodded.

"Which part do you want first?" I asked, letting my hands fall to my lap as I sat up.

"Our Lady of the Night." He tapped the card against his knee.

"This is going to take us into early Celtic myths," I warned.

"I don't care where it takes us, just as long as it makes this note understandable."

"Oh, it's perfectly understandable. In fact, it comes across clear as a bell. It's a good thing Rhan wasn't out there, he would've treated you to a full blown cow."

"No one has seemed happy about it."

"I'm not surprised." I stared at my hands for a moment, collecting myself. "Okay, here goes. 'Our Lady of the Night': Pwyll, king of Dyvet was at the Mound of Arberth when he saw a young girl riding toward him. He sent one of his men after her, but she disappeared."

"When did this happen?"

"In antiquity."

"Is this necessary?"

"I'm trying to give you the short version. If you prefer a different version, I suggest you wander back down the stairs and I'm sure Grandmama would be delighted to give you a course in Celtic Myth. It should only take five or six days."

"I'll be quiet."

"Thank you. The same thing happened the next day. On the third day, Pwyll went after her himself, calling for her to stop. She did, telling him her name was Rhiannon, daughter of Hyveidd Hen, and that she'd come to the mound out of love for him.

"The upshot is they finally got married. Rhiannon had a son who was mysteriously abducted. It was claimed that Rhiannon herself had killed the child and her punishment was to sit beside a mounting block and tell her story to anyone ignorant of it. Then she was to suggest that she carry them on her back to court.

"The child, in the meantime, had appeared in the stables of Teyron, who raised the boy, naming him Gwri Gwallt Euryn. When the child was three, Teyron took him to court, passed by the mounting block and Rhiannon told her story, ending with her offer to carry them to court.

"The boy refused and Teyron told how the child had appeared in his stable. Rhiannon and Pwyll recognized their child and Rhiannon was freed of her trouble, which in Welsh is Pryderi, and that name was added to her son's name.

"Pryderi became king after his father's death and married Kicua. He returned from Bran's expedition to Ireland as one of seven survivors, bringing with him Manawyddan, son of Llyr, who married Rhiannon." I took a break, getting up to refill our coffee. I settled back into the window seat before continuing.

"So, there you are. Of course, I don't think I need to go

into the part about the spill and how the land became barren and how it was fixed."

"Thank God. Can I assume that somewhere in your explanation is the reason why this particular lady is 'Our Lady of the Night'?"

"Of course. There are several Welsh women who could be called Our Lady of the Night. But, in this case, Rhiannon is a horsewoman. She comes out of the Mound of Arberth. The horsewoman is an image of death, but mounted on a white horse, the color of daylight, she's the image of resurrection. Rhiannon is Our Lady of the Night."

I laughed at the expression on his face. "Trust me. I cut my teeth on Welsh myths and legends. Rhiannon is the right one."

"But you said there were others."

"There are," I agreed. "But since this whole fiasco is aimed at me and my name is Rhiannon, I think we can assume I have the right woman."

"Did anyone make sacrifices to her?"

"Not that I'm aware of."

"Wonderful. So how do you explain the part about being 'beloved of the God of Death'?"

"Since he's alluding to Rhiannon as Our Lady of the Night, I suppose with her images of death, you could consider her 'beloved of the God of Death.' Of course, it could just be a twisted play-off on our name."

Dan frowned. "Your name?"

"Beltene. It's one of the names of the Cymric God of Death." I took a deep breath and looked up at him. "Basically that note is the killer bragging that he's killed for Rhiannon Beltene."

There was a lengthy pause as he digested the implications of what I'd told him. "Okay. Why did your brother appear not to understand what this meant? Everyone else did."

I pulled my legs up and wrapped my arms around them, wishing I knew a way to rid myself of the sudden chill that enveloped me. I'm not one of the mystics in the family, but I could almost visualize the tendrils of death wrapping themselves around my county and my people. A shudder rippled through me and Dan leaned forward and put a hand on my arm.

"Are you okay?"

"Yeah, I'm fine."

"Rhodri?"

"My brother, the research scientist? The one who's sure nothing important happened before nineteen forty? You can't expect him to know anything about the legends."

"Why a sacrifice?"

I contemplated my coffee cup and possible trajectories long enough for Dan to rest his hand on top of my cup. "Because the man is a bloody lunatic."

"Agreed, but why use the phrase if there's no meaning to it?"

I took the time to consider his plaint seriously. "Sacrifices are made for a number of reasons," I said. "They can be made out of fear or gratitude, out of want or love. Of course, sucking up to the gods has always been a good reason, too."

Dan slid down in the chair, with his legs stretched out in front of him. "With only what we have to go on, I'd say the sacrifices have been made out of love and admiration, with a bit of sucking up for good measure."

"I'm not a god."

"No, but chances are, the killer has put you on a pedestal and the end result is the same."

"Lord and Lady, Daniel, I spend more time in the doghouse than on any pedestal."

A small smile lit his face. "Now, why would you spend time in the doghouse?"

I shook my head and turned to look out the window. "I spend almost as much time in the doghouse as Trystan."

The moonlight gleaming over the forest was making me feel claustrophobic, closed up within the walls of my tower. I love being out in the woods on moonlit nights. I love the expanse and the air and the peace and—I needed to get outside.

"Come on." I stood and grabbed Dan's hand and waited until he got to his feet before I started up the stairs.

"Rhiannon." He jerked his hand away.

"We're just going up to the roof, Danny m'boy." Did he really think, in the middle of the family homestead, I was going to drag him, kicking and screaming, into my bed? I don't think so.

"Oh." Slowly, he followed me up the stairs.

I was already kneeling on the bench on the eastern side of the roof when he arrived. "Isn't it beautiful, Daniel?" I asked, spreading my arms wide to include the lake, forest and starlit sky around us.

He sank onto the next bench and gazed out over the moonswept lake. "Yes, Rhi, it is. Thank you."

We sat in silence; watching and listening to the waves play in the moonlight, until the two cups of coffee I'd had demanded my attention. "Be right back," I said, getting up.

"Rhi?"

"Bathroom," I answered. "Too much coffee."

He stood. "I need to go home and get some sleep."

"Okay." I bounded down the stairs ahead of him, leaving the trap door for him to shut.

I have, to this day, sworn that I only spent about five minutes in the bathroom that night. When I reentered my bedroom, it was to find the sheriff sound asleep in my bed. To give him credit, it looked like he'd sat down for a moment, fell asleep and tipped over. Now, the question was should I wake him up and send him on his way or take pity on the man, cover him up and let him sleep?

I took pity on him. He looked exhausted and I didn't have the heart to wake him up. I pulled his boots off, wrestled his forty-pound equipment belt from around his waist and pushed him into the middle of the bed, so he wouldn't roll off the side. He never even twitched. I pulled the covers up over him and shook my head.

Collecting the telephone, so it wouldn't wake him when it rang, I went downstairs and turned off the coffeepot. Then I lay down on one of the couches and pulled the afghan over me. Tomorrow was going to be a very active day and I had the feeling I was going to need all the sleep I could get.

Chapter Thirteen

Friday, sometime after seven AM

Dan slept through the phone call from Roseanne, which woke me up at seven. Lord and Lady, I almost slept through her phone call. I stumbled up the stairs, firmly reminding myself that I was getting too old to sleep on the couch and didn't remember that the sheriff was occupying my bed until I noticed the blond head on my pillow. Muttering to myself, I veered away from the bed and any thoughts I might have harbored about getting into it and managed to get into a clean pair of jeans and a tattered sweatshirt before zeroing in on the coffeepot. I drank my first cup hovering over the pot, urging it to perk faster.

Nursing my second cup, I sat in the window seat and tried to remember what was supposed to happen this morning and why it was important enough that I had Roseanne call and make sure I woke up. I was still trying to remember when my door buckled slightly, then reverberated gently.

I stared at it in horror; I'd forgotten my parents arrived home this morning. I'd also forgotten that Cris had been sure Dan would meet my parents before our ten o'clock meeting. Someday I would learn to insist on a detailed explanation of her prophecies. I sent a brief, appalled look upward and with a sigh, opened the door to become enveloped in my father's arms.

"Hi, Dad," I said, returning his hug and kissing his cheek.

"Rhiannon, my love, how are you holding up? That's quite a computer setup you've got there," he boomed, kissing me on the cheek and looking over my shoulder.

"Not too bad, I suppose," I said.

"Where'd they come from?" He turned his piercing gaze on me.

"I purchased them," I returned.

"On whose authorization?" Too many years of being the Beltene and the Mayor were evident in his voice.

"The Beltene's," I said smugly, turning to greet my mother.

"Ignore him," she said. "You know how he hates flying."

"Did they make him get in a crop-duster this time?" The notion that someone the size of my father—something just this side of a grizzly bear—could be terrified of flying was a subject broached lightly. The smaller the aircraft, the worse he got.

"No, dear. It was larger than a crop-duster by at least several feet. The problem was Teleri. She insisted on organizing a group sing-along of Buddy Holly hits. You know how she adores teasing him," Mom explained over Dad's growling.

Only the fact that Teleri had raised him after his parents died saved her from imminent death when they flew together.

I managed to keep a straight face. "Someday they'll put an international airport in Marquette," I promised him.

"Not bloody likely," he grumbled. He'd barely finished speaking when my bed creaked.

Now, my bed always creaks. It's an old-fashioned brass bed with the original springs. But it was painfully obvious that I wasn't the person making it squeak.

My parents looked upward; Mom with interest and Dad with a pensive glare.

"It's a long story," I said.

"I'm sure it will be," my father murmured as a series of creaks floated downward.

"Damn," I swore.

"Problems, dear?" Mom inquired.

"Would you believe my tower's haunted?" It was becoming a distinct possibility. The only question was who would be doing the haunting.

"Not unless you killed Trystan while we were gone," Dad returned.

"No, but there is promise for the future if he doesn't behave."

"Is this our daughter making noises as if she were the Beltene?" Mom teased.

"I don't believe this," I muttered as footsteps crossed the floor above our heads. When Cris had said Mom and Dad were going to meet Dan before the meeting, I'd kind of envisioned running into them in the hallway, not sitting in my living room listening to Dan stumble around my bedroom. I definitely was going to have to insist on details next time.

"Interesting," Dad said, heading for the stairs before Mom headed him off and pushed him toward the couch.

"It's going to be a long day," I complained, closing my eyes as water began to run in the bathroom.

"This is going to be an enthralling explanation," Mom confided to Dad as she settled in beside him on the couch.

"It had better be a complete explanation," Dad growled.

I spent several minutes hoping Dan heard them come in while attempting to articulate some sort of explanation for my parents. I was still searching for the proper words when explanations became redundant as Daniel sauntered down the stairs, barefoot, clad only in jeans, with his gunbelt over his shoulder and carrying his boots and shirt. This I would never live down.

"Lord and Lady," I groaned, dropping to the window seat.

Daniel was blithely unaware of my parents' presence. There was no way for him to see them as he came downstairs. The couch sits under the ceiling of the upper floor and his back was to them.

"Morning, Rhi," he rumbled softly. "Coffee ready?"

"Morning, Danny m'boy," I answered in a somewhat distracted tone. "Coffee's ready."

Behind him, my parents rose and walked toward us.

He turned to pour himself a cup of coffee and froze.

"Introduce us, dear," Mom instructed; her timing, as always, impeccable.

"Good morning," he said, his eyes widening as he recognized my visitors.

"Good morning," my parents said, looking him over with interest.

"Rhiannon," Mom prompted.

I intently watched a spider web in the window and limply waved a hand in the air. "I know you all have met before, but if you insist. Daniel, these are my parents, Pwyll and Branwen. Mom, Dad, this is Daniel Thorpe."

Dad narrowed his eyes, then raised his eyebrows. "Our new sheriff was in your bed?" he asked incredulously.

"Yes, sir," Dan agreed stiffly, thankfully making no attempt to try to explain what he had been doing in my bed.

Dad made his way back to the couch in silence and sat down. Mom looked from Daniel to me to Dad.

I took a deep breath. I knew what was coming. Daniel, on the other hand, couldn't possibly have been prepared for their laughter.

I avoided his eyes as he silently questioned my parents' somewhat unusual response to finding a man in their daughter's bedroom.

"The sheriff," Dad managed to say between fits of laughter. "Does Rhan know?"

I ignored both men, turning to appeal to my mother.

She responded to my wordless plea by pulling Dad's helpless body from the couch and propelling him toward the door.

"Rhan said to tell you there's a meeting in your office at ten," she told me over Dad's laughter.

"The sheriff," he chortled.

"I thought we were having it in Grandmama's room."

She shrugged. "He said your office."

"Has he told Eula so she can have everything ready?"

"I would imagine he has."

"Maybe I should call and make sure," I mused.

"If you like." She contemplated me for a moment, then smiled. "Don't forget, your office. Ten o'clock."

"I'll be there," I promised.

"It was very nice to meet you, Daniel. Welcome to Brennen County." Mom closed the door behind them.

I covered my eyes and muttered to myself in Gaelic.

"Those were your parents." Dan's voice was distant.

"Yes."

"What was so amusing?"

I uncovered an eye to find he'd already filled his coffee cup and was about to refill mine. "I don't think you really want to know."

"Your father was laughing so hard when he left that he could barely walk. That's a peculiar way for a man to react when he finds a man in his daughter's bed." Dan sat down in Roseanne's chair and leaned an elbow on the desk.

"I don't think I'm up to any sort of explanation," I said, resting my head against the stone wall.

"And why did he want to know if Rhan knew?"

"Lord and Lady," I muttered. Rhan knew. I was sure of it. I also had every confidence that the Brennen County Osmosis Line was functioning properly and everyone in the county knew he'd spent the night in my bed. And they would assume that I'd spent it in bed with him.

"What kind of meeting is the Beltene conducting this morning at ten?"

I peered up at him. "At ten? Hell and damnation, I have two of the bloody things this morning; one at ten and one at noon. Everyone got home from Wales late last night or early this morning. So we get to have a core group meeting and a family meeting so I can acquaint the family with the chaos currently eddying about their home." And the Beltene's growing feeling that the new sheriff needed to be Welcomed in order to stave off the increasing danger to the family. And sometime before joining everyone in my office, I needed to do a quick survey to see if I was part of a majority or a minority.

"That's it?"

"Can you think of anything else I should tell them?" I could. My list was getting longer by the minute.

"No," he said, after a lengthy pause. "I suppose not."

There really wasn't any way for me to explain that my dad had dissolved into hysterical laughter because I'd lost this round to a stubborn man, just barely past his first half millennium. Nor could I go into anything about a Welcoming. Not only would he think I'd lost what was left of my mind, but I, along with every other Welcomed person in the county, was unable to explain any of it to him until he'd been Welcomed.

Having been a fairly sheltered child and adult, I'd never been closely involved with an Unwelcomed person. It was rather a pain; this skirting around subjects, unable to articulate your thoughts, was probably responsible for more Welcomings than anything else. You could only take so much of it before starting to lose your mind.

"I'm sure I should insist on a thorough explanation," Dan said, leaning over to put on his socks and boots. "But I really need to get to the office."

Thank the gods, I thought.

"I'm really sorry about falling asleep upstairs and getting you into ..." he floundered, obviously wanting to use the word *trouble*, but in the face of my father's laughter, not sure it was the right word.

"Don't worry about it. They'll get over it and you needed the sleep."

"Thanks, Rhiannon. For the coffee and your bed." He smiled until he caught sight of his watch. He shrugged into his shirt. "Damn, I've got to get moving."

I stayed, cross-legged on the window seat as he moved to the door. "See you later, Dan."

He paused with a hand on the door and turned to face me, the seriousness he and Righdhonn had had earlier returning. "If you have to leave the house today—and I'd much prefer you didn't—Righdhonn, Eric, Luke or I are the only acceptable choices to accompany you. Don't leave the house alone."

I chewed on my lip. "Is it really that dangerous for me?"

"We don't know. That's what makes it dangerous for you. We don't know what he's planned and we don't know how much he intends for you to be involved. Your safety is real high on the priority list right now. If Righ isn't around, and he should be, beep one of us and we'll come to you."

Jerkily, I nodded. "Okay."

He started down the stairs, but stopped and looked over at me. "By the way, I have a present for you." With an underhand throw, he tossed something at me.

Too much baseball as a child, I thought as my reflexes took over and my left hand shot out and neatly caught the object. "It's a beeper." I frowned at him.

"Yes, ma'am. And we will be paging you on a regular basis."

"Lord and Lady."

"And I expect you to call the number displayed."

I sighed and frowned.

He shook his head. "Not a negotiable item, Rhiannon. We need to know you're safe. Later, you and Eric work out a danger word, so if you're forced to call in, we know you're in trouble."

Forced to call in? I could feel my eyes getting bigger. "Dan—"

"There's a good chance that none of this is necessary but, as Righ put it last night, we'd rather be overly cautious and keep you from getting hurt. Okay?"

I looked from the beeper to our earnest-looking sheriff.

"Okay, Rhi?"

Nodding, I agreed, "Okay."

"The word of the Beltene?"

The man learns fast what we consider to be important, I thought, lifting my chin into the air. "You have the word of the Beltene."

"Good. Could you call the office and tell them I'm on my way?"

"Sure." I shook my head as he disappeared from my sight. Call his office, indeed.

Chapter Fourteen

Friday, 10 AM

I should have known they'd put Rachel in charge of beeping me. By the time I reached my office, she'd already beeped me a half dozen times. We were currently in negotiation about how many times a day was adequate. Daniel hadn't told either of us. Rachel's view was at least three or four times an hour; I thought three or four times a day was sufficient. The jury was still out.

Everyone looked up as I entered.

"Where have you been?" Rhan asked, his level tone an indication of pique.

"Attending to the duties of the Beltene," I returned in an equally level tone as I settled behind my desk. Righ smothered a smile from his position next to the window.

"We looked for you in the tower."

I checked my watch. "I promised to be here and I'm only five minutes late. So why would you be looking for me?"

"Rhiannon Argadnel," my father remonstrated.

I leaned back in my chair, crossed my arms and stared at the members of my family scattered around my office. Besides my parents and Rhan and Righ, we'd been joined by Morgan (the family priest), Gwendolyn (the family nun, complete with traditional habit), Cris, Gwydre and Grandmama. Since I had decided to really be the Beltene, I was going to have to nip this tendency of theirs to direct and restrict my movement in the bud. "I have not been the most attentive of Beltenes since my appointment. That has changed. I am the

Beltene, with all the whistles and bells that entails. I do not need to be led to my duties. If I require assistance or instruction, I will ask for it." I held up a hand to stem the flow of comments I could see coming. "We have more important things to discuss right now."

Righ dropped a kiss on top of my head. "Excellent, *cariad*."

Cris, Gwydre and Grandmama all beamed at me. My parents, Morgan and Gwen looked stunned. Rhan nodded his head once, then smiled.

"As of last night, there have been three murders. All three have been set up to look as though a vampire killed them. In actuality, they were embalmed with their blood packaged and stored in Coleman coolers. The first cooler was found in the bushes by the road in front of Beltene House, the others have all been found with the bodies. The embalming, by the way, was the cause of death." I stopped speaking when I noticed the color draining from my mother's face.

"They were alive when the embalming began?" my father questioned, his arm around my mother in support as well as protection.

I nodded. My chat this morning with Eric had been far more enlightening than I'd planned. I forced myself to explain the horrifying, seemingly impossible precept. "From what I understand, the victims were drugged and then hooked up to embalming equipment. They didn't die until the embalming fluid hit their heart."

"God protect us," Morgan murmured as he crossed himself.

"And, just to keep our attention, this maniac left a note on last night's body. It said, 'A sacrifice for Our Lady of the Night, Beloved of the God of Death'. It's as unfortunate as it is inescapable that these men were killed for me. We still haven't identified any of the victims. The killer has been very careful about leaving evidence behind and we still don't know why he's gifting me with these bodies.

"I found the first body, and met our new sheriff, Tuesday night. He was somewhat annoyed to discover the tabloids had the story on the streets first thing Wednesday morning. In their usual weekly issue, no less. As of this morning, the press has had advance notice on all three bodies. It's a democratic killer, too, because a different paper has had the news of each murder before we've even found the body. Lord and Lady, they've had the information before the killer had even begun to kill the victim. I gather it's making the sheriff's department a little cranky.

"Righ and I went out to check on the Gwynn O'Keefes Wednesday morning and we have no reason to assume they have anything to do with these deaths. Diuran did have Niall's bags packed and waiting, so I was subjected to the 'Throwing A Child To The Wolves' ritual, on top of everything else. I fostered Niall with Jody and Erin.

"Righ has pointed out, more than once, that there are no computers at the sheriff's department. So I purchased two new systems, which are currently set up in my tower, and conscripted Roseanne and Elaine to take care of them. It's past time for computers to be put on the sheriff's department budget." I directed a firm glare at Rhan and my father.

"We'll put it on the agenda for the next budget meeting," Rhan said.

I sucked in my cheeks and stared at him for a moment. "Never mind. I'll take care of it."

Ignoring the startled looks, I continued, "The information is funneled through the sheriff's department and Eula. Only direct communiqués, like faxes or modem transfers, come to the tower. Everything else is delivered by messenger. And, near as I can figure, I am in protective custody. If I leave the confines of Beltene House, I am supposed to be in the custody of Righ, Daniel, Eric or Luke. It seems there is a possibility that I could become an important part of the killer's game plan. And there is every indication that we will continue to receive bodies until the killer is either caught or completes his unknown agenda." Righ's solemn nodding did more to convince the assembled family members of the seriousness of this situation than my words.

"But," I waited until I had the full attention of everyone in the room before continuing, "our main concern, right this minute, is Daniel."

"You think he needs to be Welcomed," my mother guessed.

"Close. I know he needs to be Welcomed. Dealing with this situation without the information he'll get from his Welcoming is like driving blindfolded. Reckless and foolhardy. We don't need either."

"He's been incounty, what, two or three weeks?" Gwen asked, hands clasped serenely in the sleeves of her habit.

"Something like that," I agreed.

"It's not really long enough, is it?"

"Not by a long shot." Even I knew that.

"Couldn't you be a bit biased?"

"Biased?" *Biased about what?* I barely knew what the hell I was doing, and she wanted to know if I was biased?

"Well, he did spend the night in your bed, didn't he?" she asked.

Ah, sex. I should have known. I rested my chin in my hand and studied her. Did I even want to attempt to dissuade them from their misconception? With a barely perceptible shake of my head, I decided to ignore the entire matter. "I don't believe Dan will be able to solve these murders without the information received in his Welcoming. Not without endangering all of us."

Gwen, only the surface of her serenity ruffled by my refusal to discuss Daniel's night in my bed, said, "You don't even have a clue what happens at a Welcoming."

"I think," Cris' soft voice commanded everyone's attention, "in this case, Rhiannon is correct. There are too many areas of this case where Daniel is barred from knowledge. He needs to know."

"I agree." Rhan, unexpectedly, came to my defense. "I spoke with Luke and Lige a little while ago. They were out until after three this morning with this latest body. Fighting with the compulsion and trying to keep Dan from chasing red herrings is driving them all loopy. Trust me, Daniel needs the information."

Gwen tilted her head in his direction. "I withdraw that particular objection."

Mom leaned forward, tapping her fingers on my desk. "How will he respond?"

"Don't look at me," I said. "I haven't a clue. But it's a moot point."

"It'll be hell on wheels getting him to believe it," Rhan admitted.

"Will he accept it?" Morgan asked.

"I believe he will," Rhan answered.

"He will," Cris said, her tone confident. "It will be difficult at first, but his belief will come soon and be strong."

Cris could go months without a single prophecy. I'd lost count of the number she'd had in the last three days.

"I took a poll this morning," I informed them. "I'm sponsoring Daniel's welcome into Clan Beltene and I have a unanimous unchanged vote. It's time for the changed vote."

Silence filled the room, as much with their contemplation as with their shock at my announcement. I studied the dust floating gracefully in the sunshine as they formulated their votes.

I gave them ten minutes. "His Welcoming needs to be done promptly. This afternoon, if possible, or tomorrow morning at the latest. It's time to vote. Grandmama?"

"I agree the young man needs to be Welcomed."

"Rhan?"

"By all means, let's get it over with."

"Gwydre?"

He shared a look with Cris and Grandmama. "There's too much to be done to have it this afternoon and while I'm sure midnight would be a most auspicious time, the regularity with which we've been finding bodies leaves me no doubt that we'd be short a full attendance. So, tomorrow morning, at seven a.m. is our best bet. My vote is for Welcome."

"Righdhonn?" I looked over my shoulder at him. He was still standing by the window, where he'd been when I entered, watching the southern lawn with an intensity that frightened me.

"For, *cariad*."

My beeper went off. Over Righ's chuckle, I pulled it off my belt and punched the button to view the incoming phone number. I deleted it and set the beeper in the middle of my desk.

"Cris?"

"He's perfect."

I didn't ask. "Gwendolyn?"

She pressed her fingers together and studied me. "You seem to be settling into your rank better."

Better than what? Not knowing where she was headed, I ignored her comment. "Gwen, your vote, please."

She studied Righ's tense form. "Welcome."

"Morgan?"

"I vote for Welcome," he said.

"Dad?"

He leaned back in his chair and smirked at me. "Oh, definitely for."

I closed my eyes. "Mom?"

"Are you sure, Rhiannon?"

"I'm sure Dan needs to be Welcomed to be able to effectively combat this killer."

"I vote for Welcoming him," she said, nodding.

"Nine votes for, none against. The vote carried unanimously on the changed side. Voting on the unchanged side were Lige, Doc, Rachel, Eric, Luke, Sam, Daffyd, Tom and myself. It, too, was carried unanimously. Daniel Lincoln Thorpe has been approved for Welcoming. Tomorrow morning?" I asked Cris.

She stared off into the distance, then turned to me. "Gwydre's right. Seven a.m. is perfect. How many shall we expect?"

Here's where my lack of knowledge could get me into trouble. "I haven't a bloody clue. What is the optimum number?"

"Twelve is the best number," she said.

"Okay."

"As the sponsor, you are required to choose the witnesses, Rhiannon. One of whom will preside as Daniel's guide."

"Oh." I got a pen out of the middle drawer of my desk and began making a list on the desk pad. I ignored my father's pained look. Desk pads were made to scribble on. "Okay, I would assume you, Cris and Gwydre need to be part of the changed quorum." I paused to look at Grandmama for confirmation. "Then I think we need Mom, Dad and Righdhonn. For the unchanged, it'll be Lige, Luke, Doc, Eric and me. And, of course, Daniel. Will that do?"

"I couldn't have chosen better myself," Cris said.

"Wonderful," I returned, wondering just what she'd done to make me choose exactly the people she wanted at Dan's Welcoming or how she knew I'd choose the right people before I'd even thought about it.

"Is the rest of the family waiting?" I asked, standing.

"Ready and waiting in the library," Dad said.

"Not so fast, Rhi."

"What? Did we forget something?" I looked at Cris in consternation.

"Yes, dear. I'm going to need about three hours of your time this afternoon."

I nodded. "As soon as the family meeting is over." My beeper went off again and as I watched, started wobbling around on my desk as the vibrator kicked in. I pushed the button, looked at the number and deleted it. Reaching over, I pushed the intercom for Eula.

"Yes, Rhiannon?"

"Could you call the sheriff's department for me and inform them that I will be in meetings the rest of the morning and most of the afternoon and would appreciate it if they could refrain from beeping me in the middle of them."

"I'll take care of it," she assured me.

"Thank you, Eula."

Cris smiled. "And you need to pick a guide for Daniel."

This was one question that needed very little consideration. "Grandmama."

"Excellent."

I was going to be a nervous wreck before they found the killer if she didn't stop making it sound as if I was following a preordained script. "Now is there anything else?"

"Not a thing."

"Thank the gods. Now let's go have meeting number two."

The meeting in the library was short and sweet. I didn't go into any details, just gave them the high points and warned them to be careful. I accosted Trys on his way out the door.

"I need to talk to you."

He flipped his hair out of his face and looked haughtily at me. "Yes?"

"I have a meeting with Cris for the next couple of hours, then I need to come up and talk with you and Pete."

"I'm not taking my website off the Net."

"I'm not asking you to."

"What is it, then?"

"I don't have time to go into it right now. I'll be up later. Stick close to home, okay?"

"All right." Turning, he flounced out of the library.

I smiled at his back. Trys was going to give me all kinds of grief over searching his website, database and file cabinets for the killer's letters. And forcing him and Pete to do the search was really going to send him into orbit. But, he would do as I asked. Because I had something that—after seeing what he'd done with my hate mail—I knew he would very nearly sell his soul to possess.

Chapter Fifteen
Friday afternoon

Cris, Righ and I spent the afternoon going over the far too numerous things I needed to know for Daniel's Welcoming. I had a sinking feeling that I was never going to remember all of it. Whatever Eula had said to Rachel was more effective than anything I'd said, since my beeper was thankfully silent.

I discovered that there was a tremendous amount of information, beyond the normal amount family members received (and that I'd spent years avoiding), that the Beltene was privy to. Most of which was fascinating to someone as steeped in history and traditions as I was.

"I can't believe this was all here, just waiting for me and I've been passing it by for years," I mused, sprawled on the couch in Cris' office.

"Well, not all of it was available until recently," she reminded me. "And you never were one to be led or pushed into anything."

Righ snorted. "I told Pwyll to leave her alone and let her become accustomed to her duties."

Cris smiled. "I knew you'd be perfect. They just needed to give you space and time."

I slanted a glance at her. "Are you prophesying more or am I just noticing it more?"

Her slight smile and Righ's grin gave me my answer and I turned on my side to study Cris. Next to Grandmama, I considered her the most important person in the family. She was the first one to become a druid, following in Grandmama's footsteps, and had been born four years after Richard the Lion-Heart died at Chaluz. Her dark hair is just beginning to show silver strands in its midst and her eyes are her power. Dark and full of mystery, they're her windows into a world of Druidic mysticism I can barely comprehend.

Most people assume she's in her early forties, and indeed, she does seem to be aging more slowly than most of the changed members of the family. It is, however, considered bad taste to ask her how she manages it.

I moved my gaze over to my mercenary cousin, who was wielding more weaponry than I'd ever seen him carry in the house. "Righ?"

"Yes, cariad?"

"Are you on guard duty?"

"Are you being beeped?"

I sighed. "You know, under normal circumstances, I leave the house for ice cream, books and Mass. I've never minded spending days on end in my tower, but I have to tell you, right now, I feel trapped. My claustrophobia is kicking up and I feel like if I don't get out of here, I could do something really irrational."

"Like chewing your back leg off?" he teased.

"Maybe." I returned his smile.

"Try not to think about it," he advised. "Then it won't seem so bad."

"Gee, thanks."

"You're very welcome."

"Now, back to the question at hand ..." I waited expectantly.

"Are you referring to the Beltene Osmosis Line?"

"That and your prophesies and Righ seems to be reading my mind. I mean, I'm sort of used to you and Grandmama and Jody doing it, but Righ?"

"Righdhonn was one of our most powerful Beltenes, child, and one who carried his post with him when he changed, for there was no one to pass it to," Cris explained. "His ability is not on a par with Grandmama or myself, but is easily on par with Gwydre. Not all Beltenes are gifted with such powers; your father wasn't. You are."

I stared at her. "You're joking."

"I never joke about tokens of power, Rhiannon. Your ability is capable of taking you to heights you've never imagined and are only shared by a handful of your family peers."

I looked wildly at Righdhonn. He laughed and hugged me. "It's not all going to come crashing in on you today, *cariad*. It comes with time and with instruction."

"Lord and Lady."

"You'll be fine."

"Not the slightest doubt." Cris stood and stretched. "Can you remember everything I've told you?" she asked me.

"In the beginning, God created the heavens and the earth, Grandmama and Father Kennedy," I answered promptly.

"Behave yourself," she scolded.

"Sorry."

"What are your plans for the remainder of today?" she asked, not taken in by my automatic apology.

"I need to have some lunch, I need to check on Roseanne and Elaine, let Rachel know she can go back to beeping me every ten minutes, and set Pete and Trys to searching their files, databases and website for suspicious letters." I flung my arms into the air. "Can you think of anything else I should do before bedtime?"

"No, *cariad*," Righ said, struggling to hold back his chuckles. "I think that's more than enough for you to do."

"Try to keep in mind the salient points of today's lesson," Cris added.

"When's the pop quiz?"

"Tomorrow. Seven a.m."

"I'll go over it again after I track down Trystan," I promised. "You probably should make a chant out of it, then I could repeat it until it's permanently stuck in my brain."

"Don't tempt me," she laughed.

I rolled off the couch and stood. "On that note, I'm outta here."

Righ joined me by the door. I frowned up at him. "Righ?"

"Just up to Trystan's room, Rhi."

I shook my head. "See you in the morning, Cris."

"Five, here."

"Right," I answered. "Five." Muttering to myself, I exited the room with Righ close at my heels. Needing to be outside, even for a moment, I chose to go up to Trystan's room via the courtyard. I stopped near the fountain and looked seriously at my cousin. "Have you spoken to the sheriff's department today?"

"Yes, ma'am."

I looked at him for further enlightenment, but he seemed content to wait for my questions. "Have they identified any of the bodies?"

"Nope."

"Has the State Police lab come up with anything?"

"Nope."

"Have they had any luck finding where the coolers were purchased?"

"Nope."

"Has the canvass of funeral homes dug up anything?"

"That was a really nasty little pun."

"It was an unintentional little pun. Has it?"

"Nope."

I thought for a moment. "Are we still expecting to find a body today?"

"Yep."

I took a deep breath and let it out slowly.

"Don't get your knickers in a twist, *cariad*. We'll find him."

"I hope so," I said, catching his eyes. "I hope so."

"Come, my Lady Beltene, let us find our cousin Trystan."

I looked pained at his use of the imperial plural and led the way up the stairs. We were nearly to the third floor when a banshee wailed and a small furry bundle flung itself into my arms. A well-placed shove from Righ kept me from tumbling backward down the stairs.

"What are you doing with Hamlet?" Trys asked, peering over the railing at us.

I tried to coax the small kitten out from underneath my chin where it had curled up, shaking and chirping frantically. Unable to coerce it into moving without getting pierced by four tiny sets of razor sharp claws, I stroked it gently. "What have you been doing to this poor little kitten?"

"Give him to me," he demanded.

I hid behind Righ. "Why is the poor thing so terrified?"

"He's not terrified."

I raised an eyebrow at him.

"Well, I don't think he liked being in my coffin."

I closed my eyes. "Trystan, you can't be putting a kitten in your coffin."

"I wanted him to sleep with me."

Too late, I opened my eyes. For a flash of a second, I'd seen Trys, one of his ladies and the kitten, all cuddled into his coffin.

"I think the Humane Society would have a conniption if they found out you were forcing a kitten to sleep in your coffin with you."

"And who's going to tell them?" he asked belligerently.

"I might," I said. "If I intended to return this poor creature into your keeping."

"You're going to keep my kitten?"

"Lord and Lady, but you do pathetic really well. Yes, Trystan, I've just confiscated your kitten." The kitten was settling down, his shaking gone and his chirping turning into a raucous purr for one his size.

"I think he likes you, *cariad*," Righ said, reaching over to stroke him.

I managed to get the kitten out from under my chin without drawing blood. "It's a seal point Siamese," I said, holding him up where I could see him. He reached out and patted my cheek with his paw. I laughed at the expression on his face. "No wonder he was fleeing in fear of his life, Trys. This isn't a Hamlet, this is Puck. You're in the wrong play."

Trys peered into the tiny face. "Fine," he huffed. "He's Puck. I'll send his things over to the tower."

"Trouble in paradise already?"

I looked over at Pete, who was lounging in the doorway of his room. He and Trystan had adjoining suites, although it appeared to me that Trys had taken over both suites and Pete had retained only a tiny corner. "You let him get a kitten?"

"He wanted one."

"In his coffin?"

"I assumed the kitten would have the good sense to disabuse him of that notion."

"He tried to name it Hamlet."

"I was confident that he wasn't a Hamlet, but I hadn't decided just who he was. I do believe you're right. Now that he's safely ensconced in your keeping, he does look like a Puck."

I shook my head and set the kitten on my shoulder where he draped himself so he could give me kitty nudges and pat my face when he felt the need. "I have a project for you two."

"Beeper," Righ said.

I looked at him and rolled my eyes. "Oh, all right. Pete, I need to use your telephone."

"Beeper? The sheriff's department gave you a pager? And you're actually carrying it?"

I popped the technology in question off my belt and held it up. Obligingly, it beeped and vibrated.

"I want the number," Trystan demanded as I pushed the button and looked at the display.

"Not in this life," I said to Trys as I pushed his keeper back into the room and headed for their telephone.

I meet Righ's questioning gaze and silently mouthed, "Rachel."

Rachel had decided that in Righdhonn's company or not, I had been out of communication with the sheriff's department for too long and was delighted to be notified that I was done with my meetings for the day. She didn't seem to hear my repeated demand that she keep the calls to a minimum—like every four or five hours instead of every four or five minutes. She merely gave a wicked chuckle and hung up on me.

"Rachel will give me your beeper number," Trys exclaimed gleefully from the depths of his bedroom.

Life as I had always known it was at an end. I could only hope that the murders would cease and I could return the beeper to the sheriff's department before I was forced into a small murder spree of my own. Rachel and Trystan, along with the originator of the beeper, would be high on my list. I wondered absently if Righ had an Uzi that I could borrow.

"Trystan," I called after counting to ten, "get your cute little tush in here."

Righ gave me a hug. "No, *cariad*, I don't have any weaponry you can borrow."

"Now, why would I be wanting to borrow a weapon or two from you?" I asked, refusing to acknowledge where he'd gotten such an idea.

His grin widened and he looked at Trystan. "Patience," he counseled. "And don't leave home without me."

"Never," I promised, watching as he left the room. It was a shame he was family, because I disagreed with Roseanne and Elaine. I didn't think Trystan was the most attractive man in our family. I thought the prize went to Righdhonn; even though he was born before the turn of the first millennium, he usually appears to be in his mid-forties. It's not considered kosher to ask him how he manages to look so young, either.

I dropped the kitten into Pete's lap, then flung myself down on his waterbed and contemplated the two incredibly innocent-looking men in front of me.

"How's the sheriff?" Pete asked before I managed to put my questions into coherent form.

"The sheriff?"

"Well, he did spend the night in your tower."

"That's no one's business."

"In Beltene House?" He chuckled quietly. "You know better than that, Rhi."

"The family osmosis line is far too efficient," I grumbled.

"It always has been," he returned.

I shared a grin with him. "Yeah, it has, hasn't it?" The news of the tryst, which had rid both of us of our virginity at the ripe old age of sixteen had traveled the Beltene Osmosis Line and reached our parents before we'd even returned home. We had been grounded until we were fifty. "We did finally gain our freedom—in time for the senior prom, wasn't it?"

"Our chaperoned senior prom."

"You were promiscuous children," Trystan interjected.

I raised my eyebrows at the truly promiscuous one in the family. It's a good thing that Rhodri is convinced that changed members of the family are immune to most viruses. In Trystan's case, especially the sexually transmitted ones. Only the gods know what he's messed with. But his interruption did remind me of what I'd come up here to discuss with them. "Your website—"

"No, no, no," Trys burst out. "I'm not taking it off the Net. It doesn't conflict with any of the compulsions and I'm just not going to," he repeated stubbornly, crossing his arms and glaring at me.

I waited until he'd finished his minor fit, then continued, "Is very nice—a bit eclectic and I'm not sure I care to be co-starring in it with you, but it's a moot point now. The escape tunnel we'll discuss at a later date. What I'm interested in is the fact that you have taken my hate mail—which I'm going to point out, I've thrown in the trash and you've retrieved—"

"I never play in the trash," Trys protested while Pete put Puck on the floor and bowed gracefully at me from his sitting position. Like I didn't know who did Trystan's dirty work.

"And stored in those file cabinets and tossed out on the Internet for everyone in the world to read."

"They're simply lovely."

"I want you to sort through them for the sheriff."

"No."

"This is not negotiable, Trystan, nor was it a request," I said sternly, turning my best imitation of Grandmama's serene but compelling stare at him.

Pete sat up in his chair. "My Lady Beltene?"

I ignored his query and rescued Puck from his frantic attempt to scale the bed frame in order to get up to me. I rolled onto my back and set him on my stomach. "It is possible that the killer has written to me and considering what he's leaving as presents, I'm sure I would have tossed his letters. So, I want to you to go through"—I waved at the file cabinets lining the walls—"all of those and see if you find any letters similar to the note we got."

"And how would we know they were from the killer?" Pete inquired. "Don't be letting that kitten loose on my water bed. If he punctures it, you'll wish Noah lived here."

"You're going to be a good boy, aren't you?" I asked Puck, who had curled up on my stomach and obviously had no intention of doing anything that might get him wet. "I'll bring you a copy of what we've received so far. Need I mention that what I bring over is highly confidential and is not to be repeated, copied, or put out on the Internet?"

"Aye, aye, *mon capitan*." Trystan saluted me.

I was more than a little surprised that I hadn't needed to bribe Trys with the Alabama letters, but maybe between the murders and Grandmama's little chat, he realized just how much danger the family could be in. I looked over at him and shook my head. He looked barely thirty, was soon to be an even one hundred and acted younger than the kitten napping on top of me. Nope, he was running with some agenda I couldn't see—or perhaps he was just so glad I hadn't made him shut down his website that he was willing to do whatever Herculean chores I gave him. Whatever his reasons, I didn't think I really wanted to delve too deeply into them. I held the sleepy Puck out to Pete and levered myself out of the waterbed. Puck settled onto my shoulder and I turned to look at my renegade cousin. "Are the ones on the Web just copies of these?"

"Yeah," Pete answered. "In fact, they're only a small portion of what we have here in hard copy and the ones I've scanned and saved." Trystan, with Pete's assistance, did his pre-production drawing in the privacy of their suite and their computer setup rivaled mine.

"I'll be back later with the copy you need. And I'll take a stroll through the ones you've got on the website. Maybe between the three of us we can find what Dan's looking for." I paused in the doorway and looked pensively at both men. "Bedtime stories?"

Trystan's grin was one of the reasons that he had a waiting list of ladies wanting to share his coffin. "They're delightful. Such perverted enthusiasms, dedicated fervor and passion. Uplifting. I read at least one every evening."

"Lord and Lady." *I had to ask*, I thought as I backed out the door and headed for my tower. *I had to ask*.

Chapter Sixteen
Friday evening

Surprisingly enough, since it was after six before I found my way back to my tower, there was still a fair number of people loitering about. I had taken the long way to the tower, via the kitchen where I combined a bite to eat with a checkup on Niall with Erin and Jody. All was rising fair on that front. Which left Trystan, Daniel and the bodies as the stars on my horizon.

"Lord and Lady," I exclaimed as Puck and I entered my domain. "Shouldn't you have departed for your homes ages ago? It's Friday night."

"The Beltene's a slave driver," Roseanne returned from behind her computer.

"I find that difficult to believe," I said.

"Truly," Elaine said. "The fervor that has enveloped this household this afternoon has been a sight to behold. I only wish I'd been present when you announced your intention."

I waved a hand at her and dropped onto the couch next to Cris. "I didn't expect to see you, either."

"I thought I might assist you in your chanting."

Roseanne chuckled as I wrinkled my nose at Cris. "I have to find Righdhonn."

Slowly Cris straightened, never taking her eyes from me. "Why?"

Puck gauged the distance and attempted to jump from my shoulder to hers. She caught him before he disappeared into the depths of the couch. "And who is this?"

"This," I held out a hand and Puck delicately sauntered up it to return to my shoulder, as if he'd planned on falling into the couch, "is Puck."

"Where, since you're not allowed out of the house, did you find this delightful little kitten?" she asked, putting out a finger and cooing at Puck.

He was not taken in by this ploy and executed a move worthy of *The Eiger Sanction*, landing on my other shoulder. "I took him away from Trystan."

"She certainly did," Pete confirmed from the doorway, loaded down with a tremendous amount of cat stuff.

"Did Trys buy out the local pet store?"

"Almost."

"What am I supposed to do with all that stuff?"

"It's Puck's."

"What is he going to do with it?" It included a cat condo, a condo style litter box, a bag of toys, dry food, canned food and ... "Kitten milk?" I looked at the superior expression on Puck's face. "Isn't he weaned?"

"Yes, he is. In fact, he's eight weeks old. Trys seemed sure we needed some in case he wouldn't eat anything else." Pete dropped everything but the litter box on the other couch and collapsed next to it after setting the litter box on the floor.

Puck skittered to my other shoulder. Given a choice between being close to Cris or Pete, he had chosen Cris. After his recent exposure, I couldn't say that I blamed him.

"When did Trystan get a kitten?" Cris looked sharply at Pete, her *why did you let him buy a kitten?* look as loud as if she'd said it.

"This morning. He wouldn't have hurt it, you know."

I sighed. "I know he wouldn't have hurt him. But what possessed him to get a Siamese kitten? I would have expected a delightful little black domestic kitten, that he really could name Hamlet, would have suited his purposes just fine."

"I think that was the intent, but Puck was so cute."

Roseanne shut down her computer and dropped onto the coffee table. "Did Trystan really try to name this poor baby Hamlet?"

"He certainly did."

"And how did you end up with him?" Elaine asked, lowering herself onto the couch next to Pete, which he'd gallantly cleared off by flinging all the cat stuff on the floor behind the couch.

"Righ and I were on our way up the courtyard stairs to have a chat with Pete and Trys and this poor baby was attempting to reenact *The Great Escape*. He flung himself over the edge and into my arms." I plucked him off my shoulder and held him up so I could look into his face. "Is this the face of a Hamlet?"

"Not a bit," Cris assured me. "He looks like—"

"Puck," Roseanne finished.

"Of course," I agreed. "He's most definitely Puck. And as such, there is no way he could live in Trystan's coffin."

"Aw geez," Elaine moaned. "He was going to make the kitten sleep in his coffin?"

"That was his intent," Pete confirmed.

"Ladies," I interjected, changing the subject and putting the kitten on my shoulder, "Are you walking home, driving home or getting picked up?"

"We were supposed to be picked up, but we've heard little from the sheriff's department today. Tom's last run was a couple of hours ago and if all went well, he thought that he and Eric would be back about now. But we're still husbandless."

"I'll drive you home," Pete volunteered.

"Thank you, kind sir." Elaine leaned over and kissed his cheek. "The children and I both thank you."

"Cool," I said, getting to my feet and dropping Puck onto

the couch. He glared at me for a long moment before stomping over to a nearby pillow. After kneading it thoroughly, he curled up into a catball and went to sleep. "You can drop me off at the sheriff's department."

Pete looked incredulously at me. "Not in this life, Rhiannon, my love. I will help you find Righdhonn before I take the ladies home. I will offer you and Righ a ride, but I am not, repeat not, going to fly in the face of a direct order from the best armed man in the state and take you anywhere outside this house."

My steadfast stare should have melted his resistance, but in truth had little effect on my childhood companion.

"Sorry, Rhi, but they're right. You're much safer in Righ's hands."

"Fine." I gave in ungraciously. "You take the ladies home and I'll find my cousin all by myself."

He kissed me on the cheek. "See you later, my Lady Beltene."

I made a rude gesture at his back as he disappeared down the stairs, Elaine and Roseanne close behind. I turned at the sound of a chuckle behind me and raised an eyebrow at Cris. "I'm going down to the kitchen."

"Have fun, *cariad*." She stretched out on the couch. "I'll be here when you get back—to help you with your chanting."

I looked pointedly at my watch. "Cris, if you're really going to insist that I drag myself out of bed at five tomorrow morning, I doubt that I'll be doing anything when I get back except going to bed."

"We'll see," she said, waving me from the room. "Go find Daniel, he'll be needing to talk with you tonight, anyway."

That sounded suspiciously like a prophecy. I stopped on the top step and thought about demanding an explanation.

"You don't have time," Cris' voice floated into the stairway. "Don't forget to tell him about tomorrow morning."

As I completed my trek down the stairs, I wondered if I couldn't just emigrate to Russia.

"It's awfully cold in Siberia this time of year," Jody said conversationally as I entered the kitchen. I just stared at him. "You're becoming more aware. And you've always been easy to read."

"Problems, Rhi?" my mercenary cousin asked from his reclined position on the couch.

"I need to be accompanied to the sheriff's department."

You could almost see the tentacles of power flowing to him as he tensed and sat up. "Why?"

I resisted the temptation to say *because I want to* and answered, "I need to get a copy of the note for Pete, so he and Trys can rummage through my hate mail for the letters from the killer. If he doesn't know how the man writes, he'll never be able to recognize them."

"Good point," he conceded. "Come along."

Following obediently, I was surprised when he headed out into the hallway, toward my tower.

"Where in the hell are you going?" I asked, having expected that we would ride in his truck to the sheriff's department.

"Just come with me. We don't want you exposed."

"I understand that. Aren't we going in via the courthouse?"

"Nope, there's a better way."

Once we got to the tower, Righ led me down into the dungeon and past Rhodri's lab into the older part of the basement. We passed the storerooms and were, as near as I could tell, somewhere under the courtyard. "Righ?"

"This way."

I stopped dead. I trusted this man implicitly, but I still wanted to know what we were doing in the dungeon. "Righdhonn Dafydd Beltene, where in the hell are we going?"

He turned and grinned at me. "To the sheriff's department."

"Through the dungeon?"

"Now, Rhiannon, would I be bringing you down here if I didn't know we could get to the sheriff's department from here?"

I narrowed my eyes and frowned at him.

"There's still a lot of information that our new Beltene needs to know."

"There's another tunnel, other than the one that leads down to the bay?" Perhaps I had been too quick to judge Trystan and his escape tunnel—maybe there was one that went out into the forest, sans Keanu Reeves, of course.

"I've always maintained that you were quick, *cariad*."

"Why in the world would we have a tunnel from the house to the sheriff's department ... No, never mind. It connects with the tunnel that runs from the courthouse to the sheriff's department. A bolt hole, all things considered, for the family if threatened." I nodded. "Makes sense."

He patted the top of my head and led me into the grungiest storeroom I'd ever seen in Beltene House.

"We need to get Indeg down here," I said, batting at cobwebs.

"No, we don't."

Now, cobwebs make my skin crawl when they're in corners. I'm not at all happy when they're sticking to me. I put out a hand and wiped them off on Righ's shirt.

"Cobwebs are good. We want to discourage people from wandering around down here, Rhi. There are a very limited number of people who know about this access. The current Beltene and, of course, former Beltenes, and one or two other select individuals, like the sheriff."

I put my hands on my hips. "Are you trying to tell me that an Unwelcomed sheriff has knowledge of this little escape tunnel of yours? I don't think so."

"No, *cariad*, he doesn't know about this tunnel. It's just one of the many things that he'll find out about after his Welcoming. He's almost as ignorant as our Beltene."

"Thank you very much," I muttered, making rude noises under my breath, and followed closely on his heels as he passed through several rooms, each getting smaller and grimier. The last had no obvious exit except the doorway through which we'd come. It contained nothing except a floor-to-ceiling bookcase and a trunk.

"Lord and Lady, Righ, a secret tunnel behind a bookcase—isn't that a bit too much of a cliché, even for us?"

He grinned and kicked the trunk. It moved maybe an inch. A six-foot-wide section of the wall beside the bookcase slid silently open.

"Cute." I peered into his tunnel, noting that it did not originate at this opening, but went off in two different directions. It was also significantly cleaner than the room in which we stood.

"Lights?" I prompted.

He obligingly reached in and flipped a switch. "And God said 'Let there be light.'"

I smacked him as I moved into the relatively cobweb-free tunnel.

"This way, my Lady Beltene," he said, closing the door behind us as he joined me.

My sense of direction, in the best of times, is nothing to brag about. I followed Righ to the right.

These were not natural caverns we were wandering through, as was most of the public tunnel to the bay. This was a man-made tunnel, arched in traditional Gothic methods and paved all around with stone. Electric lights were strung along the ceiling.

This is definitely not the place to be when the electricity goes out, I thought.

"There's an emergency generator that kicks on, *cariad*," Righ said. "You'd never be without lights down here, unless you decided to stay down here for more than a month."

"Righdhonn, have I mentioned how creepy this mind-reading stuff is?"

He flashed a grin at me just as we stopped. He peered through a crack in the wall, then pushed a stone. At least, that's what it looked like he did. The wall slid open just as silently as the first one and we found ourselves in the tunnel between the courthouse and the jail.

Our appearance into the chaos in the sheriff's department was not greeted with open arms.

"Jesus, Righ," Eric swore as he stared at me in amazement. "Tell me you didn't bring her through that mess."

"I didn't bring her through that mess."

"Dan's going to have a fit. There's been another one, you know."

"The gods have mercy on us all," I said and, without knocking, entered the sheriff's office.

Three heads snapped toward the door as I closed it.

"Hi, guys," I said, dropping into the only empty chair in the room. Lige, Luke and Daniel all stared at me in what was patently not amazement. "What?"

My tongue-lashing was forestalled by Righ's entrance into the room.

"Well," Daniel said, relaxing back into his chair, "at least we don't need to make a trip over to Beltene House."

"Another note, too?" Righ leaned against the doorway.

"Yeah. But before we get into that, would you like to tell me why you brought Rhiannon here?"

"She asked."

"I need a copy of the note you showed me this morning." I explained.

"For what?"

"Do you remember asking me about my fan letters?"

He nodded. "You said you threw them out."

"Yeah, well, I did, but someone else retrieved them and saved them."

"Who?"

"I've put them to work sorting through the file cabinets looking for a letter with a similar feel, but they need an example."

"Who retrieved your hate mail?"

"Does it really matter who it is?" I really didn't want to wave Trystan, or Pete, for that matter, in front of our new sheriff like a red flag.

"Yes."

Lige appeared to be reciting a mantra or a prayer. It was obvious to me, at least, that everyone in the room, with the exception of Daniel and me, knew that Trystan had been collecting my fan mail. Why no one had mentioned it to Dan was beyond me.

"Trystan and Pete," I answered.

He stared at me. I couldn't really blame him. Trystan had all the makings of becoming our new sheriff's prime suspect—an excellent reason, all on its own, for his Welcoming.

"They have them neatly filed in file cabinets in Pete's room," I explained, perhaps not as helpfully as it was intended. "Hell and damnation, they've scanned tons of them and even put some out on the Net."

"Why?"

I started to answer, but stopped, unsure of just what it was that he wanted further explanation on.

"Why have they dug your hate mail out of the trash, filed it, scanned it and put it out on the Internet?" he clarified.

I chewed the inside of my lip for a moment. This was going to be tricky. "Trys collects my hate mail because he's warped and, in general, quite a pain in the ass."

"I think perhaps I need to speak with them." He put out a hand to push his intercom.

"You're way off base, Sheriff Thorpe." The ice in my tone stopped his hand in midair and brought his eyes up to meet mine.

"Really? Every time I turn around he keeps popping up."

"He keeps popping up because he's a complete and total idiot." Well, that probably wasn't the most diplomatic way of describing Trystan, but it was one of my more polite descriptions.

"Generally, when someone keeps popping up like this, they're involved in some way with the crime."

I could see help was not going to be forthcoming from the men around me; they were waiting to see how the Beltene handled this situation. After all, that was one of the main precepts of my job description. "Trystan is a lot of things, but as I told you yesterday, being a legal pain in the ass isn't one of them."

"You're asking me to trust you."

I refused to wince at the flat, emotionless note in his voice. In his place, I'd probably be a little cranky if all this kind of weird stuff was going on and the person who appeared to be my prime suspect was being protected by his family. And the person for whom the bodies were piling up was asking me to ignore this particular suspect. I was batting a thousand. "I'm ... oh, hell; yes! Yes, I'm asking you to trust me. I'm asking you to not only trust my instincts but the instincts of the men working on this investigation with you." I waved a hand at the silent trio.

He crossed his arms.

"Ask them."

"You're asking me to turn my back on what appears to be two perfectly good suspects on your word."

"No, you idiot." I winced as my inappropriate choice of words set his teeth on edge. "I don't want you to waste your time trailing Trys around the county, a useless task at best. Besides, that's what we hired Pete to do. I want you to spend your time hunting down this killer. I can guarantee that no one in Beltene House is responsible for these murders."

"I see. Do you understand what the likelihood is that you know the killer?"

Lord and Lady, I really did not need to hear that.

"Just how can you guarantee no one in Beltene House is responsible?"

I walked myself right into that corner. There was no way for me to answer that question. I lifted a shoulder and dropped it in frustration. "I, ah, umm ... hell and damnation, Daniel, you've been here three bloody weeks, can't you just take it as a given?"

"No."

Lige stepped smoothly into the charged silence. "I think we've gotten a bit off track here. Dan, are you seriously considering Trystan as a suspect?"

The sheriff clenched his teeth and took a deep breath. "Seriously, no. But he does pop up far too often to make me comfortable ignoring him."

"Well," Righ drawled. "As Rhi so tactfully put it, he is a pain in the ass. I'll keep an eye on him, just in case."

"Thank you." Dan retreated gracefully in the opening Righ had given him. "Do you consider this Pete responsible enough to keep the note a secret?"

"I'll personally reinforce Rhiannon's instructions regarding the note. It will be safe."

"All right." He went to the door and yelled for Eric.

"You needed me, Dan?" Eric appeared at the door, hesitantly looking in.

"Make a copy of last night's note for Rhiannon, please."

Eric raised an eyebrow at me, sketched a salute at Dan and vanished from the doorway.

"Now," I slid down in my chair, stretched my legs out and crossed my ankles. "What had you planned on coming over to Beltene House for?"

"Translation of the latest note."

"Oh." I straightened in my chair and Dan approached me, plastic-covered card in hand.

"Can you read this?" he asked, handing the card to me.

I stared at the printing on the card for a long moment before slowly reaching for it.

"Well?" he asked impatiently.

"I can read it."

"And?"

I bit my lip and rubbed a hand across my face. Turning, I handed it to Righ. "It's Welsh, sort of."

"Sort of?"

I shrugged. "The person who wrote this note isn't fluent in Welsh or doesn't want us to know he's fluent in Welsh. It's almost as though someone wandered through a dictionary or phrase book and picked out words, without knowing if they fit together properly. The words are correct, but the sentences aren't structured right. They don't flow. It's the language equivalent of clipping words and letters out of magazines and newspapers to paste on paper."

"What does it say?"

I put a hand to my mouth and chewed on a fingernail, intently watching Righdhonn's expression. He lifted his eyes to meet mine and the sympathy in them almost started the tears lurking behind my tightly controlled façade. "It says, 'Did you enjoy your late night tryst with the sheriff? Are you pleased with my efforts on your behalf, My Lady of the Night? It's so easy. They come to me gladly, for your sake. Until the next, my beloved of Beltene.'"

The shocked look on Dan's face was matched by the looks on Lige's and Luke's faces. There was a very small circle of people who knew about Daniel's visit to my tower early this morning.

"We went up on the roof." I spoke almost without realizing what I was going to say.

"He's watching Beltene House." Righ's hands on my shoulders kept me from bolting from the chair and stiffened my resolve not to break down in public. At the very least, Rachel would enjoy it too much.

"How did you get here?" Dan asked.

Righ's hands tightened on my shoulders. Lige looked at us, at Luke, then back to me. Obviously Luke wasn't among the chosen few and, as I very well knew, neither was Daniel. This was a decision for the Beltene. I could feel the question just as surely as if he'd spoken aloud. There was no question about Daniel receiving the knowledge, albeit early. I looked at Luke and nodded once.

"There's a tunnel," Righ explained. "From Beltene House and it intercepts with the tunnel between the courthouse and the sheriff's department."

Luke's small smile told me he understood the ramifications of what he'd just become privy to and Dan's barely perceptible acknowledgment told me he appreciated the benefits of this knowledge.

"So no one knows you're here." Dan said.

"No one knows we've left Beltene House," Righ confirmed.

"Except ..." my voice died off as everyone turned to look at me.

"Except," Lige prompted.

"Except Cris, Roseanne, Pete, Elaine and Jody all knew I was coming over here."

He shook his head at me. "Don't scare us like that—we meant, people outside of Beltene House."

"Oh, sorry."

"I don't know that someone watching Beltene House is of any real assistance," Luke mused. "You can see Rhi's tower from all over town. And Sevyrn is bursting at the seams right now."

"True." Dan frowned at me.

I scrunched up my face, sure what his next order would be. "Now wait a minute ..."

"You have to stay off the roof of the tower."

That was the one I'd been sure he'd mention. I jettisoned out of my chair and Righ's grasp. "I hate this, I just hate this. I'm confined to the house like *I* was under arrest—" I held up a hand to forestall the protests I could see forming. "That's what it feels like. Some idiot is decorating my county with bodies, dead embalmed bodies, for me. Presents," I choked on the word, but forced myself to continue. "Gifts to please me. I'm under a bloody siege here. Is it ever going to end?"

"Under normal circumstances, I'd say that the more time that passes the less chance we have to catch him. But, he keeps leaving new bodies every day, he's confined himself to a relatively small area and he's fixated on a stationary target—you." Dan's voice was modulated at a smooth, soothing level.

"I'd say our chances are fairly good," Luke interjected. "And once the identities of the victims start coming in, I think we'll start to pick up speed."

"How will identifying the victims help?"

"Once we know who they are," Dan explained, "we can trace their movements. I think we'll find that each of them has some sort of link to you."

I shook my head. "But I don't know any of them."

"You only saw the first one," Lige reminded me.

"True," Dan said, pulling open a desk drawer. He spread

four pictures across his desk. "Do you recognize any of these men?"

I approached his desk slowly. I knew I did not want to look at pictures of dead men, especially men who were dead simply because someone thought I wished them to be dead. I kept my eyes on Daniel until I reached his desk. Taking a deep breath, I dropped my eyes to the pictures and my hands to the desk. Carefully, I examined each of them. Shaking my head, I raised my eyes back to our sheriff's. "I don't know any of them."

Turning abruptly, I leaned against his desk and closed my eyes. I clenched my fists, barely feeling the nails digging into my palms as I struggled for control. "I don't know how much more of this I can take."

"More than you think, *cariad*." Righ's hands were unclenching mine and gently rubbing the nail marks from my palms.

I leaned against him for a moment, then opened my eyes and turned back to the sheriff. Thankfully, he'd removed the pictures from his desk. "Okay, Dan, I'm under house arrest and I'm not to go up on the roof. Roseanne and Elaine are taking care of your incoming information and I have Pete and Trys looking for similar letters in their files. My plan is to look at the letters out on the Net and to wade through the, as Trys puts it, 'tons of e-mail' I've gotten since he put the new site up. Have I missed anything?"

"If you've gotten e-mail from the killer, how useful is it in helping us locate him?"

"Well, you're a little out of my line of expertise, but it will give you his user name and the service he's using. Which you should be able to track down, but since all you need to do to get on a service is call and give them a user name and a password, I think you're kind of out of luck."

"Billing," Luke said.

Dan nodded. "Credit card or invoice—has to go to some-one, somewhere. Even if it's not the right person, it gets us that much closer."

"You should talk to Jessie. I think there are ways to tie into the Net without using a service," I added.

"Jessie?"

"Jessie Blackthorne. He owns and runs ojibway.net, our local computer place. If you've got a computer question, he's the person you need to talk to."

"Thanks," Dan said wryly.

"No problem. Anything else, or can I toddle back off into my house arrest?"

Dan looked pained. "I wish you wouldn't call it house arrest. And, yes, there is one more thing. Can you take a copy of this note and see if you can match it up to a dictionary or phrase book and then write it out properly, so I can see the difference?"

"Yeah, I can do that. We have copies of most of the books out on the Welsh language in the library. If I can't find it, Grandmama might be able to put her finger on which it came from without having to look it up."

With only a breath of a sigh, Daniel let my bringing in one more person pass without comment. He was learning. This boded well for his Welcoming.

"Lord and Lady, I almost forgot. Daniel, you need to come over to Beltene House tomorrow morning for a meeting. About quarter 'til seven."

"You're kidding."

"Nope, Lige, Luke and Eric will be there, too."

"And who else?" Our new sheriff had a funny look on his face.

"Mom and Dad, Rhan, Righ and a couple others." I shook

my head slightly. Dan relaxed as he apparently got my message that this wasn't about him being in my bed.

"Is it necessary?"

"Yes."

He exchanged a look with Lige. "Very well, quarter to seven, Beltene House. Coffee klatch?"

I'm sure I looked skeptical. "Grandmama will meet you at the door."

Righ grabbed my arm and hauled me toward the door.

"Here." Dan handed me the latest note. "Have Eric make a copy of this for you. I'll see you in the morning."

Sure, he'd see me in the morning, at least briefly. I now knew what a Welcoming entailed. Our Saxon sheriff was not going to be happy with me, not at all.

Chapter Seventeen
Saturday Morning

Righ and I delivered copies of both notes to Pete upon our arrival back in Beltene House. My suggestion that they regard the contents of the notes as a state secret was reinforced by Righ's causal examination of his current weapon—all I know is it looked huge and I was suitably impressed. The guys did seem to get the point.

Trystan, on bended knee, promised to never divulge the contents of the notes, even under torture. Like I believed that. Threaten to send him to Wales to herd sheep for a millennium and he'd spill his guts. Threaten to cancel his hundredth birthday party and he'd not only spill his guts, he'd sell his soul and any nearby ones as well.

My rooms were blessedly family-free when I finally managed to get to them. The only sign of Cris was a note requesting my presence in her office at five AM. I immediately called Roseanne for the added security of an outside call and went to bed.

We began the cleansing ceremonies—for me, the Welcoming Chamber and all the accoutrements that we were going to be using—at precisely 5:13 AM. I assembled all the ingredients needed for a Welcoming, brought them into the chamber and mixed them, each with their own chant, color and properties.

Six-thirty found me sprawled in the Beltene's chair, still damp from my ritual bath, feet on the table and the floor-length gold silk robe pooled at the top of my thighs.

"Tell me again, Cris, just how we're going to convince Dan to suck up that much wine at this time of the morning? He thinks we're having some sort of coffee klatch."

"Grandmama will convince him."

Did I want to know? No, I decided, shaking my head.

"She's very good," Cris added, knocking my feet onto the floor. "Get ready, everyone's coming."

"Ow," I complained as my bare feet bounced on the oak floor.

The Welcoming Chamber is a stark, unadorned room. Its only furnishings are a worktable on the east wall and the huge, oval oak table and chairs that dominate the room.

After all the witnesses had straggled in, Cris watched as I completed the final stage of the cleansing. First I seated everyone, one by one, binding them irrevocably into Daniel's Welcoming. I completed the ritual by placing mistletoe on the ledge of each window and above the door.

Quickly, for I was running out of time, I assessed the assembled ingredients on the workbench and went over my checklist one more time.

"You've done everything," Cris' soft voice assured me. "Sit."

I had barely seated myself when St. David's began to toll the hour and the doorknocker boomed, both promptly at seven.

I stood, overly conscious of the flowing gold robe as it swept the floor, and walked slowly to the door. Cris followed, slightly to my left and behind me.

I swung both halves of the door open and, with my hands clasped tightly in my sleeves and my eyes firmly on his shoulder, asked, "What is your wish?"

Daniel rolled his eyes and looked down at Grandmama, who nodded encouragement to him. "I wish to be Welcomed."

"Do you come to this chamber unencumbered, free of influence, blandishment and conscription?"

"I do."

"Do you agree to abide by the laws of the clan?"

"I do."

"Do you enter this chamber and attend this Welcoming of your own free will?"

"I do."

I moved to one side, allowing Cris to move forward with a gold basin held on her palms. Pushing back my sleeves, I rinsed my hands. First Daniel, then Grandmama followed my example. Cris returned the basin to the worktable, bringing a soft cloth back with her.

After drying my hands, I passed it to Daniel. Grandmama returned it to Cris and smiled reassuringly at me. Cris made another trip to the worktable, returning this time with a chalice.

Trying not to wince, I took a swallow. It was easily as horrid as Cris had promised it would be. Taking a deep breath, I passed the chalice to Dan. He did wince as he handed it to Grandmama.

"Enter and be welcome," I said, moving out of the doorway. I gestured at the empty seats on the west end of the table. "Kith and clan welcome you."

"I am honored," he answered, bowing his head and entering. "That tasted like shit," he said, *sotto voce*.

"Tell me about it," I agreed in the same low tone and gestured again to his seat.

Grandmama followed him to the supplicant's end of the table.

Taking a deep breath, I closed the doors and dropped the latch into place. As sweat trickled down my back, I leaned against the oak for a brief moment, trying to draw strength from it. Pushing away, I composed my face and returned to my seat.

Flattening my hands on the table in front of me, I began.

"We are gathered here today to Welcome Daniel Lincoln

Thorpe into the community residing in the town of Sevyrn, in the county of Brennen, in the state of Michigan, under the auspices of the family of Beltene.

"The witnesses have gathered, not only as attestors to this ceremony, but as vouchers to Daniel Lincoln Thorpe's readiness to be Welcomed.

"For the record, witnesses, state your name and occupation." I began the role call. "I am Rhiannon Argadnel Beltene, authoress and the Beltene. I am both the moderator and the sponsor of this Welcoming."

Daniel looked unsurprised by my pronouncement—I wondered just what Grandmama had done to him in fifteen short minutes to make him so accepting of our Druidic ceremony.

Grandmama finished the roll call. "I am Rhiannon Tangwen Beltene, Matriarch of the family Beltene and guide to our supplicant, Daniel Lincoln Thorpe."

"Let the Welcoming begin," I intoned.

Cris doused the electric lights. She moved gracefully from sconce to sconce, lighting candles. When she'd finished and the room was bathed in soft flickering light and the smell of vanilla, she handed the taper over to me.

Chanting in Gaelic, I touched the taper to the middle candle in the triple-branched candelabra in front of me. With a whisper, the candles, the two in front of me and one in front of each witness, lit themselves in a slow, sweeping progression toward Dan. He raised his eyebrows as the flames stopped, leaving the middle candle, on the candelabra in front of him, unlit.

Breathing a small sigh of relief that it had actually worked, I waited, taper in hand for Cris to bring a small brazier to the table. I touched the taper to the coals and leaned back as they burst into flame.

I exchanged the taper for the tray she was now holding. On it were two bowls and what appeared to be a piffle iron.

One bowl was filled with the mix for the cake and one with an herbal mixture. Carefully, I buried the iron in the coals to warm it and waited.

It had been made at the Metalworks, specifically for the Welcoming Ceremony and to Grandmama's exacting standards. It would make a flat cake scored into twelve pieces, covered, top and bottom, with a variety of symbols, which I'd been assured would help in the completion of our purpose. One of the sections of the iron was made of a different metal so the piece coming from it would be scorched.

I filled the heated iron with batter and set it back in the coals, flipping it after twenty seconds, removing it entirely after another fifteen. Cris held a gold plate ready as I opened the iron and let the finished product drop out.

I let it cool for a moment before attempting to break it along the scores. Cris took the plate, ceremoniously offering Daniel the first piece.

Without hesitation, and with a great deal of amusement, he took the charred piece. Whether he was following Grandmama out of respect for her age (and wait until he knew how old she really was) or because she'd done something to him, I was relieved not to have to deal with a hostile supplicant.

Cris then offered the plate first to me, then to each of the witnesses, serving herself last. Everyone put their piece on the small gold plates to their left.

Before seating herself, Cris made one last trip to the worktable to get a bottle of wine and a large gold chalice. She set them on my right.

Chanting in Gaelic, I filled the chalice and handed the bottle to Grandmama, who'd approached me for her part in the ceremony. She filled each of the tiny wine cups, then discarded the empty bottle on the sideboard.

I placed the chalice to the right of the brazier, then picked up the bowl of herbs. Pushing my sleeves back, I ceremoniously dipped a small ladle into the mixture and dusted the charcoal. A fragrant white smoke billowed toward the ceiling. I counted to thirty and dusted the charcoal again. I would need to do it once for each witness, then three times each for Grandmama, Daniel and myself. Even as ignorant as I was, I knew the strength of three tripled.

When I was finished, I returned the bowl to the sideboard and resisted the urge to sneeze as I moved to stand behind my chair. I hadn't realized how invasive and confining this type of incense would be. I could feel it hemming me into my place at the table and as I inhaled its fragrance, the melange of scents and tastes seeped deep within me, leaving a dizzying feeling of response. Like some ancient priestess ...

With a snap, I pulled my wandering mind back to the business at hand. Dan's look of annoyance was tinged with awe and came across loud and clear through the haze. Grandmama and Cris, on the other hand, looked quite pleased with themselves.

Cris had neglected to mention how the haze effected your mind. Nervously, I tried to remember if there was anything in the herbal mixture that could possibly be hallucinogenic or if it was simply the combination of the herbs. If it was a hallucinogenic mixture, I wondered how Dan was handling it. Firmly, I gathered all my senses and concentrated on keeping my mind from wandering off into some trip through antiquity.

I held my silence for the prescribed three minutes before pulling the plate toward me.

"To the family Beltene, kith and clan alike," I said thickly, my tongue having lost most of its connections with my brain. I saluted everyone with my cup and plate before popping the tiny triangle of cake onto my tongue and tossing back the thimbleful of wine. Around the table, everyone followed suit. Letting the wine absorb into the cake before I swallowed, I could feel the rush as the wine hit my bloodstream and merged with the tendrils of incense. I closed my eyes for a moment, wishing I wasn't required to do this on an empty stomach.

I watched, making sure everyone was finished before walking toward Daniel, taking the chalice with me. Merlin had made the wine; this special wine, a brew of both grapes and herbs, was used only for Welcoming Ceremonies and was made once every ninety years. This particular brew had been bottled in 1908.

I knew perfectly well that Rhodri and Pentraeth had isolated the ingredients which changed the appropriate letter in a supplicant's genetic code. I had suggested slipping the potion into Dan's coffee as an alternative to getting him drunk and forcing him to participate in mystical voodoo. Cris had simply pointed out that while Rhodri's serum worked exceptionally well in computer simulation, it had never been tested on a human being. Had I wanted our new sheriff to become our first guinea pig?

I'd declined. So here I was, rotating the bowl of the chalice over the flame of the candle to Dan's left, carefully maintaining my distance from him. When the wine was warmed to my satisfaction, I looked directly at him as I lifted the chalice and saluted him.

"Welcome, Daniel Lincoln Thorpe. I, Rhiannon Argadnel Beltene, the Beltene of the family Beltene, bid you welcome. You and your heirs from this day forth will forever be members of this community, bound by the laws and traditions that bind us all. Welcome." I lifted the chalice and drank, then handed it to Dan.

With a wry look, he saluted me and said, "I thank you for your Welcome." Then he lifted the chalice and drank.

The startled look on his face told me that the minute

sample he'd already drunk hadn't prepared him for the wine's dangerous potency. He returned the chalice to me, his look warning of the storm to come.

I passed it on to Grandmama. This part of the ceremony, once Dan and I had completed the first salute, was age-related. Eldest on down.

I returned to my seat and watched as, one by one, the witnesses saluted Daniel and returned to their seats. By the time Eric had finished, Dan was leaning against the table. With a sip of wine required with each salute, he was perilously close to being incapacitated.

With misgiving close about me, I stood and returned to Daniel's end of the table.

He saluted everyone with a sweeping gesture with the chalice. "Once again, I thank you all for your gracious Welcome." He spoke in the carefully precise manner of the inebriated. "I have accepted this Welcoming of my own free will. I agree to abide by the laws and traditions of the clan." He sipped one last time before handing the chalice to me. I suppose it would be more accurate to say I rescued the chalice before he dropped it.

I took a moment to study him. He was aware only that we'd filled his belly with lethal wine and his lungs with the perfume of our herbs during our archaic little ceremony. All too soon I would be required to explain to him that we'd taken the liberty of changing his DNA in ways I couldn't comprehend. Neither of us was going to enjoy the remainder of the day much.

Raising the chalice, I performed my last remaining speech. "This Welcoming has been attested to by the attending members of the community, both kith and kin alike. The attending members of the community have vouched for this supplicant, both kith and kin alike.

"You, Daniel Lincoln Thorpe, are now a member in good

standing of the clan residing in the city of Sevyrn, in the county of Brennen, in the state of Michigan under the auspices of the family of Beltene. All records, information and history closed to the Unwelcomed is now available to you. Use it well," I finished.

Grandmama stood and unobtrusively urged Daniel upright. Touching my hands to his shoulders, I quickly kissed his cheeks. "I, Rhiannon Argadnel Beltene, Head of the family Beltene and the clan which dwells within the auspices thereof, bid you welcome."

As I uttered the word *welcome*, the unlit candle in the center of the candelabra in front of Dan burst into flame. Daniel and I both jumped and eyed the candle warily.

Before he could do more than turn his somber and irritated gaze on me, the others surged forward to add their good wishes and tidings to mine. Nodding, I accepted his look of censure.

With a smooth, absent-minded gesture that did little to soothe my rattled wits, Grandmama extinguished the candles while Cris moved to turn on the electric lights and an exhaust fan which began to pull the smoke quickly from the room.

Eric and Luke maneuvered their way into place on either side of Daniel as he swayed. The time it took for the ceremony and exactly when the supplicant would collapse was defined down to the second. He fixed his eyes on me.

"Rhiannon?" he managed.

Eyeing him warily as I unobtrusively checked my watch, I answered, "Yes?" His thirty-three minutes and three seconds were just about up.

He took a deep breath and collapsed. The guys caught him before he hit the floor.

I sighed and raised my eyebrows. "He's going to be really

cranky when he wakes up with a roaring hangover," I observed.

"Everything went perfectly, Rhiannon," Gwydre said smugly.

"Well, if you consider getting your new sheriff wasted at seven o'clock in the morning successful, then yes, it all went perfectly."

"He'll be fine," my mother assured me.

"He'd better be."

Grandmama rested her hands on my shoulders. "The beginning will be rocky."

I laughed. "Rocky? I bet they hear him in Miami."

She smiled. "I hardly think so. Detroit, maybe."

I turned to face her. "I can't believe that you're going to make me tell Daniel about us all by myself."

She looked shocked. "Rhiannon, why would you think you have to explain the family to him by yourself?"

"I don't?"

"Of course not. Even if this weren't your first Welcoming, in general or as the Beltene, you wouldn't be explaining anything to the supplicant by yourself. There is always another person involved in that stage of the Welcoming."

"Oh, then who ..."

"I think you'll find that Righdhonn, both as someone Daniel respects and as a former Beltene, already plans to stay with you and assist you in your explanations."

"Thank the gods," I said, looking around for him and heaving an inappropriately heavy sigh of relief.

"Righ went upstairs with the guys," Cris said as she joined us.

"Well, I suppose I should get out of this," I plucked at the sleeve of the robe, "and join him."

***

Rhodri was waiting for me when I arrived upstairs. "Don't forget, it'll take a little time for him to adjust."

"Adjust? Now there's a misleading term. I'm sure he's going to have a bloody cow."

"I don't think it will be quite that bad."

I raised an eyebrow at my brother.

"Okay, he's going to be pissed."

"To say the least."

"Righ's going to be here to protect you and the ladies are going to be working and keeping you company until Dan wakes up."

Did he think I'd missed seeing Roseanne and Elaine? "Yes, I know."

"I'll check on him again."

"Fine." I collapsed on the window seat as he went upstairs for one last check on our catatonic sheriff.

"He'll be fine," he assured me as he rejoined me, watching as the excess family trooped out. "He'll wake up right on schedule. Give him this tea and the headache will go away."

I made an inarticulate sound. "He might take it from Righ, but I can't imagine that he'll be wanting to accept any liquid beverages from my hand."

Eric cruised back in. "When Dan wakes up and is fairly coherent again, tell him we've got a positive identification for the first body."

"What!" I sat up. "Who is it?"

"Just tell him."

"Who is it?"

"It's only polite to let Dan know first. He is the sheriff, you know."

"I'm the Beltene."

"That's nice."

"Get stuffed," I told him to the vast amusement of his wife.

"'Bye, Rhi," he tossed over his shoulder, kissing Roseanne before leaving.

"Has anyone seen Puck?" I had left the tiny kitten sleeping on the couch. Of course, that was nearly four hours ago and since I'd found him in bed with me this morning, I knew he could climb the stairs.

"He's sleeping with Daniel." Rhodri paused in the doorway and pointed at me. "Leave them alone, they're both fine."

I stared into the empty hallway for a long moment before turning to look at my friends. "Someday," I threatened idly. "So where's the family mercenary?"

"Upstairs, he said he was going to take a nap while Dan was unconscious," Roseanne said.

"Now that's the best idea I've heard all morning," I said.

Chapter Eighteen
Saturday, not quite 11:00 AM

The amount of time it takes for the supplicant to regain consciousness is also a given. It took Daniel three hours and thirty-three minutes to wake up. Druidically speaking, three threes are deeply cool. Well, Cris did have a mystical explanation that lasted forty-five minutes, most of which went right over my head, about the significance of that particular amount of time in this ritual. Maybe someday I'll understand exactly what it was she was trying to tell me.

Righdhonn woke me up about fifteen minutes before Dan was due to resurrect. Having a kitten dropped on your chest does get your attention. I transferred Puck to a pillow and sat up.

"Is he awake?"

"Nope," my cousin answered from the couch across from me. "He's got twelve more minutes."

"Where are the ladies?"

"I sent them out for an extended lunch. Dan doesn't need company during his orientation."

"You get to officiate and I get to watch?" I asked hopefully.

"I'm here to keep you out of trouble."

"Keep me out of trouble?" I really did think it was unfair of them to allow an inexperienced Beltene to be giving any kind of explanation.

"You'll be fine," he assured me. "Just remember that in normal cases the compulsion takes the better part of twenty-four hours to settle in. But in Dan's case, it will be within fifteen minutes of when he drinks the tea. I had Rhodri slip a dose of his elixir into it. Dan's going to need a hell of a lot more information than we'd normally be able to give him."

I frowned. "Isn't this the same stuff that's never been tried on a human before?"

"Yep."

"We've changed the man's DNA, got him crocked on his ass, he's going to have one hell of a hangover when he wakes up and now, you've given him Rhodri's serum on top of it all—Lord and Lady, Righ, if we were going to give him the serum anyway, why didn't we just slip it into his coffee and forgo the mystical voodoo?" I distinctly remembered discussing this very subject with Cris yesterday. I also remembered that we rejected it because the serum had never been tested on a human before.

I glanced upstairs as his laughter rang through my rooms. "The mystical voodoo is important, too," he assured me. "It prepares his subconscious so that what we tell him rings true."

I rolled my eyes and stood. If I was to be at all coherent, I needed coffee. Cris had been adamant that fasting meant nothing but water. No wonder I'd taken a nap.

I'd just juggled the first cup out of the pot when my bed creaked as a restless, sick body shifted. My eyes met Righ's before lifting to listen to the next series of creaks, which were followed by a rush of unsteady footsteps across the ceiling to my bathroom. I winced at the sound of retching.

Actually, I could commiserate with Daniel. Merlin's wine has a well-deserved reputation for having a number of varied and vicious side effects on anyone unsuspecting or stupid enough to indulge in more than a small glass. And Dan had been required to not only have a large amount first thing in the morning, but had also been required to have it on an empty stomach.

At age fifteen, having dared each other into it, Eric, Roseanne, Pete and I each drank an entire bottle of Merlin's wine. Eric had dandelion, Roseanne had blueberry, Pete had rhubarb and I had red raspberry.

For my part, I think dying would have been the easiest solution. I had auditory hallucinations for a week. Pete lost the feeling in all his extremities for two days. Roseanne and Eric were incommunicado for seventy-two hours and to this day have refused to discuss any of their symptoms. We all swore off liquor for weeks.

I waited for the sounds of physical distress to quiet before heating the tea Rhodri had left. Righ waited on the couch.

My appearance at the bathroom door, tea in hand, was not greeted with enthusiasm.

"How are you feeling?"

He didn't bother looking up. "I died."

I didn't attempt to explain that he was supposed to feel like he died. Cris had gone into great detail yesterday about his symbolic death. "Rhodri said to drink this tea."

"I don't want it." Dan looked a bit green as I sat the tea on the counter.

"Rhodri said it will take the headache and nausea away."

"Only death could take them away."

"I know. Drink the tea. You'll feel better."

"No, thank you."

"Drink it."

"I have some serious reservations about my ability to keep anything down. Even the aspirin returned from whence it came." He wasted energy lifting a hand to wave at the over-turned bottle on the counter.

"Trust me. It works and it won't come up."

"Trust you? *You?* You were the one who poisoned me."

"I didn't poison you."

"Really? I'm afraid I'd call wine at seven in the morning a form of poisoning. It would've been simpler to shoot me."

"Nonsense."

"It would've been kinder, too."

"You'll be just fine."

"Fine? Just fine? What the hell do you call this, this ..." His words died off as his green tinge deepened.

I bit my lip. "It's a hangover."

"I don't have hangovers."

"You've never had Merlin's wine before." I surveyed him objectively. "You're actually in pretty good shape for the amount you consumed."

Daniel moaned as he straightened.

"You really should drink the tea. It will make you feel better in a very short period of time. You're lucky Rhodri left it. He always makes sure his concoctions taste good. Cris, on the other hand, is a firm believer in the worse it tastes, the better it is for you."

"What was in that wine?"

"Black raspberries."

He cast a bleary glare in my direction and flushed pale beneath the green.

"Drink the tea," I encouraged, pushing it closer.

"Take . . ." Whatever he intended to say went unsaid as he quickly turned away from me.

I departed the bathroom with haste, closing the door on his discomfort.

Leaning over the railing, I gave Righ my best imitation of Grandmama and motioned for him to join me. If he was supposed to keep me out of trouble—

"Righ, if the serum will work in fifteen minutes, then the compulsion's in place at that point, so why do you have to keep me out of trouble and who else knows that you and

Rhodri decided to make Dan a guinea pig for expediency's sake?" I asked softly, meeting him at the top of the stairs.

He shook his head and with an eye on the bathroom door, answered, "We need to give Dan a lot more information than we'd be able to give him with just the ceremony; I'll keep you from getting too sidetracked onto unimportant subjects. You and Rhodri and I know."

"Lord and Lady," I muttered

Righ patted me on top of the head and settled into my papa-san chair. He's one of the few people I know who can actually get in and out of it without looking ridiculous. He also manages to look relaxed and perfectly comfortable when he's in it. I love the way the chair looks, but I never sit in it.

I settled into the window seat next to the stairs and was waiting, cross-legged, when Dan stepped out of the bathroom, tea in hand. He sipped slowly as he looked from me to my cousin. I was relieved to see that he'd begun to regain his normal coloring.

"A coffee klatch? I'd hate to see your version of a drunken brawl."

"You were the one who referred to it as a coffee klatch."

"That's true," he agreed after a moment's thought. "You merely, by your silence, let me assume that was your intention."

His level look forestalled any protest. I lifted a shoulder and dropped it, nodding. "I did not correct your assumption."

"Why?"

"You needed to be at this meeting and if I had explained, you might not have come."

"Good point, I probably wouldn't have come. After all, I do have a multiple murder investigation in progress. But, still and all, I had assumed that a seven a.m. meeting would be accompanied with coffee and donuts. I think I can be excused for not expecting to get sloshed with the county's leading family at that hour of the morning."

Silence seemed to be my best bet. He hadn't finished the
tea and I wasn't going to start the fifteen-minute countdown
until that cup was empty. I could now tell him anything I
wanted. Once he had regained consciousness, my inability to
discuss family matters with him had ceased. Unfortunately,
until the compulsion kicked in, he could turn around and
tell anyone he wanted, welcomed or not.

"What time is it?"

"Not quite eleven-thirty."

He looked blankly at me for a moment. "I passed out?"

My eyes darted around the room. "Yeah."

"We all had that devil's brew of yours. Who else passed
out?"

Maybe they were right and I was getting more sensitive. I
could almost see his thoughts; about how embarrassing and
undignified it was to have passed out in front of everyone,
how angry he was with me for setting him up and how uncer-
tain he was about why I'd set him up. Righ's encouraging nod
prompted me to stick my foot in my mouth. "It's all right, we
knew you were going to pass out at the end of the meeting."

I didn't need Righ's wince to realize that wasn't exactly
what I should have said. Dan's face darkened with anger as
he swallowed the last of his tea before responding. I checked
my watch.

"You deliberately plied me with wine—enough wine to make
me pass out. On purpose. Why?"

I looked over at Righ. My brief flash of ESP had deserted
me and I stalled for time. "Umm ..."

"Would you *please* give me some sort of explanation?"

"Of course," I answered. My cousin leaned his head into a
hand and muttered something silently to himself.

"Good. Why don't you start at the beginning and explain
why you insisted on an alcoholic stupor and mystical nonsense

in the middle of a murder investigation." It wasn't a question. Dan left the bathroom doorway and settled onto my bed, relaxing against a pillow and the headboard with a sigh.

The beginning? Surely he wasn't ready to hear about Grandmama and Brenainn yet. Of course, in his weakened state there was no way for him to get out of my rooms until the fifteen minutes had passed. I nodded and began my explanation. "First of all, what you participated in this morning is called a welcoming."

"Getting someone drunk enough to pass out is one hell of a Welcoming."

I paused with my finger still in the air. He had a valid point. "It's a very important ceremony for us. It is virtually unchanged from the first one ever held in seventy-one A.D."

"What is the purpose of a Welcoming ceremony?"

"A Welcoming is held after a newcomer to the area is judged to be a person who can adapt and accept the hidden knowledge of Clan Beltene. There is a vast amount of information about the county and the Clan that is not available to the Unwelcomed. Your Welcoming opens you to the knowledge and places a compulsion on you to keep the knowledge hidden. And it is your position in this community and these murders that necessitated your Welcoming."

"What kind of knowledge and how is it hidden? And what the hell kind of compulsion are you talking about?"

I looked at Righ. He shrugged. Either I was doing okay or I was doing so badly that he was incapable of speech. Encouraged, I began, "The knowledge specifically, and in particular, deals with my family. I suppose you could refer to it as unveiling the skeletons in our closet." Righ made an inarticulate sound. Dan and I both looked at him. He waved a hand at us, so after a moment, I continued, "The compulsion is what hides the knowledge and is what prevents you from discussing it with an Unwelcomed person."

"You have skeletons in your closet?" He nodded. "Somehow, Rhiannon, that doesn't surprise me."

Relieved things were going so well, I flashed a grin at him. "Tell me about the candle."

"The candle?" I echoed.

"I do remember the entire damned ceremony. Tell me how you did the candle trick—both of them."

"I lit them," I temporized.

"You lit one of them."

"I did exactly as instructed. I lit the stupid, bloody thing and repeated the chant that Cris made me memorize and concentrated on an image of the flame sweeping along the table lighting the other candles. I was probably as surprised as you were that it worked."

"You lit a candle, chanted and thought about lighting the rest," Dan repeated dubiously.

"Yeah."

"And just what made it all work?"

"Cris probably. Although she did keep telling me that I was the one actually doing it. But I'm most definitely not one of the druids of the family. Lord and Lady, I became the Beltene by default."

"Druids?"

"Cris is a druid," I agreed.

"And Rhodri is a Nazi-Quaker."

"Don't be ridiculous. Rhodri's an occasional Catholic. Cris, Grandmama, Gwydre and Daffyd are the druids."

"You think that your grandmother, a perfectly nice, respectable woman, is a druid?"

Righ groaned. I frowned at both men. "Grandmama and druids are not mutually exclusive terms. She's been a druid for a very long time."

Dan rubbed a hand across his chin. "You lit the candles

with some sort of Druidic hocus-pocus. Oh, hell, why not? I've got embalmed, bloodless bodies popping up all over the place. Why not druids? Just try not to clutter up the county with too many of your blood sacrifices ..."

His voice died off and he got an odd expression on his face. He closed his eyes, then shook his head abruptly. "No," he muttered, "their hearts were intact."

"Their hearts were intact?" I questioned. "What are you talking about?"

"Wasn't it the druids who took hearts from living sacrifices?"

"There are a number of religions which advocate the taking of beating hearts from ... Lord and Lady, Daniel, you're wandering way the hell off the subject. Please try to pay attention."

"I am paying attention," Dan said. "You left that one candle in front of me unlit until I was thoroughly drunk and you'd finished your pretty little speech. Then, pouf!" He gestured with the teacup. "It lit itself."

This did not seem to be a point where I should say anything.

"I don't care how it happened. It was impressive and I'm willing to admit that. But my one question is, why? I'm in the middle of a multiple murder investigation and you hauled half the officers working on the case into a meeting that you *claimed* was of the utmost importance that turns out to be some sort of mystical claptrap. I really don't have time for this shit and neither do my men. So why?"

"Time out," Righ said, forming the classic 'T' with his hands.

Dan and I both looked at him.

"It was because of this multiple murder investigation, Dan, that you were Welcomed this early in your residency here. We believe that the information that you'll gain from being Welcomed is necessary for you to fulfill your duties as the sheriff of Brennen County. *Especially* in light of these murders."

Dan took Righ's explanation a hell of a lot better than he'd taken mine. It was probably some sort of male bonding thing.

"It was Rhi's decision. As the Beltene she proposed your entrance into the community, officiated at your Welcoming and," Righ looked over at me with something akin to despair, "is conducting the post-Welcoming festivities."

Dan's expression as he stared at me was perilously close to Righ's. "Somehow I'm not the least bit surprised that Rhiannon is directly responsible for this."

"Now wait a minute," I protested. "Grandmama started this."

"How did your grandmother start this?"

"She's the one who performed the triad sacrifice and officiated at the first Welcoming." The words were out of my mouth before I noticed Righ's head shaking and I remembered that I'd already mentioned that the first Welcoming was in 71 AD. I winced and dropped my head into my lap.

"Rhiannon Argadnel Beltene." As many times as I've heard my name uttered in anger, this was the first time it sounded like a curse.

"Sorry." I lifted my head and shrugged apologetically.

"Wait a minute." Dan's words as well as his upraised hand stopped Righ. His gaze shifted from me to Righ and back again. I moved nervously in the window seat as we waited for the conclusion that was obviously churning about in his mind. "I'm sure it has to do with the fact that I'm losing my mind, but this all has the feel of truth. Answer this one question—what is the Beltene family hiding that requires such elaborate protection?"

I stole a look at Righ. He gestured for me to finish my explanation. With my first real attempt to direct the Beltene psychic communication, which supposedly I inherited, I queried the feasibility of the whole truth. Righ nodded.

"Most of the family have extended lifetimes. The protections are to keep us from discovery, from the predations of scientists, from the implacable condemnation of the churches and from society in general. That's why we have these protections, why we own most of the county and why we are very careful to whom we reveal this secret."

"You said there is a compulsion on those with this knowledge that forces them to keep the knowledge secret?"

I nodded. I had hoped that the compulsion and the changes it necessitated would have been one of the last things I had to explain—or even better, that it was one of the unnecessary things Righ didn't think we needed to bother with. I checked my watch and thanked the gods that we had gone past the proscribed fifteen minutes. I also sent up a small, fervent prayer that Rhodri was right and the serum really did take effect in fifteen minutes.

"How?"

"It begins with your acceptance into the community. The obvious result of this is someone nominating you for a Welcoming. The fact that you were hired to be sheriff is tacit approval to begin with. They wouldn't hire someone for the position without being sure that he would fit into the community and be Welcomed at a relatively early date. Sheriff is a position that needs a Welcomed person in it. Under normal circumstances you would not have been Welcomed this soon, but it would have been within the next couple of months.

"Once you have been put forward as a candidate for Welcoming, a quorum of family and community members must agree that you're ready."

"You decided I was ready?"

I grinned wryly. "No, we decided that, in this case, circumstances were conspiring against us and we *had* to Welcome you. Everyone agreed to that supposition."

"Continue."

"Once the quorum is taken, a date and time is decided in conjunction with the Druidic element of the family." Dan scowled. "I'm sorry, Dan, but you're going to have to come to grips with the fact that not a hell of a lot gets scheduled around here until Cris, Grandmama or Gwydre have been consulted."

He stared at the ceiling for a long moment. "Okay."

"After the date and time have been set, then the witnesses are picked. They are generally people who are close to or work with the supplicant. They are never Unwelcomed persons. It's also generally evenly split between community and family members. One of the witnesses serves as the guide for the supplicant—usually Grandmama.

"The ceremony is very archaic. As I mentioned, the first one was held in seventy-one A.D., and the one we hold now is virtually unchanged from that first one. You must come into the Welcoming of your own free will and must state your desire at the door. The washing of hands and the drink at the doorway are symbolic of the peaceful intentions on both sides. It is at this point that the tendrils of the compulsion begin. The incense, coupled with the cake and wine, sink the tendrils deep to bring about the changes within you. The change is physical and makes it impossible for you to ever betray the clan." I stopped speaking as Dan held up his hand.

"Physical?"

"It changes a letter in your DNA."

"Excuse me?"

I lifted a hand, spreading my fingers wide. "I can't even begin to explain how it happens, Dan, or why or what it is we do that manages to accomplish this change. For that kind of detail, you need to talk to Rhodri or Pentraeth. They're the ones who insisted on screwing around with the ceremony until they figured out just what the hell was happening."

"You've changed a letter in my DNA?" he repeated.

I nodded as Righ slowly straightened in his chair. Dan looked over at him. "Extended lifetimes?"

Righ nodded, a muscle in his jaw jumping as he clenched his teeth.

"Is yours extended?"

Righ nodded again.

"When were you born?"

"November tenth in the year eight hundred and seventy."

Chapter Nineteen
Saturday, mid-day

It took several minutes for Daniel to recover from Righ's pronouncement. Lord and Lady, I knew Righ was over eleven hundred years old but hearing it put that bluntly took even me aback. Righ just leaned back and smiled at us.

"Well." Dan drew the word out, raising a knee and lacing his fingers around it. "How old are you?" he asked, looking at me.

"Thirty-two."

"Born in thirty-two?"

I shook my head. "Nope, thirty-two soon to be thirty-three. I'm the eldest unchanged member of the family. That's what makes me the Beltene."

"What exactly does the Beltene do?"

"The Beltene is the family protector, the liaison between strangers and the Unwelcomed dwelling within the community and the family. All the property, businesses and financial matters are kept in the current Beltene's name. My job is to make sure that we remain a nice, quiet northern community where nothing much ever happens."

Dan rolled his eyes.

I laughed. "Okay, it's not been very quiet this week, but even with my fans coming out of the woodwork, keeping a lid on things has never been very difficult. After all, without any physical proof, who would believe that District Court Judge

Rhys Beltene III is the same Rhys Beltene who's been our District Court Judge twice before in the last one hundred and twenty years."

"His third tour?"

"He likes being a judge," Righ interjected lazily.

"And you?" Dan asked pointedly.

"He's a mercenary," I answered.

"For eleven hundred odd years?"

"On and off," Righ answered.

"He's a very good mercenary," I assured Dan. "There are a number of incredible legends about this man. Want to hear about the battle of Agincourt?"

Rhiannon," the legend interrupted.

I peered at our new sheriff. "The King was Welsh, you know," I said innocently.

"What about your cousin, Trystan?" Dan asked, pointedly ignoring me and getting back to the heart of his concern.

I sighed. "Trystan—now there's a horse of a different color."

"How old is he?"

"Three."

"Three?" Dan raised an eyebrow at me.

"Well, emotionally he's three. Although that is probably casting the maturity of your average three-year-old into doubt. His birthday, believe it or not, is October thirty-first and this year he will be exactly one hundred years old."

Dan snorted. "Halloween. That's appropriate."

"Trystan is unique even amidst our family," I explained. "He is the only one of us born of changed parents—and I might add, the sole reason that people of child-bearing years must be sterilized before they take their change. The main reason, among other things like Cris and Grandmama having had a chat with him, that I know he's not involved in these crimes is that he'd sell his soul to keep his hundredth birthday party on line. He knows if he gives me too much shit, I'll cancel it in a heartbeat and send him to Wales for the next millennium."

Our sheriff stared at me thoughtfully.

Righ laughed. "You'll not be wanting to get on the wrong side of our Beltene, Dan. She'll zero in on the most sensitive spot you have and rub it raw."

Now that was helpful. "Thank you very much, Righdhonn."

"It's a talent you have, *cariad*."

"If it's so important for the sheriff to be Welcomed and have possession of this knowledge, then why did they hire me?" Dan stared at me. "I can't believe I'm discussing this like it was perfectly normal."

"It is," Righ said. "For Brennen County."

"There have always been a number of positions here in Brennen County that are supposed to be filled by a Welcomed person. I don't know where their brains were when they hired you." A discreet choking sound came from my cousin's direction. "All right, that's not true. I do know what they were thinking about. The idiots. They hired from the outside because there wasn't anyone qualified in the county who wanted the job. So, my dear sheriff, here you are; chock full of Merlin's wine, Cris' incense, some Druidic voodoo, an odd concoction of Rhodri's and some slightly altered DNA. Relatively painless, hmm?"

My light tone drew a censorious glance from Righ.

"Thanks for the recap, Rhiannon," Dan said dryly.

"No problem."

"Who's Merlin?"

I frowned. "You haven't met Merlin yet?"

"I don't think so."

"Have you been over to Keltia Bank?"

"Of course. It's the only bank in town. I set up my accounts there."

"Okay. Then you met Merlin. He's the distinguished-looking man in his fifties and a three-piece suit who wanders aimlessly around the bank."

"I met the president of the bank. He was a Beltene."

"That was Merlin."

"I would have expected Merlin to be a mighty sorcerer."

"Oh, I wouldn't be saying things like that too loudly. Merlin gets annoyed by references to King Arthur, sorcery and especially about getting walled up in trees by tarts and his paybacks are always a bitch."

Dan looked sharply at me. "Is he really in his fifties?"

I gave him a brilliant smile. "No."

He started to say something, but stopped, staring at me with a puzzled look on his face, then he changed the subject. "How did you know I was going to pass out?"

"Everyone does. It's a Druidic equivalent to dying and arising new within the community."

"How do you get endowed with an extended lifetime?"

"Only family members qualify. Once they turn thirty-five—it was twenty-five at one time—"

"It was sixteen if you go back far enough," Righ murmured.

"A family member can opt to go through the changing ceremony. It takes the better part of eighteen months—"

"It does take eighteen months, exactly," the person who wasn't going to explain anything murmured.

"And it takes up a fair amount of your time, so if you decide to change and you happen to be the Beltene, the position passes to your heir."

"Who's your heir?"

"Olwen."

"Sex isn't an issue here, is it?"

I chuckled. "We're a matriarchal community, Dan. No,

sex has never been an issue in assumption of the role of the Beltene."

"Who else has been the Beltene?"

"Rhodri, before me and Dad before him. Rhan, Cris, Righ," I waved a hand at the former Beltene. "Just to name a few."

"How extended are the lifetimes?"

I lifted a shoulder and shook my head. "We don't know. Grandmama, who was the first, is still going strong at a mite over nineteen hundred."

"And the Gwynn-O'Keefes?"

Righ burst into laughter as I moaned and dropped my head back against the cool stone.

"Rhiannon?"

"They're in exile."

"Oh, yeah. Sure they . . ." His words died off as he met my serious gaze. "Exile? In the United States of America?"

"Well, this wasn't the United States of America when they were sent into exile. No," I hastened my explanation at the horror in his expression. "None of them have extended lifetimes."

"Thank you," he murmured.

"This is difficult to explain, Dan. In a lot of ways, with our holdings both here and in Wales, we operate on a style of self-autonomy that governments frown on. Kith and clan are the most important thing and to endanger them is the worst form of treason.

"There were ten families who joined in the uprising. It was shortly after we'd moved here and before Beltene House was finished. On Beltain—which we do consider a holiday—during the festivities, they attacked. Over there," I gestured toward town. "St. David's and the cemetery sit on the location of the attack. The day was ours, but the fatalities were horrifying. After all the dust had settled, and the attackers had been rounded up—with their families—they were offered a choice.

"We had plenty of land, and you are supposed to consider charity in these matters, so they were offered death or exile. The family members who hadn't been involved in the actual attack were offered a place within the community where they could be watched. They all took exile, down to the last child. We took them out to the site where they live today and left them, with their weapons and building materials and supplies. And there they've been for the last two hundred odd years."

"Two hundred years?"

"The rebellion was in seventeen eighty-five."

Dan shook his head. "You don't hold a grudge, do you?"

"Not a bit," I returned, smiling. "However, I do believe that the Gwynn-O'Keefes are a problem the Beltene is going to need to rectify. I'm sure they're nowhere near as ignorant as they want us to think they are. It's time they were brought back into the clan and I suppose Diuran and I are going to have to have a wee chat about the matter. This 'Throwing a Child to the Wolves' ceremony of ours sucks."

"Throwing a child to the wolves?" Both the sheriff's eyebrows were up as he stared at me.

"You've gotten sidetracked," Righ interjected.

"I'll explain later," I promised Dan. "I think this is one problem that can wait until after you catch the murderer. But it does explain why the Gwynn-O'Keefes, whether still in exile or repatriated, couldn't be responsible for these killings and why we were so surprised to see a body within the confines of the wall."

"How does it explain that and what the hell kept them barely across the river?"

"It was after the uprising that Grandmama and Cris put up the wards. Warding is a Druidic thing—"

"Thing?" he interrupted.

"Okay, warding is a spell set in a specific area to coincide with similar spells to encompass a designated area. We have general warding set around the county, a Gwynn-O'Keefe warding around the town, and then there's the Beltene House warding which is set into the wall that encircles the forest, beach, part of the bay and the house."

Dan was giving me an *I-know-I've-lost-my-mind-and-now-I-know-she-has-too* look.

Righ shook his head and laughed. "*Cariad*, it's time to be letting the man get back to what we pay him for. You're going to send him into information overload."

"How are you feeling?" I asked, turning a worried face toward our sheriff.

"Much better. All other ingredients aside, your brother's tea did get rid of my hangover."

"Good. You've got a ton of stuff waiting at the office for you and I'm sure Rachel has a semi load of stuff to send over here and it's probably just about killing her that she couldn't call or beep me today." I sighed. "You realize that she's going to try to make up for it and beep me every ten minutes."

"What is waiting?"

"Lord and Lady," I exclaimed and bit my lip.

"What?" Dan sat up, sliding to the stairway side of the bed and dropping his feet to the floor.

"Eric said to tell you that they've identified the first body."

He looked at his watch. "Jesus Christ, woman, we've been screwing around here for the last hour and of all the things you've been intent on telling me, you forgot that one of the victims was identified?"

I spread my hands and decided, once again, that silence was my best recourse.

"Never mind," he said, standing. He paused as if testing to make sure the change in altitude wasn't going to send something else into overload. "I've got to get back to the office."

He stopped at the head of the stairs and looked thoughtfully from me to Righ. "This tunnel system of yours—you brought Rhiannon to the office yesterday via it, correct?"

"Are you asking for the easy way back to your office?" Righ asked.

Dan's face broke into a smile, "That's what I'm asking."

"Let's be on our way." Righ rose and joined him at the stairs.

"Daniel."

He turned to look at me.

"We told you about the tunnels yesterday because we had to. Normally this is information open only to the sheriff, the Beltene and, of course, former Beltenes and a select few. A select Welcomed few. Luke joined those ranks yesterday with you. This is not information for public consumption."

Righ nudged Dan and beamed at me. "Doesn't it make you proud to see her taking on the role of the Beltene like she was born to it?"

Dan wisely chose not to answer.

"Men," I muttered as they hurried from my tower.

Elaine and Roseanne returned from their extended lunch with the news that the natives were restless in town. Rachel was annoyed that I had been incommunicado for so long (it obviously made no difference to her that I was with both Righ and her beloved sheriff) and my agent, Kate, had been trying frantically to get through to me all day. I declined to respond to either Rachel or Kate and spent the afternoon searching through my on-line hate mail for letters similar in style to the ones found with the body. About five, I took a break for dinner with the family and sent Elaine and Roseanne home for the evening.

I arrived back at my tower shortly after six, looking forward to a long, quiet evening when the phone rang. Rachel, true to form, had been beeping and calling all afternoon. I eyed the phone like it was a cobra with its hood spread and ready to strike. At fifteen rings, I acknowledged defeat and answered it.

"What?"

"Where have you been, why aren't you working and what the hell is going on over there in the back of beyond?"

Kate Grenwall has been my agent since the beginning of my writing career.

"Hello, Kate."

"Your book sales are *up*, a lot! I just love free publicity."

I winced and put her on the speakerphone. We were going to have another discussion about publicity. Kate seems to think that if she talks loud and fast enough, she might get me to change my mind. For years, the only signings I've done are local and I never do publicity tours, interviews or television.

"You and your delightfully backward little town are on the cover of nearly every magazine and paper in New York," she continued.

"Lord and Lady."

"All the lovely, trashy magazines which the citizens of this wonderful, free-market country read."

"I don't want to know."

"You'd better listen," she advised me firmly. "They want to do another reprint, in paperback, of your first three novels. Yesterday, if not sooner. I should have the contracts ready tomorrow—we're working overtime on this one. You'll have them Monday and I expect them to be back on my desk by ten, Tuesday. Vampire murders in the home county of the Vampire Queen." I could almost hear her hands rubbing together gleefully.

"People are dying," I interjected.

"I'm really sorry about that," she said unconvincingly. "When do I get the new package? They'd like to move up the print date."

"When I'm finished with it."

"Rhiannon, love, I don't like the sound of that."

"It'll be on time."

"I don't want it on time. I want it by the end of next week."

I laughed shortly. "Good luck."

"They want a tour with it."

"No."

"Rhiannon, a tour right now would—"

"No."

"They want to budget a couple hundred thousand for it."

"No."

She sighed. "Well, I said I'd try."

"Umm." I sat down to continue looking through my hate mail.

"You should have let me know this was coming."

"I didn't have any idea that someone was going to start decorating my county with dead bodies."

"I know that. I meant when you knew it was going to hit the news big time. With a little advance notice, you'd be surprised how much you can herd them along in the direction you want."

I rested my elbow on the desk and my head in my hand.

"Are you going to be doing any interviews?"

"Have you lost your mind?"

"Pity. Call me first, if you change your mind. Be sure to get me that manuscript as soon as you can. And don't forget to sign the contracts when you get them Monday and Fed Ex them back to me immediately. I want them Tuesday morning. Ciao, dear."

"'Bye, Kate."

I hit the button to shut the speakerphone off and continued paging through the files and talking to Puck, who had awakened and condescended to sprawl across the papers on the desk. "The dungeon is beginning to sound really good. I'm sure there is a nice, quiet room down there where I could hide. Or perhaps a deserted island might be a better option ..." My voice died off as I stared at the words on the screen.

For you, my lady of darkness. All of this is for you.

Chapter Twenty
Saturday, throughout the evening

They were right. He had written to me. In all, I found ten letters in Trystan's on-line bedtime stories.

I read them as I printed them off, knowing why Pete hadn't caught the implications in them. They detailed the crimes of each victim, but only one letter spelled out the punishment decreed. They had been in six different categories in Trystan's website. It was only when you were looking for similarities between the notes and the letters in the writing itself that these stood out. Just to complicate things, not one of them was signed by the same person.

I reached out and dialed the kitchen as the last of the letters printed.

"Jody."

"It's Rhiannon. Is Righdhonn down there?"

"Certainly. You want to talk to him?"

"No, just have him come up here, please."

"He's on his way. Are you all right?"

"Not really."

"Everything will be fine."

"Thanks, Jody."

His chuckle warmed the fear I could feel gathering around me. "You want someone cursed?"

"Trystan?" I asked hopefully.

"No, Rhi, I can't be cursing that boy, they bounce right off him."

"I'm not surprised."

"Now, anyone else—just bring me a rooster and some rum and I'll see what I can do."

"Chicken fingers and a hot toddy?"

"Get away with you," he scolded. "What's taking that cousin of yours so long?"

"Well," I said as Righ burst through the door, "he's over eleven hundred years old."

"Now you're in trouble," Jody warned me.

"I'm his favorite."

"Be safe," he said before hanging up.

"What?" my cousin asked, sliding his pistol back into its holster after making sure there was nothing dangerous in the room. Puck ignored the fact that Righ didn't consider him dangerous.

"I found the letters. All of you were right. He had written to me." I gathered the papers into a pile and concentrated on neatening the corners.

"*Cariad*." The sympathy in his voice brought my tears perilously close to the surface.

"We need to take these over to the sheriff's department."

"They can't wait until morning?"

I looked up at him and shook my head. "No, they can't."

"Let's go. I'll let you kick the trunk this time."

"I'm honored."

Our trip through the tunnels was uneventful, although our arrival was into chaos that rivaled our previous visit. Having an identity for one of the bodies had evidently kicked everyone into high gear. I grabbed Tom as he sped past me. "Daniel?"

He jerked a thumb over his shoulder in the direction of the sheriff's office and continued on his way.

Righ and I entered the sheriff's office, I must admit, abruptly and without knocking. The specter of Rachel bearing down on me was more than I could bear at that moment. Once inside, I leaned against the door as if that would keep her out.

Luke, Dan and Lige turned from the worktable on the far wall with identical expressions of irritation on their faces. I looked everywhere in the room but at them, rolling and unrolling the papers in my hands. My gaze fell on the letters and I held them out in the men's general direction. "He did send me letters," I managed before my throat closed up.

"What?"

Luke beat Dan to my side, plucking the papers from my grasp.

Looking up to meet Dan's gaze, I took a deep breath and explained, "They were out on the website. There are ten of them."

Righ watched as Luke handed out the letters. "So who was the guy Rhi found?"

"Charles Arnay."

Everyone in the room turned to look at me.

I shook my head. "I don't recognize the name. Who is he?"

"He was a journalist. A tabloid journalist. They were all tabloid journalists."

"All?" Righ looked sharply at Daniel. "You've identified the others, too?"

Our sheriff nodded, looking up from the letter he was reading. "All but the one found this afternoon."

I closed my eyes as Righ asked, "Another one?"

"The vet called it in just after Dan got back from his Welcoming," Lige explained.

"Yes," Dan said, "Embalmed, male, two incisions on the neck, blood in bags in a nearby cooler. No note this time, just a cover from one of Rhi's books."

"Mother of God," I murmured.

"Is there a point to the identified ones being journalists?" Righ asked.

"Oh yes," Dan answered. "There certainly is. Arnay's best-paying story was an exposé of North America's best-known vampire novelists. Guess who was in the top five?"

I stared at the floor. I'd read the letters, each of which detailed a separate crime against humanity—humanity, in this case, going by the name of Rhiannon Beltene. I have always considered my writing to be a form of entertainment, both for me to write and for my readers to enjoy. I've always looked with benevolent amusement upon the misguided souls who visit Brennen County. To discover that there was someone who took the nonsense in tabloids so seriously that they felt a need to extinguish another human being's life over them was almost beyond my comprehension.

Dan's voice continued inexorably, "The second one was Drew Brohaugh, whose best paying stories were a series of nasty critiques on every single book—which, as far as I could tell, he'd never read—written by a certain vampire novelist. Now, mind you, he did this particular series on several different novelists, but Rhiannon's was the highlight of the series.

"The third was Marshall McDonnell, whose top story—I can't grace these artistic endeavors as articles because they fall much more gracefully into fiction—was an in-depth interview with a high-ranking Satanist on the involvement of certain vampire novelists in black witchcraft and how it affected them, their books and their readers."

Righ pulled me close against him as I shivered, a chill settling in my bones.

"Yesterday's body was Wayne Leighton, whose only story was about how he killed his entire family under the influence of Rhiannon's books. He was convinced that he'd been attacked by a vampire and was forced to sustain himself with his family's—all sixteen of them—blood until he was strong enough to go out into the world. According to the story, he is currently in hiding from the law."

The blood drained from my face. This particular incident hadn't been included in the letters I'd brought over. "What? He did ... he killed ..." I stammered.

"Purely fiction," Dan hastened to assure me. "At least I can't find any reference to that crime in anyone's computer."

"Thank the gods," I said fervently. I moved away from Righ and slid into a nearby chair.

"I have no doubt that when we identify today's body we'll find that he, too, did a story which was detrimental to Rhiannon."

My stomach rolled. I pulled my knees up to my chest and wrapped my arms around them. "These people have been killed over stories that I've never read and didn't even know existed?"

"Motives are strange things."

"I'm going to be ill." I dropped my head onto my knees.

"We had just decided, before the vet found today's body, that these murders were a definite violation of the journalist's first amendment rights. The ultimate censorship,"

I lifted my head and looked at our Saxon sheriff. "That is really sick, Daniel."

"Eric thought we should turn the entire mess over to the ACLU," Luke interjected, barely looking up from the letters he was reading. He'd been steadily collecting and reading all ten of them.

"You're all getting slaphappy," I said.

"I agree." Lige was slumped on the couch.

Luke lifted his head as he finished the last letter. He straightened the pile, watching me thoughtfully. I wasn't sure how to decipher the expression on his face as he turned and looked at Dan and Righ before moving his gaze back to me.

He cleared his throat and waited until everyone looked at him. "You said you found these on Trys' new website?"

I nodded.

"Are they identical— No, no, do you know if Pete scanned them in or keyed them in?"

I stared at the corner of Dan's desk as I tried to remember what Pete had told me about Trystan's bedtime stories. I looked back up at Luke. "I think he told me they'd scanned them in. Why?"

He didn't answer. He picked up the phone on the desk and tersely asked Pete the same question. He stared at the closed curtains and slowly put down the receiver. He ruffled through the papers in his hand, putting one on top and staring at it like he expected it to give him an explanation.

"What is it, Luke?" Lige asked, sliding forward to sit on the edge of the couch.

There was anticipation in the air. Even I felt it. Like we were poised on the brink of finding the answers we wanted, the answers we needed.

"They were scanned," Luke muttered, still looking down at the letters.

"Okay, fine, Pete scanned them." I unwound myself and stood. "What makes that so important?" I asked, wondering what the bloody hell I'd missed when I'd read them over.

"The dates."

I frowned and moved to join him, taking the letters from his hand.

"What's wrong with the dates?" Dan asked.

"Oh, shit," I muttered.

"What?"

"The date on this letter is August second, fourteen-fifteen."

Righ's head snapped up. "What?"

"Signed by Thomas Grey," Luke supplied.

"Lord and Lady," I whispered, holding the letter out for the sheriff while all the color and expression drained from my cousin's face, leaving only a visage seemingly carved from stone.

"Who is Thomas Grey?"

Obviously Daniel wasn't a history or Shakespeare buff. Was it only hours ago that I'd teased Righ about Agincourt? "Sir Thomas Grey was a knight of Northumberland."

"He was a traitor," Righ said. The implacable tone in his voice scared me. I'd never seen him so distant and pitiless.

"Who?" Dan looked frustrated, confused and angry.

I sidled close to the family mercenary and reached out to touch his arm. My hand never connected. Had it been any-one else, I'd have sworn that he bolted from the room.

"What the hell?" The men stared after him in surprise.

Once more into the breach, dear friends, once more into the breach ... I seemed to be handing out historical and mythical explanations on a regular basis to the sheriff's department lately. Well, at least I was earning my non-existent wage as an honorary deputy. "Sir Thomas Grey was in the circle of men surrounding Henry the Fifth—"

"Shakespeare?" Dan interrupted incredulously.

"Shakespeare based his plays on fact, Daniel. This now, is history. Grey, along with two others, conspired to betray Henry to the French, killing him before he could invade France." It was all I could do not to simply fall into the chorus' part:

"... and three corrupted men,
 One, Richard Earl of Cambridge, and the second,
Henry Lord Scroop of Masham, and the third,
Sir Thomas Grey, knight of Northumberland,
Have for the gilt of France, —O guilt indeed!—
Confirmed conspiracy with fearful France;
And by their hands this grace of kings must die ..."

I could almost hear Derek Jacobi's voice echoing around the office. I pulled myself back to the explanation at hand. "Their plan was discovered before they left England. Grey and Cambridge confessed. Scroop denied the charge, but admitted that he knew about the conspiracy. Grey was executed on August second, fourteen-fifteen. Cambridge and Scroop were executed on the fifth. Family rumor has always claimed that Righ and Grey were friends. And that Righ had a hand in exposing the plot. Not that any of us are actually brave enough to ask him about it."

"He's a mercenary," Dan pointed out.

I raised an eyebrow. "True, but Henry was Welsh."

He stared at me.

I lifted a shoulder and dropped it.

"The other letters?"

I shuffled through them, checking the dates and signatures. "They're all dates of executions, signed by the executed."

"More Shakespeare?"

I shook my head.

"Anyone I'd recognize?"

I picked the most likely candidate. "William Wallace, August, Thirteen-oh-five."

Dan frowned at me.

"Braveheart," I prompted

"Swords and kilts." Recognition lit his eyes.

"A fair approximation," I agreed. "Wallace was taken to London and executed. The others, unless you're into medieval history, I doubt you'd recognize."

"Like whom?"

"Charlotte Corday d'Armount, July seventeenth, seventeen-ninety-three."

He looked at me blankly for a moment. "Okay, never mind. Is it critical that I know who these people are or is it simply important that all these people were executed?"

"I don't know," I said, returning to my chair. After all, I couldn't really go anywhere until Righ came back.

"I think both points are equally important," Luke said.

"Was Righdhonn involved with all the people in these letters?"

It was my turn to stare blankly until the implications of his comment drove me to my feet. "Excuse me?"

"How far would he go to protect your family?"

"You're out of line, Daniel," I said, unintentionally lending my voice an implacable tone similar to the one Righ had recently used.

"Am I?"

"Yes."

"Perhaps," Dan returned.

I started to refute the doubt I could see in his face, but instead turned to Lige. "You explain to this newcomer just how far out of line he is," I commanded. "I am going to find my cousin and go home. Please keep us posted on any new developments in this case." Turning, I swept regally out of the room. My exit could have been improved only by a cape, which I could have swirled elegantly around me, and by a lack of amusement from the occupants of the office.

Righ was leaning against the doorway of the coffee-room talking to Eric. His face as he turned toward me was still drawn and I wondered just what had conspired between him and Thomas Grey that would provoke such a reaction almost six hundred years later.

"Ready to go back to the house?" he asked.

I nodded.

He pushed away from the wall and waved at Eric, then guided me into the tunnels. We were at the entrance into the basements below Beltene House, when I decided I couldn't face going upstairs. I desperately needed some air and I fancied my cousin did, too.

"Righ?" Carefully, I avoided touching him.

Pausing with his hand on the switch, he looked at me.

"Would it be terribly dangerous for me if we went through the tunnels down to the beach? Please?"

He sighed and reached out to stroke my cheek. "Yes, Rhi, we can go down to the beach for a few minutes."

"Thanks." I followed as he led me through the tunnels to the beach access. I leaned against the cool stone at the mouth of the tunnel while Righ positioned himself just outside the entrance. It was hard to believe that it was still Saturday. Too much had happened and as I took deep breaths of Lake Superior's air, I could feel the tension ease.

I watched my cousin as he maintained a constant vigilance. Daniel's question refused to be banished from my mind. Which, of course, was exactly what our new sheriff had intended. I shook my head and firmly pushed it anyway. I could easily imagine Righ killing someone who actually threatened me or anyone else in the family. I could even see him taking justice into his own hands if he discovered the identity of the killer. I couldn't, however, picture him killing someone over magazine articles that were not only pure fabrication, but that didn't truly endanger anyone in the family, much less me.

"Righ?"

"Yes, *cariad*?" In the blaze of the sunset, I could see him turn his head toward me.

"I'm going to go watch the paintings."

He hesitated for a moment, then nodded. "All right."

I walked the ten steps up the tunnel to the mouth of the Cave of the Paintings. Grandmama named it. Rock paintings, yes, but not of any great antiquity. Trystan decorated the cave when he was about fifteen. It has a natural set of openings high on the bay side wall, which at sundown, illuminate his drawings, turning them into something truly spectacular. With the sunset blazing into the room, I didn't need one of the flashlights near the doorway, but I did pick one up for later. I sat on the natural sandstone bench under the openings and watched Trys' drawings dance in the waning sunlight. It was finished within minutes, leaving me sitting in the dark.

I dropped a hand to the bench to push myself up and recoiled as my fingers touched something cold and wet. Not an uncommon problem, what with seabirds and male relatives with sophomoric senses of humor. I switched on my flashlight and looked down. There were dark blotches where something liquid had seeped into the sandstone and several spots where liquid was still puddled on the surface.

I flipped the light to look at my hand and got distracted by some equipment sitting at the end of the shelf. Equipment that from the doorway was invisible. A generator, an ominous piece of equipment that I couldn't identify with long lengths of tubing, and a green-and-white Coleman cooler. I focused the light on my hand, unconsciously rubbing my thumb over my fingers, testing the liquid.

My heart began to beat faster and I flashed the light quickly around the room, searching. Only half convinced I was alone, I stood and shined the light on the puddles again. The blood was still moist—obviously the killer hadn't been absent long. Who had he laid on the shelf? I closed my eyes, remembering that the victims were alive when the process began and didn't die until the embalming fluid or an air bubble reached their hearts. A shudder wrenched my eyes open. Where was he and where had he taken his latest victim? Was it the body they'd found earlier?

My eyes returned to the drying stain on my fingers. I don't think anyone expected to find that he was executing his murders this close to Beltene House—literally beneath Beltene House. I stopped cold. If he was killing them here, in the

Cave of the Paintings, then he knew about the tunnel. Therefore, he had access to at least the public areas. And he'd already shown himself to be immune to one of our most daunting security measures. I doubted he'd had access to Beltene House; there are elaborate electronic security devices at the house end of the tunnels. But could he have possibly found the private tunnels? The tunnels known only to the Beltene, previous Beltenes and a few select individuals.

Taking a deep breath, I sucked the moist air of the cave deep into my lungs; the hitherto unnoticed tang of blood assaulted my senses and I screamed as I flung myself across the room in the direction of my cousin and safety. Righ met me before I was barely halfway across the room. He enveloped me in his arms even as he shone his light around the cave.

"Rhi, *cariad*?"

"There's blood over there," I managed to get out around my chattering teeth.

One of the things I love about Righdhonn is his intuitive leaps. He grasped what had occurred in the cave without any further information from me. "Are you all right?"

A shudder rippled through me and I lost the battle to keep my eyes from the shelf. "No."

"Come on, *cariad*, you need to get some air. You'll be better once you're away from here."

I disengaged myself and stepped back so I could see his face. "This is where he's been killing them."

"I can see that."

"Trystan's going to have a fit," I said irrelevantly, tears finally starting to slip down my face.

"Yes, he is."

"The blood is still moist, Righ."

He straightened, every muscle in his body taut. "Are you sure?"

I held up my hand, palm facing him and began to shake.

"Come, *cariad*," he repeated. "You have to get out of here." He pulled me close and steered me toward the door.

"Jesus God, Righ, how are we ever going to be able to allow this to come to trial?"

"I don't know." He sighed as we moved into the main tunnel. "Maybe it won't come to a trial. That would be for the best. What I do know is that I need to get you up to the house and into competent hands before I call Lige and Dan."

The last rays of the dying sunlight followed us up the tunnel.

Chapter Twenty-one
Sunday Morning and Beyond

The telephone's insistent ringing dragged me from the drugged sleep I'd been in since shortly after Righdhonn deposited me into the competent hands of my mother, Grandmama, Rathtyen (one of my aunts and head of nursing at the hospital) and Cris. They had hustled me up to my room, got me bathed, calmed down and tucked into bed within an hour. Then, tactfully, Rathtyen and my mother left, leaving me, my fears and Daniel's veiled accusation with Grandmama and Cris.

Grandmama wasn't necessarily encouraging where our sheriff and his comment were concerned. Like us all, she knew Righ was capable of killing to protect the family and indeed, had done so in the past and would probably do so again in the future, but she didn't for a moment believe that Righ had killed these journalists.

It was during one of her assurances that I suffered one of Righ's intuitive leaps and realized that she thought there had been something in the cave, or something about the cave, that had given Righ a clue to the identity of the killer. His comment that it would be best if it didn't come to trial haunted me.

Cris, her prophetic nature ominously silent, finally insisted that I drink one of her concoctions. As usual, it tasted horrible and I was asleep before I finished all of it.

I opened an eye to discover the telephone was actually on its base beside the bed. My attempt to push the right button to stop the noise and connect me with the soon-to-be deceased person on the other end succeeded. A distinct click as the line disconnected was the only reward for my efforts.

I stared at the phone's silent form irritably, then flung it toward the end of the bed. Still drowsy from Cris' tisane, I started to snuggle back into my blankets. My eyes were just beginning to close when I noticed the wall clock.

"Lord and Lady," I yelped, flinging the blankets away and jumping out of bed.

It was Sunday. The ringing had been an insistent wake-up call because it was twenty minutes to twelve and noon Mass was the last of the day. I opted for no makeup, jeans, an Aryan sweater and Reeboks. In less than ninety seconds, I brushed my hair and my teeth, splashed water around and was headed down the stairs, sure I had forgotten something.

I had. The realization struck me just as I was about to open the front door. Unless I could find a nearby police officer or my mercenary cousin, I wasn't going to Mass. Grumbling to myself, I stomped down the hall toward the kitchen. With the discovery of the cave the previous evening, I judged my chances of getting to Mass slim to none.

Jody and Erin were the only people in the kitchen.

I draped myself across one of the islands and stared at the cinnamon rolls cooling on a counter.

"Good afternoon, Rhiannon," Erin said.

"Ah, Erin, it's still morning, by a good three or four minutes," I returned.

"You're going to miss Mass."

"Where's Righ?"

"Down at the cave," Jody answered, slathering frosting on the cinnamon rolls.

"Daniel, Eric, Luke and Lige?"

"At the cave. They went to chapel here at six, I served them breakfast at six-thirty and they've been down there since. How are you?"

"Worried." I lifted my eyes to meet his.

He waved my worries away with a flick of his frosting knife. "All will be well."

I propped my elbows on the counter and frowned at him. "You know, prophecies are really irritating."

He flashed a grin at me. "I know."

"Do you see only the end result or everything in between as well?"

He dropped the knife into the bowl and moved to stand across from me. A finger lifted my chin so he could look into my eyes. "You are worried."

My nod was almost imperceptible.

"I see only the end. Which tells me that this fussing of yours is for naught."

"Since you found the evidence in the cave, I would imagine there's an excellent chance they'll find the killer," Erin said.

"It's possible," I agreed. "But if they find him, there'll be a trial. How are we going to survive a trial?"

Jody shook his head. "There'll be no trial."

"Why will there be no trial?" I whispered.

His eyebrows shot into the air. "Is that what you're fussing about?" Smiling, he patted my cheek and returned to his cinnamon rolls.

I straightened. "I think that's a reasonable thing to fuss about."

"All will be well," he repeated. "And the time 'twixt now and then will be manageable. You're the Beltene after all, in truth and action as well as title."

I should have stayed in bed, I thought as I shook my head and accepted a glass of milk from Erin. A plate with two cinnamon rolls followed and I retired to one of the nearby couches to consume my breakfast.

I deposited my glass and plate in the sink and turned to

look at Jody. "If anyone's looking for me, I'm going to be in chapel for a while."

"Dinner's at two."

"Yes, sir," I saluted as I exited the kitchen, taking the route that would take me past my office, where, to my surprise, I found the Beltene's secretary busily at work.

"Eula," I said from the open doorway.

"Good afternoon, Rhiannon."

"What are you doing?"

She smiled at me. "Keeping Rachel from aggravating my boss."

I closed my eyes in pain and tried to remember what had happened to my beeper last night. "I don't have my beeper, but I'll be in chapel for a while, if anyone needs me."

She nodded.

"Don't stay too long, Eula, it is Sunday, after all."

"I'll take Wednesday off instead." She waved me out the door.

I dipped my fingers into the holy water at the door and genuflected before sliding into one of the middle pews. Flipping the kneeler down, I slid off the pew, rested my forearms on the pew in front of me and dropped my head onto my forearms. A fairly comfortable pose for praying, if only one doesn't fall asleep.

I still hadn't come up with any answers to my many questions when a hand dropped onto my shoulder.

I jumped and collapsed back onto the pew. "Lord and Lady, Morgan, don't be sneaking up on people like that."

"I didn't sneak," he returned. "I wasn't sure if you were praying or sleeping."

"I don't know if you could call it praying," I mused. "Looking for answers, perhaps."

"Isn't it the same thing?" With a hand under my elbow,

he gently urged me from the pew, waiting while I genuflected and escorted me to his office.

"Is it the same thing?" I asked.

"You should have been a Jesuit," he teased.

"Do I ask that many questions?"

"Always. What questions are troubling you now?"

I stared off out his windows for a long time before answering. "Morgan, I don't think discussing them is going to help."

"The Beltene is not required to make decisions all on her own. You do have benefit of council."

I nodded absently. "I know, but the ultimate decision must be mine."

"Are you planning to join the family for dinner?" He changed the subject, leaving the decision of if and when I'd discuss my worries to me.

I flicked a glance at his clock. I'd been in chapel much longer than I'd thought. "No," I answered. "I'm going to be in the library."

With the Old World charm and manners ingrained in the men of my family, he escorted me to the door of the library. "Shall I have Jody bring you a tray?"

"No, I'll get something later."

"If you need to talk?"

I kissed his cheek. "Thanks, Morgan."

Wandering aimlessly around the library did little to settle me. Finally, coming to a decision, I went up one of the spiral staircases and rummaged around in the family histories until I found the volume I was looking for. I was ensconced in one of the library chairs with my feet on the railing when an entourage from the sheriff's department came looking for me.

"Rhiannon?" Luke called.

I dropped my feet to the floor and leaned over the railing. "Up here."

"What are you doing?"

"A little research." I gazed down at Lige, Luke and Dan. "What can I do for you, gentlemen?"

"How about coming down and answering a few questions?"

"Okay." With a quick look to memorize my location, I gently closed the illuminated manuscript I'd been reading and put it back in the case before joining the men. They had gathered around one of the library tables and while they'd left a space for me, I chose to sit in one of the overstuffed chairs nearby. "What can I do for you?"

I was a bit daunted when Luke set a small tape recorder on the edge of the table by me and turned it on. He recited the date and time before turning to me. "Could you give us your name, address and occupation, please?"

I took a moment to seriously contemplate the three police officers in front of me. "My name is Rhiannon Beltene. I live at One Hundred Llanthony Road, Sevyrn, Michigan, and I'm a novelist."

"Please tell us what happened yesterday afternoon after you left the sheriff's department."

Leaning over, I pushed the stop button. "For whose edification am I giving this information?"

"The sheriff's department," Dan said tightly.

"The tunnels are not public information."

"They may be before this is over," he returned.

I leaned back in my chair and considered this side effect of our recent rash of crime.

"The information will only be used if absolutely necessary," he assured me.

"Who defines the necessity of it?"

"I do."

"Daniel, realistically speaking, as soon as I put voice to that tape, these secret tunnels of ours are no longer secret.

After all, who's going to transcribe the tape? Rachel. Who's going to have access to it? Nearly everyone at the sheriff's department."

"It can be restricted."

"But will it be?"

My bald question did not sit well with any of the law enforcement officers. I could tell their immediate response was to tell me *of course it would be restricted*, but fortunately, they were all honest enough to admit, at least to themselves, that it wouldn't be.

Sighing, Daniel popped the cassette out of the machine, leaving its door open and the machine off. "Satisfied?"

"Thank you, Dan." I pulled my feet up to sit cross-legged in the chair. Luke, unobtrusively, had his pad and pen ready. "I left the sheriff's office and rejoined my cousin, Righdhonn Beltene, and we went down into the basement of the jail with the intention of returning to Beltene House. When in the tunnels, I asked Righ if we could take a minute and go down to the beach. He—"

"You suggested it?" Dan asked.

"Yeah. Righ was all ready to go into the basement at Beltene House and—" I stopped speaking and reran his question. I crossed my arms and looked stonily at him. "May I ask the purpose of that question?"

"No."

"I think I need an answer to it before I continue."

"Please continue with your statement."

I shook my head. "Nope, answer my question."

"It's possible that Righdhonn Beltene could be a suspect."

I did not lose my temper. I took a deep breath and started counting silently. "Simply because of the dates and names on those letters?"

"Are you telling me that your cousin, an acknowledged mercenary, wouldn't kill to protect your family?"

Luke and Lige shifted uncomfortably in their chairs.

"No, Daniel," I said calmly. "Righ *would* kill to protect the family."

He spread his hands wide. "Well?"

"These killings have nothing to do with protecting the family. Do you really think that Righ is stupid enough to think that the ridiculous bullshit that they print in tabloids is a danger to us?"

"Sometimes ridiculous things set people off."

"Daniel, did you read those bloody letters? They're love letters." This particular observation was something I had steadfastly, to this point, been refusing to acknowledge. "Love letters. I think that in itself sets Righ aside."

"I don't."

My mouth dropped open.

"He's obviously very attached to you."

"Mother of God," I muttered. "He's my cousin."

"Is he?"

That stopped me cold. "Are you asking me to define the consanguinity of our relationship?"

"Yes."

"There would be no legal or papal constraints if we chose to get married. Is that what you're asking?"

"Yes."

"However"—I raised a finger to illustrate my point—"the emotional and familial constraints are as if we were first cousins. We do not marry within the family. Ever."

"I don't mean to upset you, Rhiannon, but he—"

"Daniel?"

"What?"

"What did Righ have to say?"

He looked bewildered. "When?"

"When you asked him about the consanguinity of our relationship."

Luke choked and stood, moving across the room to look out the window.

Dan had the grace to look abashed. "I haven't."

I rose to my feet and walked across the room. The smile hovering near the surface defeated the formidability of my stance. I thanked the gods that he hadn't broached the subject with my mercenary cousin. Of course, I wouldn't have approached him with that particular question, either. I have a healthy sense of survival. "I would suggest you not speak with him about it, but the choice is yours." I turned and moved serenely back to our sheriff. "I understand the need to examine every possible suspect, but it's time to quit looking in Beltene House. Neither Trystan nor Righdhonn is your killer."

"Is that a direct order from the Beltene?"

I shook my head and allowed my smile to surface. "No, Dan, it's not. It's merely a suggestion."

"Well, hell," he muttered. "It sounded good."

"Did Righ know everyone in the letters?" Luke asked.

"I don't think so. From the records I've been checking, I can only isolate three. Grey, Wallace and Corday d'Armount. I do believe it's time to ask Righ about them, however. Perhaps he can help shed some light on them."

Dan nodded. "You're right. We've got maybe two or three more hours down at the cave. Shall we meet in your tower at eight? That will give us some time to get cleaned up and have a bite to eat."

"Eight is fine. Do we need anyone other than Righ to join us?"

Dan exchanged a look with Lige and shrugged.

"Your father, Grandmama and Cris," Lige said.

"We'll see you at eight, gentleman." I stood, holding onto the back of the chair, and watched the men file out of the library. I took a moment to run into my office and request

that Eula take care of a few details for me before following the
spiral back upstairs to finish the history I'd been pursuing.

Feet back on the railing, comfortably slumped in the library chair, I continued looking for the information I needed
for our eight o'clock meeting.

Chapter Twenty-two
Sunday Evening, Eight PM

By eight, I'd had a brief conference with Gwenddydd, the family historian, found the information that I'd been looking for and was ready for the conference in the tower. I shuffled through the papers on my desk as I waited for the participants to show up. Jody had already been and gone with refreshments.

They arrived in a group, like they'd been milling around the foot of my stairs to make sure no one backed out. I waited until they were all seated and comfortable before coming out from behind my desk and joining them. I looked at the pages in my hand before looking up.

I put my feet on the coffee table and settled comfortably on the couch next to my favorite mercenary. Obviously I was chairing this meeting because no one had yet said a word. "Okay, a recap for those not fully up-to-date. These letters"—I handed the sets I'd made for everyone to Righ. He took one and passed the rest on—"are from the killer to me. I found them on Trystan's website. He had them listed as his bedtime stories. We started looking for them after Daniel pointed out that the killer had probably written to me. I gather it's unusual to escalate to this sort of violence without some preliminary groundwork. I set Pete and Trys to looking through their files while I looked on their website. I found these ten.

"The truly disturbing part of these letters are the dates and signatures. The one we noticed first was signed by Sir Thomas Grey with a date of August second, fourteen-fifteen. August second was the day he was executed. I've spent most of the afternoon in the library tracking all these names down. Any questions before I give you what I've found?"

Grandmama sighed before putting her hand on Righ's arm. "I'm sorry, Righdhonn."

My cousin slid down in his seat and put his feet up beside mine. "It had to be done."

Silence filled the room as we contemplated what circumstance had forced my cousin to do.

"Continue, Rhi," Righ said, waving a hand in the air. "Fascinate us with your expertise."

I swatted him as I took a breath to begin.

"Wait a minute," Dan said, his gaze firmly on Righ. "What had to be done?"

Righ met the sheriff's eyes. "It was not acceptable that Henry be betrayed. I found out about the plot from Thomas. He seemed to think that since I was a mercenary I would have no problem taking French gold. For familial reasons I could not be the one to tell the king. History has a way of immortalizing men in the spotlight. I simply made sure the plot was discovered and the king warned. Thomas was my friend and while I could not stand by and condone what he planned, neither did I want him dead."

Dan nodded. His acceptance went as far as his nod. His expression, on the other hand, told the story of the conflicting thoughts in his mind. Our potion might have changed the man's DNA and convinced him of our truth, but his own innate common sense was battling it out with Rhodri's serum for all it was worth. I had every confidence that Rhodri's witch's brew would win out and smooth the wrinkles from our new sheriff's mind.

I waited a moment to see if Dan or Righ had anything further to say, and when they stayed silent, continued, "Okay, here's the rundown on the letters. Thomas A'Becket, beaten and cut to death by four of Henry II's knights in Canterbury Cathedral on December twenty-ninth, eleven-seventy.

"Charlotte Corday d'Armount was guillotined in Paris on July seventeenth, seventeen ninety-three for killing Jean Paul Marat.

"John Fisher refused to acknowledge that Henry VIII was the head of the new Church of England and lost his head on June twenty-second, fifteen thirty-five.

"Jan Hus was burned at the stake for urging political and religious reforms in Constance, Germany, on July sixth, four-teen-fifteen.

"Girolama Savonarola tried to show the truth of his belief and doctrines in an ordeal by fire. Unfortunately, it rained that day and he was taken into custody by the Medicis for heresy. He was tortured and forced to confess, then was burned at the stake on May twenty-third, fourteen ninety-eight, in front of the Medici palace.

"William Wallace was hanged and drawn as a common outlaw in August of thirteen-oh-five. He'd held out against Edward I for eight years before Edward resorted to buying Wallace, who was then taken to London. It was one hell of a sentence. 'You shall be carried from Westminster to the Tower, and from the Tower to Aldgate, and so through the City to the Elms at Smithfield, and for your robberies, homicides and felonies ... you shall be there hanged and drawn, and as an outlaw beheaded, and afterwards for your burning churches and relics your heart, liver, lungs and entrails from which your wicked thoughts came shall be burned and finally, be-cause of your sedition, depredations, fires, and homicides were not only against the King, but against the people of England and Scotland, your head shall be placed on London Bridge in sight both of land and water travelers, and your quarters hung on gibbets at Newcastle, Berwick, Stirling, and Perth, to the terror of all who pass by.'"

"Edward was—"

"An asshole," Righ muttered.

I nodded. "That's a fair description. Robert Devereau was beheaded on February twenty-fifth, sixteen-oh-one for treason. He let his insecurities get the better of him and decided to clear Elizabeth's court of his enemies. She took exception to this move. He was the last prisoner executed in the Tower of London until World War I.

"William Fitzosbert was a self-appointed champion of the oppressed. The king's men attacked him and his men and Fitzosbert killed one. They took refuge in Bow church, claiming sanctuary. The Justiciar of London refused to observe sanctuary and had him dragged from the church. He was hanged April sixth, eleven ninety-six.

"Guilford Dudley & Jane Grey were executed for treason by Queen Mary on February twelfth fifteen fifty-four. It probably wasn't necessary, but they didn't call her Bloody Mary for nothing. Jane is usually referred to as the Nine-Day Queen.

"That's our ten signers. Now, I've broken this down every way I can think of. All ten of these were considered executions. But, six were in London, one in Southampton, one in Florence, one in Paris and one in Germany. Four were beheaded, two were burned at the stake, one was hanged, one was hanged and drawn, one was guillotined and one was beaten to death.

"There were two Williams and two Greys. Two of the executions were in February, one in April, May and June, two in July, two in August and one in December. Two were in the twelfth century, one in the fourteenth, three in the fifteenth, two in the sixteenth, one in the seventeenth and one in the eighteenth.

"One was French, one was Scottish, one was German, one was Italian and six were British. Four were arrested for treason, one for killing a king's officer, one as an outlaw, three for heresy and, of course, Becket wasn't arrested, he just pissed off a king.

"And, last but not least"—I met my cousin's eyes—"Righ knew three of them. Corday d'Armount, Wallace and Thomas Grey." I shook my head. "I can't make any sense of it. Unless, of course, it's just a red herring to sidetrack us."

Lige shook his head. "I don't see any sense in it. Too many variables except that they were all executed. And that's exactly what our killer is doing. He's executing these people for their crimes."

I propped my elbow on a knee and rubbed my eyes.

"How sidetracked are we getting?" Cris asked, anger rising in her eyes as she realized who was the likely suspect in the room.

"Now, Cris," Lige soothed.

"Don't 'now Cris' me," she snapped. "That is the most ridiculous accusation I have ever heard."

"We haven't made any sort of accusation yet."

"Hah! Do you think I can't see it?"

Dan looked askance at her.

"We have to look at all the angles," Luke interjected. "Just because we don't believe them doesn't mean we should ignore them."

She surged to her feet and looked steely-eyed at the officers. "I will tell—"

Righ's laughter cut the tension in the room like a knife. She whirled to face him. "I don't think this is the least bit funny, Righdhonn."

He waved her into her seat. "Of course it is," he said.

Her eyes snapped at each officer before sitting.

Righ draped his arm around my shoulders. "Did they ask about the consanguinity of our relationship?"

I chuckled while the police looked sheepish. "They did."

"And what did you tell them?"

"That the law and the pope wouldn't object, but that the family would raise hell."

His eyes twinkled at me. "It might be worth it."

For one wild moment I considered that he was right. It would certainly take Trystan out of the doghouse. Shaking my head, I closed my eyes. I really didn't need to have the family in a tizzy right now because Righ and I—*Lord and Lady*, I thought explosively, *what in the world am I thinking about?* I opened my eyes to find my cousin watching me, his mirth barely repressed. My father, Cris and Grandmama, on the other hand, looked like they weren't sure if he was kidding or not.

Daniel cleared his throat to divert everyone's attention. "It would have worked out so neatly if Righ had been guilty," he said regretfully. "But it was too neat and as everyone has pointed out to me, very much out of character. Does anyone have any ideas on these?" He waved the letters absently.

My father pressed the tips of his fingers together, still studying Righ. I could almost see the thoughts running through his mind about his daughter—first he'd found the sheriff in her bed and then, only several days later, innuendoes about her relationship with her cousin. Consanguinity aside, a man who was still her cousin. "Do I want to know what— Mother of God!" he exclaimed.

Suppressing my smile, I stood and removed Puck from the top of his head. "Sorry, Dad."

"When did you get a cat?"

"I took him away from Trystan. This is Puck."

Dad stroked the top of his head with a finger. "Heads are not to be bounced, young man," he said firmly.

Puck responded to his scolding by purring madly. I dropped the vibrating kitten into my father's lap.

"Anyway." Dad collected himself as Puck got comfortable. "Do I want to know what these letters were doing on

Trystan's website? And I assume we're not talking about the website I know about."

"He and Pete made a new one, just for Trys. Were you aware that he's been collecting all the hate mail I've been throwing out over the years?"

"Yes."

"Well, he put them on the Web so he could share them." Dad shook his head. "I'll never understand that boy."

"I don't think we're meant to," Grandmama said softly.

I didn't think I wanted to understand Trystan. "The letters?" I prompted. "Other than their content, which is far too close in content and context to the notes found with the bodies, does anyone see any real value to the dates and signatures?"

One by one everyone shook his or her head. Lige answered for all of them. "Luckily, with you finding the cave last night, we didn't have any time to spend on them. If the cave hadn't turned up, we could have easily spent too much time trying to find answers in them."

"You missed Mass this morning," my father said casually in my direction.

"The police and Righ were all busy," I answered, rather more shortly than I'd intended. Being the dutiful Catholic that I am, I try to catch Mass at least once or twice a month. However, it seems that the Beltene is supposed to catch Mass once or twice a week.

"St. David's is across the street—and accessible through the tunnels."

I raised an eyebrow and looked thoughtfully at him. I hadn't considered that St. David's would be tied into the tunnel system but now that I thought about it, I wasn't surprised. Idly I wondered just how extensive this tunnel system of ours was.

"I'm sure Morgan understands," Dan interjected into what had the potential of becoming a nasty situation. "I had a chat with him this morning, so he knew Rhi wouldn't be at Mass."

I transferred my glare to our sheriff.

"The Beltene is—"

I missed the remainder of my father's somewhat pomp-ous statement because Righ stuck his elbow in my ribs.

"Ouch," I hissed in his ear.

"Don't be fussing at them, *cariad*."

"I'm thirty-two years old and the Beltene. I think it's just about time for ... What the bloody hell are you laughing at?" My voice was low, indecipherable over the discussion raging across the room.

"You, *cariad*. Cris is right. You are going to be the finest Beltene we've ever had."

Chapter Twenty-Three
Monday, late morning

It was on that note that I had gathered myself and flung everyone out of my room, the better to prepare for the dawning of a new day. No one seemed appreciative of my gesture or my reasons, but they went.

The ladies arrived at eight, slightly after dawn, and settled down into their routine. My laptop and I went down to the privacy of the Beltene's office. Not that it was private for very long. Morgan and Gwen were my first visitors.

Gwen sat stiffly on one of the chairs (she boasts of never letting the back of a chair touch her spine) while Morgan settled comfortably onto the couch. They waited for me to figure out what they wanted. Morgan has always felt lessons in ESP should be mandatory.

I declined. "And to what do I owe the honor of this visit?"

"When is the marriage?" Gwen asked bluntly.

I stared blankly at her, then looked from her to Morgan. "To whom?" I asked finally.

"Are you planning more than one?" she snapped.

Well, at least they hadn't heard about Righ's suggestion of the previous evening. That would really send her into orbit. "I'm not planning even one."

"You'd better."

"Again, with whom and why?"

"Sheriff Thorpe. He spent the night in your bed."

Morgan was watching our exchange, moving his head from side to side as he assessed our volleys.

"I have no intention of marrying a man I've barely met."

"You'd better," she returned grimly.

I could just picture her holding a flaming sword over Dan's head while Morgan performed the ceremony. I shook my head to dispel the image.

"Don't you think you're jumping to conclusions here?"

"Your own parents were witness to his presence in your bed."

I sighed. "Yes, they were witness to the fact that he was in my bed."

"Well?" Gwen is a nun and thus trained not to make sweeping gestures, but her voice called forth the image of sweeping gestures.

"He was alone in my bed."

She frowned at me.

I frowned back at her. "I will explain this once and only once because of the respect I bear the two of you and your positions in the family. Daniel fell asleep on my bed, I covered him up and slept on the couch downstairs. I don't expect this subject to come up again."

A slight twitching of the lips was the only indication that Morgan was amused by my response to Gwen's line of questioning.

"Is he Catholic?"

I covered my mouth with a hand and contemplated her, then shrugged. "I don't know."

"*You ... don't ... know?*"

I don't know how she managed to get so much incredulity into three words. "Someone told me he was the youngest detective in Las Vegas history," I offered.

Morgan sighed. "We know that. If he's not Catholic, will

he convert? Has he ever been married?" At my repeated shrug, he said forcefully, "Good Lord, Rhiannon, what have the two of you been talking about for the last week?"

"Murder. His religious affiliations haven't entered the conversation."

Gwen shook her head. "Rhiannon."

"It didn't cross my mind. Wasn't he at chapel yesterday morning?"

"Yes," Morgan answered.

"Well?" I spread my hands.

"He didn't take communion."

"That doesn't necessarily preclude his being Catholic."

"True," Morgan admitted, his hand following the shape of his beard.

"However, if it is truly critical to your emotional well-being, why don't you ask Rhan or Dad? They're the ones who vetted Daniel. I'm sure being a good Catholic was on their list of important things to check. Probably right up there with 'Is he married?' and 'Will he suit Rhiannon?'"

Gwen raised her eyebrows. "Now why didn't I think of that? Of course they'd know." Rising, she swept out of the room.

"How is the investigation going?" Morgan asked, staring fondly after Gwen.

"Last night, they had all the bodies but one identified," I answered, wondering how he managed to run St. David's without killing Gwen.

"What about the cave?"

"All I really know is that they spent all day yesterday down there and it wouldn't surprise me to find they're back down there even as we speak."

"Are there any ideas as to the identity of the murderer?"

I exchanged a worried glance with him. "Not that I know of. You know, of course, about the letters I found."

He nodded. "I've heard."

"Thankfully the cave kept them busy enough not to worry about the letters and their meanings."

"What was the verdict?"

"Red herrings. Only three of the executed were directly involved with anyone in the family. I think their sole purpose was to throw Righ out as a suspect and send the sheriff's office off in the wrong direction."

"To involve Righdhonn in such a manner, then you must recognize that the killer has to know the family. In fact, it almost certainly makes the murderer a Welcomed member of this community."

I stared open-mouthed at Morgan. "Lord and Lady, that hadn't even crossed my mind."

"Did it cross anyone else's?"

"Not that they mentioned last night."

He glanced at his watch and whistling softly, stood. "I have to go hear confessions, now. I'll talk to you later."

"I'll be here," I assured him.

He closed the door on this latest revelation, leaving me to stare sightlessly at the screen saver on my laptop and stew about "it almost certainly makes him a Welcomed member of this community."

Maybe it was Daniel. None of this started until after he arrived. Rolling my eyes, I was in the process of trying to convince my screen saver to depart when the devil strolled in.

"Morning, Rhi."

I gave up the battle and let the screen saver win. "Morning, Dan. What can I do for you?"

"A little chat."

"About what?" Now that had to go down in history as one of the stupidest questions I've ever asked. Dan refrained from pointing that out.

He stared over my shoulder at the forest. "There are a hell of a lot of trees here."

"There are."

"They make it too damned convenient for the murderer."

"I'm sorry, Dan, but I really can't allow you to log the entire county, just so that this man is easier to trail."

A smile lit his face. "Naw, we don't want to do that. Besides, it would take far too long. I just wish he didn't find it so easy to slide in and right back out again. He leaves almost no trace of anything behind except for a body and a cooler, and occasionally a note. It's frustrating."

"What about the cave?"

"Oh, hell, we found lots of equipment, but very little evidence to tie it to anyone. Of course, he's limited in his killing options now. We have his equipment. He either quits, gets new equipment or takes to a new format."

I liked the first option best. "What do you think he's going to do?"

"I don't think he's going to quit."

I knew he was going to say that. "But what *do* you think he'll do?"

Dan shook his head. "I'm not even going to try to second-guess him."

Morgan's comment drifted back through my mind. "Dan?"

"Yes?"

"Morgan was in here a bit ago and we were talking about ..." my voice died off under Dan's scrutiny. "Lord and Lady, Daniel, he's a priest."

"I didn't say anything."

I frowned and then continued. "He pointed out that for someone to do those letters and try to point a finger at Righ, that they'd almost have to be a Welcomed member of the community."

"That just occurred to you?"

"I'm not a cop," I flared. "I hate puzzles."

Dan smiled. "I love puzzles. I don't think I would've become a cop if I hadn't. I always intended to be a detective. Of course, my dad is a cop and we've had Texas Rangers in the family since they were formed."

"What made you to come to the back of beyond?"

"The back of beyond? That's not a very nice way of describing where you live."

"Don't get me wrong, I like living here because it *is* the back of beyond. A big city would drive me crazy. Why did you leave Las Vegas?"

"I was looking for peace and quiet. Las Vegas has neither."

I winced. "Sevyrn hasn't been very quiet lately, either."

Dan chuckled without humor. "True, but it still doesn't hold a candle to Vegas for violence. This spree of violence will end and Brennen County can go back to being a haven of peace and quiet."

My frown drew his attention.

"Is there a problem?"

"I hate to be a spoilsport, but it is hard for me to picture Sevyrn as a haven of peace and quiet. We have Trys and the Gwynn-O'Keefes and Rachel ..."

"You're definitely on her shit list. What have you done to her?"

"She's been pissed off at me for the last six months. She wanted Trystan to be the Beltene."

"About Saturday," he began, changing the subject abruptly as he gazed out the window. Just as well, Trystan as the Beltene is a thought not broached lightly and best banished completely.

Of course, Saturday wasn't a subject I really wanted to discuss, either. "Umm." I whipped my chair around to stare out the window.

"Talking about it bothers you."

I spun back to face him. "There were aspects of your Welcoming that don't bear thinking about." Rhodri's serum for one.

"Do I want to know?"

I shook my head.

"I was pretty pissed off Saturday."

"Really?"

His wry grin coaxed a matching one from me. "Well, I guess you could say forty-eight hours does wonders for one's perspective."

"How much?"

"Well, not totally. I keep having these double-sided conversations with myself. Example—Righdhonn is an excellent suspect, for a number of good reasons. And yet, I can't shake the deep-set notion that I trust him implicitly and have no reason to suspect him. Does this get better?"

"I don't know."

He closed his eyes for a moment. "That wasn't exactly the answer I wanted to hear, Rhiannon."

"I'm sorry, Dan. That's not a question I can answer. You're the first newly welcomed person I've ever had close contact with. But I'm really confident that if you find Cris, she can answer any question you can think up."

He stood. "I think then, while I have a semi-free moment, that I should go and ask my questions."

I was, once again, trying to convince my laptop to let go of the screen saver when my intercom buzzed.

"Yes?"

"Pete would like to see you if you have a moment."

I shrugged and gave up the battle with my laptop. Sending a quick prayer up to the gods of Win95, I shut it off. "Send him in."

He burst into the room, a cooler dangling from one hand. "What's up?"

"Look at this." He dropped the cooler to the floor.

"That's a nice Coleman cooler, Pete. I surely do hope you didn't drag it all the way down ..." My voice faded. It was a nice Coleman cooler. It was a white one with a green lid and I had seen one just like it several days earlier. "It can't be."

"It is." With a handkerchief-wrapped finger, he flipped the lid open. It was no surprise to see the bags of blood snuggled neatly inside.

"Where the bloody hell did you find this?" I asked.

Pete dropped into a chair and covered his face with his hands. His mumbled answer was unintelligible.

"What?"

"I said, I found it in Trystan's room."

A million thoughts flashed through my mind. Chief among them was that I was going to kill Trystan. Following close behind were how could he have escaped Pete's clutches long enough to perpetuate any of these crimes? The family was going to have a cow. I found it difficult to believe that Trystan could be the killer. I didn't know that he wasn't capable of the crimes, but I was sure he wouldn't have committed them to censor my critics. And, of course, Dan would be so impressed that Pete came to me before the sheriff's department.

"In Trys' room," I repeated. "Where?"

"Hidden underneath his coffin."

"Naturally." It's Trys' favorite hiding place. He stashes all his favorite things there, up to and including his rumored collection of vampire pornography. Personally, I didn't want to even think about the possibilities of vampire porn. "Where is he?"

"At the Metalworks. He's starting a major project tomorrow and he's over there getting all his prep work done. I expect it will be taking up a majority of his time for the next couple of weeks."

"How'd you find it?" I averted my eyes from the cooler.

"I do periodic sweeps through his room. I tidy up before the maids come. You know, make sure the vampire porn is all put away, the coffin's closed. Stuff like that. I opened up the storage area and there it was. I hadn't seen any of the coolers before, but I've certainly heard about them. I opened it carefully, then called your tower. Roseanne said you were down here."

"You should have called Dan."

"You're the Beltene."

I nodded. "True enough, but I think this falls beyond the scope of my duties."

"I can't believe Trys would do this, Rhi."

"I can't either. But if he didn't, then where the hell did he get the blood?"

Pete ran both hands through his hair. "I don't know. Maybe he found it."

It was a notion worth considering. I could easily see Trys finding the cooler and merrily making off with the blood, thinking he'd pulled something over on everyone.

"We still have to call Dan."

"Don't you think you should discuss it with someone? Grandmama, Rhan, your Dad?"

"Nope. I have to trust that Dan, Lige, Luke and Eric won't railroad Trys if he was just being stupid."

Reaching for the phone, I dialed Cris' office.

"Good morning, dear."

I really hate it when she does that, when she knows who's on the phone before she answers. It's even freakier when she answers with your name. But, who knows, maybe she has caller ID on her office phone. "Is Dan still there?"

"Yes."

"Could you ask him to come back to my office, please."

I was not surprised to find Righdhonn and Cris trailing along behind Daniel when he arrived.

We had left the cooler sitting in the middle of the room. Dan stopped dead in his tracks as he came through the door and stared at it, then at me.

"Where did it come from?" Dan asked.

Pete and I had already decided I would field Dan's questions. As the one who placed the call and as the Beltene, it was my duty. I spread my hands firmly on my desk, drawing strength from the oak it had been carved from and answered, "Pete found it."

"And why didn't Pete call me?" I was relieved to note he sounded more curious than pissed.

"Because Rhiannon is the Beltene," Pete answered.

Dan studied first Pete, then me before turning to my telephone. His conversation with his office was short and curt and as we waited for Lige, Luke and Eric to arrive, he mused, "Rhiannon's involvement as the Beltene means the blood was discovered in the possession of one of the family. Correct?"

Cris nodded.

Dan had connected the circumstance with the reasons with an unerring accuracy. I could only hope that my trust wasn't misplaced and that Trys wouldn't go to prison for the rest of his life. While the prospect of Trystan living out the remainder of his life incarcerated was tempting, the prospect of the world discovering the length of Trys' life was appalling.

"Rhiannon?"

I let my eyes dart around the room before I tried to respond to Dan's implicit question. "Would you agree that possession of the blood does not necessarily mean the possessor is our killer?"

Comprehension flashed across Righdhonn's face while Dan fought with my query.

"I would agree to that supposition," Dan admitted. "But I would have to counter it with the contention that in all probability the possessor of the blood is the killer."

I was reprieved briefly by the arrival of the rest of the police.

"Rhiannon," Dan prodded after setting Eric to printing the cooler.

Of course, Dan wouldn't have to imprison Trystan. My intention was to incarcerate him in the farthest corner of the dungeon for an exceptionally long period of time. I might let him come up for air once every couple of hundred years. "You're the sheriff, Daniel. And you're a Welcomed member of this community and as such, subject to the authority of the Beltene. I don't really know that those two entities have ever come into conflict—"

The inarticulate sound coming from Dan interrupted my speech for a moment. I eyed him, unsure if it was a response to the point of conflict I was trying to discuss tactfully or whether he'd figured out who I was talking about. A combination of both, I decided, thinking it may have been a tactical error to let Pete stay.

I continued, "In the past. However, before I tell you where the cooler was found, I do need assurance from you that you won't go off half-cocked. That you'll stay here so we can figure out how to pry loose the information of who the real killer is. Please."

Everyone in the room knew. It only needed the name to be spoken aloud.

Dan sighed and collapsed on the couch next to Righdhonn. "How do I get myself into these things?" he asked the ceiling.

"Go ahead, Rhi," Righdhonn said. "You might as well get it out in the open."

"Pete found it underneath Trys' coffin."

Dan straightened in his seat. I had forgotten he'd never seen Trys' room. "Underneath his what?"

"Trys has a coffin in his room."

"Why?"

I met his eyes and shrugged. "Who the hell knows. The bloody thing gave me nightmares for years."

Luke smiled at me from his perch on my desk. "Rhi swore Count Dracula lived here. It's probably why she writes about vampires; it's the only way she can exorcise them from her mind."

"Your cousin had this cooler of blood stored beneath the coffin he keeps in his bedroom. Correct?"

Nodding, I agreed, "Correct."

"What type of reasoning do you have that you don't suspect your cousin of committing these murders?" Dan asked. He immediately shook his head and continued, "No, don't bother to answer that. It's probably the same ones I have and it quite literally is in our genes. Damn it to hell." Dan turned to Lige. "I'm open to any and all suggestions."

"Where is Trystan?" Lige asked Pete.

"He's at the Metalworks."

"Do you want to talk to him here or at the sheriff's department?" I asked.

Lige and Dan both paused before looking at each other. Dan tipped his head, indicating his agreement with Lige's choice. "We don't want the press getting wind of this, so dragging him to the jail—pleasurable as it sounds—is out of the question. Here, we can enlist the aid of Grandmama, if we ..." Lige looked around the room and frowned. "Where is Grandmama anyway? I would have expected you to have her here."

"I didn't need anyone to point out the need to call the sheriff's department," I said. "Now, where do you want to question Trystan? If you do it here, I'm sure I can round up at least one pair of thumbscrews and maybe a scourge or two."

Dan massaged the bridge of his nose with his forefinger and thumb. "I think here is our best bet. But I don't want it to look official. Yet," he added, sparing a glance for me. "Righdhonn, could you and Pete go over to the Metalworks and haul his ass back here?"

"Certainly." Within minutes, the two of them were on their way with orders to stay away from reporters, to try to keep Trys from making too much of a scene (my suggestion of a large stick was declined) and to hurry.

Dan looked at me. "Call your grandmother."

"My grandmother?" I stammered, for a moment unsure of just whom he meant. My maternal grandmother lived in Wales and I'd never known my paternal grandmother. She'd died when my dad was very young. Teleri, his great-grandmother, had raised him.

"Yes, your grandmother. You know, the lady who's over nineteen hundred years old. I have a feeling we're going to need all nineteen hundred years of her wisdom today. Call her," he ordered.

Mindful of how effective Eula had been so far, I turned the task of finding Grandmama over to her. Once that had been accomplished, I turned to Daniel for further instructions.

"Now, we wait."

Chapter Twenty-Four
Monday, after noon

Grandmama and Trystan arrived at the same time. A look of resignation was on her face as she followed him into my office. She didn't appear to be surprised to see either the cooler or the police.

Trystan, on the other hand, was outraged. "I demand to see your search warrant," he snapped.

"I don't have one," Dan answered easily.

"You are required by law to have one. You cannot just come in here and take my possessions without a search warrant. It's a violation of my rights."

"I don't need a search warrant."

"Of course you do. Protection against illegal search and seizure is one of my inalienable rights as a citizen of this country. You have to have a search warrant!"

"Trystan," I broke into his speech before he hauled out his soapbox and got truly pompous. "A search warrant wasn't necessary."

"Why not?"

"Because the sheriff's department is here at my invitation."

"So what's your point?" he returned. "The cooler was in my room and it was not in plain view. Which means someone had to search for it. Whoever it was, they had no right being in my room." He was moving from outrage into petulance.

"First of all, the sheriff's department wasn't in your room. I had possession of the cooler when I called them and I don't need a search warrant. Second of all, if I invited them to do so, they could search every nook and cranny of this house. And not one person living here could complain.

"The sheriff's department, or whatever police agency I called, could do so, Trystan, because as the Beltene, I am the owner of all Beltene property, which does include this house. And as the Beltene, I cannot allow anything to endanger our family. Your possession of this cooler endangers us past all comprehension." My voice had been rising steadily during my lecture. "*What the hell were you thinking about, you blithering idiot?*"

"So much for tact and diplomacy," Luke said over Trystan's sputters and the awed lull my speech left behind.

"This is an invasion of my privacy," Trys insisted stubbornly, crossing his arms and glaring indiscriminately around the room.

"Where the bloody hell did you find that cooler?" I asked, my voice settling down to a mid-range howl.

He put his nose in the air and stared haughtily at me.

"Trystan," I said, trying to keep from wrapping my hands around his throat and strangling him. "You are not helping the situation. What you are doing is obstructing this investigation. I have had about all of this childishness that I'm going to take. I demand to know where you found that cooler."

"You demand?" he sneered.

"Trystan, let me put this as succinctly as I can. You *will* tell us where you found that cooler, if the body was in the same vicinity as the cooler, and what the bloody hell you thought you were doing. You *will* cooperate with us, because if you don't, I will exile you for the next millennium. You'll be herding sheep on the loneliest peak in Wales and I'll leave you there until you lose what little bit of a mind you possess.

Then, I'll have Gwen find the nastiest hole of an insane asylum in all Christendom to put you in for the remainder of your life. You won't be allowed to do any metalwork, have any female companionship and, most of all, you most definitely *will not* have a hundredth birthday party."

Trys dropped into a chair and pouted. I ignored him for a moment. He'd tell us what we wanted to know. He'd been planning his hundredth birthday party for years and would very nearly sacrifice his soul to keep it on the schedule.

Righdhonn's chuckle cut through the quiet of the room and drew my eyes. "And Rhan was concerned about you being the Beltene."

Sheepishly, I fidgeted as everyone but Trys and I joined his laughter.

"Oh sure," Trys muttered. "Everyone always sides with her."

"Trystan," Grandmama warned.

He paused long enough for us to understand he was giving us his information under duress. "I found it over at St. David's yesterday."

"Where?" Dan asked sharply.

"In the cemetery."

"When?"

"After Mass."

"Which Mass did you attend?"

"Ten-thirty."

"Where in the cemetery?" Dan had his little notebook out and was writing Trys' answers down in neat little letters.

"Next to the Beltene monument."

"Was the body near the cooler?" I barely recognized my voice.

Trys tried to look coy.

"Trystan." I didn't even bother to raise my voice.

He frowned and hurriedly answered, "Yes."

"Next to the monument?" Luke picked up the thread of questioning.

"Yes."

"Male body, embalmed, drained of its blood?"

"Yes." In the background, I could hear Daniel using my phone to tell one of his officers to leave the jail via the tunnel and check around the Beltene monument in the cemetery for yesterday's body.

"You left the body there and took the cooler home with you?"

"Yes."

"*Why?*" Lige's question was full of our frustration.

"I needed it for tonight."

No one really wanted to ask him why he needed it. We all looked around at each other, silently passing the buck, until Dan put my phone gently onto its base and marshaled the nerve to ask, "What do you plan on doing with the blood tonight?"

Trys took a deep breath and let it out slowly. "Liz is coming over."

"And?"

"Well," he snapped waspishly, "if you must know, we're going to bathe in it."

I covered my face with my hands. They were going to bathe in it. His words echoed around the room, battering us all with their unacceptable premise. A bit of history and a memory of something briefly noticed on his website flickered across my mind and I opened my fingers to peer at Trys. "Trystan, have you been reading about Elizabeth Bathoy?"

He grinned. "Delightful woman, wasn't she?"

I groaned and dropped my head onto my arms. Elizabeth Bathoy was a contemporary of Vlad Dracul who bathed in the blood of virgins to keep herself young. Her peers ignored the situation until Elizabeth began using their children for her supplies. She spent the remainder of her life walled in her room. They dropped food and water in from a hole in the ceiling. It was an idea worth contemplating; Trys' room was on the third floor.

"What if the blood's contaminated?" Luke asked. "After all, you don't know what these guys have been around or who they've been with. It might even be HIV positive."

Trys looked startled. "Good Lord, I hadn't thought about that. I'll have to have Rhodri test it for me right away."

"You are seriously warped," I muttered through my arms.

"I'm afraid we're going to have to impound the cooler and its contents," Dan said, having valiantly recovered from my cousin's outrageous confession.

Trys' face fell. I don't think the possibility of the sheriff's department confiscating the blood had crossed his mind. "You can't."

"We have to, I'm afraid."

"But Liz is expecting to take a bath in it. Tonight!"

"It's evidence in a murder," Dan explained. "We have to impound it."

"But it was going to be so much fun," Trys wailed.

"I'm sorry. We really do have to take it." Dan's voice was bemused. I'm sure he'd never been in the position where he felt it necessary to apologize for impounding evidence.

"Besides," I said without thinking, "Elizabeth used the blood of virgins."

"Rhiannon Argadnel Beltene!" There was a veritable chorus of voices reprimanding me.

I covered my mouth and lifted my head. "Sorry."

"Pfft," Trys waved my observation away. "Do you know how hard it is to find virgins of consenting age nowadays?"

"Thank the gods," Grandmama muttered.

Dan answered my phone on its first ring. He listened for a moment, then replaced the receiver gently. "The body is sitting on the bench on the eastern side of the monument."

"Rather artistically set up, I might add," Trystan said.

"They said the rigor appears to be fairly well gone and the embalming rigidity well set. He was wired into place so he wouldn't slump or fall over before he stiffened. If this blood matches the blood we found in the cave, we'll be fairly sure when and where he was killed. But we'll have to wait for the lab results. What's going to be a real pain in the ass is trying to figure out when he was put there."

"We do have a general time," Luke reminded Dan.

"Yeah." Eric rolled his eyes. "Somewhere between mid-afternoon Saturday and noon Sunday. That's damn near twenty-four hours."

"Well, wouldn't it be logical to assume he put the body there sometime Saturday night?" I asked.

Eric gazed pityingly at me. "Logical, yes. But this time of year the nights are getting longer. Somewhere between eight p.m. and seven a.m. isn't a lot of help, Rhi."

I never got a chance to protest the cavalier dismissal of my assistance.

"Two-thirty."

In slow motion, we all turned to stare at Trystan.

He ducked his head. "Oops."

"What did you say?" I asked.

"Two-thirty."

"You saw the body being placed on the bench at two-thirty Saturday night?" Dan asked.

"Yes."

"Before you picked up the cooler?"

"Yes."

"You saw who put the body on the bench?"

"Well ..." He quit dithering as I rose from my chair and took a step toward him. Grandmama was on my heels. "Yes."

"Did you recognize the person?" Dan continued his questioning. Personally, I was going to scream if he didn't ask the identity of the killer.

"Yes."

"*Who the bloody hell was it?*" My version of the question beat Dan's by a good three-quarters of a second.

"Henry."

"Henry who?"

Trys frowned. "Henry. You know, Henry Branton."

Dead silence ensued.

"That's impossible," I said flatly.

"It was Henry," Trys insisted.

"He's a repatriated Gwynn-O'Keefe," I returned.

"It was Henry."

"He did arrive at Sam's before you found the first body," Dan mused. "And he was at the park before Rhodri found the third body."

"There's no way on earth it could possibly be—"

"Wait a minute, Rhiannon," Grandmama said, interrupting me.

With a chill running through me, I turned to her. "Grandmama?"

She sighed heavily. "It is possible."

Suddenly dizzy, I stared open-mouthed at her before blindly finding my chair and lowering myself into it. "How?" I whispered.

"It has been clear all along that the murderer considered the killings gifts for you. As long as Henry meant you no harm, he wouldn't get twisted up in our compulsions."

"Lord and Lady."

"What exactly did you see at two-thirty Sunday morning?" Dan asked Trys.

"I'd been over at Liz's and was on my way home. She lives over on Bosworth Street. So I swung past the jail and decided to take the short cut through the cemetery. It wasn't necessary, but I wanted to see if anyone had removed my cherubs from the monument yet. The cherubs were still there and as I got closer, I noticed Henry and someone else sitting on the bench. I started over to see what they were doing, but I noticed Henry was tying the other man to the bench.

"I'd never realized Henry was kinky, and since they appeared to be having a good time, I didn't want to interrupt him. So I went on home."

It was a comfort to me that if Trystan ever saw me involved in something highly suspicious with a perfect stranger that he would simply assume I was into much more kinkiness than he'd supposed and go quietly on his way. Perhaps I'd send him to Wales just for the hell of it.

Trys continued, unaware of my plans for his immediate future. "On my way home from Mass yesterday morning, I stopped by the bench to make sure he hadn't left a mess. My mother and the women of the family visit there often and I didn't want them to see anything that would upset them."

Well, maybe I would restrain myself. His concern about cleaning up the alcove before anyone saw it was a mature and selfless action. What was the world coming to?

"The man was still tied to the bench and appeared to be dead. From the cooler, filled with all that delightful blood, at his feet, I concluded this was Sunday's victim.

"Liz and I have been reading about Elizabeth Bathoy and we've been trying to figure out how to get our hands on some blood so we could try one of her baths. And there it was at my feet, just waiting for me. A whole cooler full of blood. A gift from the gods. There wasn't a soul around, so I took the cooler to my room and stored it underneath my coffin. I did replace the blue ice, though, so the blood wouldn't spoil before tonight.

"Of course, then I couldn't report the body because you would have wanted to know where the cooler and its contents had wandered off to. I figured sooner or later someone would find it."

He didn't want his mother to find a kinky mess, but it was all right for her to find an embalmed corpse. And his reasons for taking and hiding the blood were selfish and immature. I shook my head; he was back to herding sheep in the back of beyond again.

"You're sure it was Henry?" Dan persisted.

"It was most definitely Henry Branton."

"What now?" I asked Dan.

"First we get a formal statement from Trystan and then we find a judge. If he agrees we have enough for a warrant—and I'm sure he will—then once he signs the warrant, we go out to Henry's."

"Rhys is in the garden," Grandmama interjected. "He didn't need to be in court until this afternoon. I'll get him for you."

"Thank you." Dan smiled at her as she moved to open the door.

She paused in the doorway. "Eula could take Trystan's statement and transcribe it for you. It would save you the aggravation of trying to get a police stenographer over here."

"That would be great," Dan agreed.

Before I could hit the intercom to summon Eula, she appeared in the doorway, pen and pad in hand. "What can I do to assist you, Sheriff?"

"You can take Trystan out to your office and get his statement. We'll need three copies. If he makes any corrections to the printed copies, have him initial each correction. When he's ready to sign it, call us because it needs to be witnessed." He turned to Trys. "Start when you left Liz's."

Trys nodded as Eula took his arm and guided him into her office.

"I still can't believe it's Henry," I said as the men clustered around my desk.

"I think we were all blinded by the fact that he's a Gwynn-O'Keefe and we're conditioned to believe anyone who manages to make it into town isn't dangerous," Lige said. "Except Dan, of course. But his hands were tied because we kept insisting it couldn't be a Gwynn-O'Keefe."

"As soon as we get the warrant, we'll go out to Henry's." Dan was sitting on the corner of my desk again. "Luke, can you start a complete background check on him? Especially since he moved into town. Eric, you'll go with Lige and me when we go out to arrest him. He lives out on Black Abbey Road, right?"

"Right. I think we'll want to include Superior Deliveries in the warrant," Eric added. "With as much time as he spent at work, I think it's possible he could have taken anything incriminating there. Either in the building or the van he drives."

I rested my elbows on my desk, my chin in my hands and let the men's technical conversation wash over me. I tried to equate Henry with the fear and horror and ruthlessness of these murders. I was still wrestling with it when Grandmama returned with Rhys.

"I understand my idiot nephew may have broken the case," he said, joining everyone standing around my desk.

"Broken the case?" I muttered. "Lord and Lady, please don't tell him he's the keypoint of solving this case. His ego will inflate well past the tolerance point and I'll have to kill him, just to put us all out of our misery."

The police officials in my office chose to disregard my comments and began explaining Trystan's presence in the latest developments of our murder spree.

They hadn't quite finished when Eula dragged Trys and his statement into the office. "He's been over these and is ready to sign them," she informed Dan.

"Sign away," Dan told Trys, handing him a pen.

"We'll need to trace as many of Henry's movements over the last week as we can," Luke said as Trys signed his statement.

With Trys' signed statement in hand, the men dispersed to begin the process of arresting one slightly myopic sociopathic murderer.

I still found it difficult to believe. Henry. Our nightmare was not ending—it was just beginning to take shape.

Chapter Twenty-Five
Monday, mid-afternoon

Dan, Lige and Eric accompanied Rhys to the courthouse to do the official paperwork necessary to the issuance of a warrant.

Luke stopped by my rooms to instruct Roseanne and Elaine on where and how to start tracing Henry via computer, before leaving to begin the physical drudgery of tracing an inconspicuous man.

Pete, who Trys never did suspect of delivering the blood into my hands, accompanied his ward back to the Metalworks with strict instructions not to let him out of his sight. Not even for a moment. Or they'd both find themselves herding sheep on a lonely peak in Wales.

The four of us were left alone in my office with promises of communication as soon as anyone knew anything. My father, even with only a touch of the mysterious Beltene ESP, arrived mere minutes later.

Rhys rescheduled his afternoon trial while he was over at the courthouse and, after signing all the warrants the sheriff's department could think of, returned to my office to wait with Grandmama, Cris, Righ and me. He strolled in barely fifteen minutes after I'd finished bringing my father up to date on what was happening. Dad was still pacing about the room threatening to send Trys to a lonely peak in Wales. His version was in Welsh.

We had agreed not to advise the family of the impending arrest. This left us little to do except watch Dad and wait for the phone to ring.

Being unable to play an active role in this phase of the case was both a relief and an annoyance. I didn't want to be there when they served the warrants. I didn't think I could bear to see Henry's madness, which must have always been there, and know that I'd never recognized it before.

The annoyance was in the waiting. Waiting for the phone to ring. Waiting to hear the arrest was complete. Waiting for the fear and horror to end—although it wouldn't. It would change; Henry would be arrested and the surfeit of bloodless corpses would cease, but then the trial would come and with it, bring its own brand of fear and horror.

When, to my relief, the telephone finally rang, it was several hours later and we all stared at it. Hesitantly, I reached for it. "Hello."

"Rhiannon, this is Eula."

My shoulders sagged. "Yes, Eula, what is it?" I'd noticed that seldom did anyone wait long enough for Eula to either use the intercom or the telephone to notify me or any of the previous Beltenes of their wish to see the Beltene. They just stroll through her office and into mine without a by-your-leave.

"Sheriffs Thorpe and Williams are here to see you."

I hadn't expected them to bring us the news first hand. "Send them in."

The door opened and both men walked in. Without a word, Dan shut the door and leaned against it while Lige sat heavily on the couch.

"Dan?" I asked after the tension had stretched too thin.

He shook his head and pushed away from the door, sitting on the opposite end of the couch. Lige exchanged an enigmatic glance with him before Dan said, "Henry's dead."

I slowly straightened in my chair and very carefully did not look at Righdhonn. "What?"

"What happened?" Rhys and Dad asked at the same time.

"He was dead when we got there. We don't really know yet when he was last seen, but I'd guess he's been dead since sometime yesterday afternoon."

"How did he die?" Dad asked.

"He, umm ..." Dan looked worriedly from Grandmama to Cris to me.

"Go ahead," Grandmama encouraged him softly.

"He hung himself," he said quickly, not quite looking us in the eye.

My mind's eye showed me the interior of Henry's cabin and tested location after location, trying to find a place that fit the criteria of hanging. "Where?" I asked hoarsely.

The silence lengthened with the shadows. Lige finally answered reluctantly, "You know the walkway in the peak?"

The access to the walkway was a spiral stairway from the loft. Henry had added both the stairway and the walkway to the design of his house after showing Dad and me the blueprints seven years ago. I had suggested both of them, along with the skylights lining both sides of the peak. The skylights could be cranked open, which is what necessitated the walkway. As far as I knew, Henry had never opened them. He loved the way it looked, but was terrified of actually climbing up there.

"Yes." I pictured the rope tied to the railing and the body dangling above the floor. I felt the color leaving my face.

"He took—"

"Lige," Dan interrupted.

"No," I told him, my arms wrapped tightly around myself. "I need to know."

"He used fishing line."

The office blurred in front of me. I closed my eyes, opening them abruptly as my imagination showed me all too clearly the result of a fall with fishing line around your throat.

"Rhiannon." Righ's voice was next to me. I hadn't seen or heard him move.

"I'm all right," I said.

"Not really," he returned.

"Did he leave a note?" Rhys asked.

"Nope."

"He didn't?"

Dan shook his head. "No, he didn't."

"But ..." Looking around the room, Rhys stopped speaking.

"Not all suicides leave a note," Lige said. "He'd already left a multitude of letters and notes. Maybe he just didn't have anything more to say."

I pushed my chair away from my desk and spun to face the window.

"I guess I don't need to be worrying about how the family's going to survive a trial, do I?" I asked, suddenly cold and not quite sure why.

"No, Rhi, there won't be a trial." Rhys' voice was level.

I bit the inside of my cheek and took several deep breaths in order to keep the tears at bay. Too many people recently had assured me that there wouldn't be a trial. Did I want to ask if they suspected that Henry might *not* have killed himself? If I did, that would immediately lead to who might have taken care of this small problem for us, which in turn would lead to my favorite cousin. Blindly I reached toward Righ and he took my cold hand in his. It took me about ten seconds to decide not to ask that question. "What happens now?" I asked instead.

"There was embalming fluid and a couple other things in the house. More than enough to implicate Henry in the murders. I don't think any of us have any doubts that he's the killer–Trystan's statement aside. We'll have an inquest. Henry's death will be ruled a suicide. He will, due to evidence, be declared the guilty party in regard to our other bodies and that will be the end of it." Our new sheriff didn't seem to have any unresolved questions floating around.

"Like, by tomorrow?" I asked hopefully.

"More like things will settle down in a couple of weeks."

"Am I off house arrest?" Not that I was going to have time to go anywhere, but this trapped and claustrophobic atmosphere I'd been living in the last few days would dissipate if only I *knew* I could go outside. Our sheriffs looked at each other then turned in unison to gaze at me.

"Yeah, Rhi," Dan said, nodding. "It's safe for you to go outside."